Ben Hobson lives in Brisbane and is entirely keen on his wife, Lena, and their two small boys, Charlie and Henry. He currently teaches English and Music at Bribie Island State High School. In 2014 his novella, *If the Saddle Breaks My Spine*, was shortlisted for the Viva La Novella prize run by Seizureonline. *To Become a Whale* is his first novel.

For Charlie and Henry

To Become *a* Whale

BEN HOBSON

ALLEN&UNWIN

SYDNEY·MELBOURNE·AUCKLAND·LONDON

First published in 2017

Allen & Unwin
83 Alexander Street
Crows Nest NSW 2065
Australia
Phone: (61 2) 8425 0100
Email: info@allenandunwin.com
Web: www.allenandunwin.com

Cataloguing-in-Publication details are available
from the National Library of Australia
www.trove.nla.gov.au

ISBN 978 1 76029 439 7

Internal design by Romina Panetta
Set in 12.5/19 pt Minion Pro by Midland Typesetters, Australia
Printed and bound in Australia by Griffin Press

10 9 8 7 6 5 4 3 2 1

MIX
Paper from
responsible sources
FSC® C009448
www.fsc.org

The paper in this book is FSC® certified. FSC® promotes environmentally responsible, socially beneficial and economically viable management of the world's forests.

There's no eel so small but it hopes to become a whale.

—German proverb

ONE

1961

He was told her headstone would be placed tomorrow. For now it leaned against the side of the church, a grey rectangle against the red brick. As family and friends wandered inside for cordial and lamingtons and small sausage rolls provided by the church, the boy gazed at it, the stone, and her name etched in front, so strange to see it written in full. Elizabeth Mary Keogh. Beloved mother and so on. This, the boy decided, would finally convince him of her death. So he stared as the muffled chatter through the wall slowly lost its restraint. But the stone failed to provide anything in the way of finality. The boy expected that, after a while, his father might come looking for him. He didn't. And so, seemingly forgotten, the boy stayed by the headstone, ran a hand along it. It had been warmed by the sun. He slid his fingers over her name. In his mind he promised he would not ever forget her and that he would pray often and listen for her voice and that she would always be with him.

Later, as the two of them, father and son, walked back to his grandparents' house from the church, a cool breeze whipped the edges of his jacket. He hugged it around him all the tighter. He struggled to keep pace with his father, who swerved on meagre drink, and every so often he jogged a little to keep up. Hard to do holding his jacket so. He caught up at a corner as his father trailed the two and a half remaining fingers of his ruined hand along a white picket fence, and the boy was finally able to catch a glimpse of the man's face. But there were no streetlamps down this dusty street and no cars at night and the moon above was mostly hidden by clouds. His father's face was ensconced in shadow.

His granddad and grandmother were already in bed as they returned, the older man's snoring loud, reverberating through the walls. His father was careful as he shut the flyscreen door, then the main. The deadlock clunked into place, far too loud in the silence between snores. They took their shoes off and placed them neatly to the side and then started across the linoleum in their socks. They had to avoid the pot plants his grandmother obsessively collected and, in the months leading up to his mother's death, had forgotten to water. They entered the bedroom and his father gently shut the door, which muffled the snoring only a bit. This room had belonged to his mother and aunty when they were girls, the aunty dead some time ago now. Her picture on the dresser in front of the mirror with his mother as a girl, posed in black and white. Both were dolled up in floral dresses, his mother's arms around his aunty's middle. Younger in the photo than the boy was now. He wondered at that.

The boy sat on his aunty's bed as his father undressed until his father said, 'Get ready for bed, mate.'

The boy removed his nice shirt and belt and his too-baggy black pants. These funeral clothes had once been his father's. When his father's parents died his old clothes had arrived in a suitcase with a note and some books and a moth-eaten piece of cloth. The boy had never met his father's parents and had never questioned their absence. The boy's mother had kept these clothes for nice but there had never been a purpose for them and they had stayed in his closet until the day she died. The boy was sad she never saw him so well dressed.

As they put on their pyjamas the boy compared the two of them in the circular mirror that sat atop the dresser. He rubbed his hands over his face and imagined his father's visage etched into his own. What would it be like to have a beard, to have it growing from the neck?

'You did well today,' his father said, drawing breath. 'Not hard shovelling dirt, though, is it?'

Earlier, at her gravesite, the herd of mourners surrounding the hole in the earth that held her coffin, his father had kicked at a pile of nearby dirt and stepped back. Arched his eyebrows at the boy. As everyone watched, the boy had begun to shovel. He had not felt up to the task and had not been prepared, and his doubt had slowed his shovelling. The sound the dirt made as it struck the wood like drumming fingers on a tree. The sun glowed against the surface of her coffin until he had covered it in thick clods and then it grew lifeless, dull, a feature of the landscape. None of the other men helped him at all, and in their stares and sorrow the boy sensed an importance about this act he could not fathom. When he had finished he dropped the shovel onto the nearby grass. The clanging sound like a slap to the ear. He looked to his father for forgiveness. Wordless disapproval instead in the man's clenched fist, the way his mouth had creased. The boy felt he'd failed whatever test he'd been set.

The father now finished buttoning his pyjama shirt, tousled the boy's hair. The boy climbed into bed and his father stood at the light switch and waited for the boy to settle beneath the blankets, burrowing in like a wombat, before he turned it off. Until the boy's eyes adjusted he could only hear his father and not see him. An animal in the dark. The feather doona was too hot, so the boy kicked it off. The boy said, 'I don't know what to feel.'

His father grunted. Then, 'Feel sad. You should feel sad.'

'I do,' the boy said. 'But it doesn't seem real.'

Another grunt. 'Go to sleep.'

Silence for a time. The boy heard his father's breathing soften and steady, which suggested slumber, but he ventured another question. 'Are we going home tomorrow?'

A murmur of assent.

'Why did Mum get buried here and not at home?'

'This is what she wanted,' his father said, and shifted in bed. 'Go to sleep.'

'Where will I be buried?'

'Be buried wherever you want.'

'What about you? Will you be buried here?'

'I'm not a bloody Werner, mate,' his father said. 'Now go to sleep.'

So even when all three of them were dead – the boy, the father, the mother – they still would not be together. His father in one cemetery and his mother in another. And the boy, in the middle, having to choose.

His father's breathing drifted into a light snore. The boy was wide awake and wished his mother was there to sort out the mess in his head. What he tried to remember now, tucked up in bed, was how soft she had been. His father, by contrast, was jagged. The boy had settled in himself that his mother would die and prepared himself for her absence, but he had never thought on what shape life might take for he and his father afterwards. Without her it was only them. To fall asleep, the boy stared at his father in the shadows, his body moving with each snore. The boy did his best to take from this some comfort.

In the early hours the boy sobbed. He did his best to hide the noise he was making with a hand clasped tight over his mouth and his head buried in his pillow.

Despite the boy's efforts, his father woke. 'You alright?'

A sniff. The boy couldn't answer.

Another moment and his father added, 'You have to stop crying, mate, and get some sleep. Crying doesn't fix anything.'

This upset the boy further, but he clenched his fingers into his palms and did his best to quieten. He was sure his father regretted what he'd said because in the shadows he saw this parent of his sit up and regard him. When the boy appeared calm, the shadow lay back down. Soon the snoring began again. The boy listened and counted the snores until he fell asleep.

The boy woke. His father's bed was already empty so he sat up. He looked in the mirror and scuffed his messy hair and yawned. Quickly he dressed from his already packed suitcase, then left the room. Down the corridor the sound of male chatter and the smell of burnt butter. The boy stumbled into the kitchen and sat at the round table. His granddad, wearing a black apron, hunched over the stovetop with smoke billowing around him. His father rested against the kitchen counter with an orange coffee cup in his hands. The boy looked at him and his father winked in his direction, sipped, and tilted his head towards the back of his granddad in mock alarm. The boy refused to add to this insult and looked crossly at his father, who shrugged.

Soon his granddad turned and, from his black and smoking pan, ladled burnt eggs onto buttered bread sitting on three plates. He plonked it down before the boy and then sat opposite him at the table and said, looking at the father, 'Have the eggs.'

'I'm okay with the coffee.'

'You want some, mate?' his granddad asked, turning towards him.

'Don't think he drinks coffee yet, Charles. He's only thirteen, God's sake.'

'What?' his granddad said, smiling. 'You're thirteen, are you?'

'Where's Grandma?' the boy asked, chewing, crunching on something unpleasant.

His granddad coughed and looked at his father and said, 'She's not feeling well. She's still in bed.'

'Won't she want some eggs?'

His granddad smiled again. 'I asked. Her loss, right?'

The boy ate. The eggs were awful, but for the sake of his granddad, he feigned delight. He forked in another piece.

His granddad leaned back from the table and said to his father, 'You still heading off today?'

'Soon as we've eaten.'

'Well,' his granddad said, and took a moment to compose himself. He shuffled his hands across the table and eventually settled them before him, clasped together. 'You look after our Sam.' There was a ripple in his voice, like he was stifling a cough.

'I will.'

'And you'll have to bring him to visit.'

His father laughed loudly. He dashed the remainder of his coffee in the sink and turned on the faucet to rinse the cup. He said, 'We're just going home. We're not running out on you. Liz died, doesn't change you and him.' He nodded at his son. 'Sam'll visit at Christmas like normal.'

The boy nodded while he chewed another forkful of eggs. His granddad's suggestion that his father might be incapable of caring for him had never struck him before and he dwelled on this as he finished his eggs, which made them taste even more unpleasant.

'We can come back before Christmas too,' the boy added. He tilted his head back to regard his father, whose smile and slow nod might have meant anything.

There had been a silence developing between his granddad and his father while the boy had eaten his eggs. Some kind of shared understanding between the two men to which he was not privy. He drank some orange juice and watched his granddad's eyes as the old man focused on the table before him and fiddled with his cutlery. There was nothing in him that suggested things were well or that anything would ever again be the same. The summers the boy had spent at this house whisked away with his mother's death. Judging by his granddad's jaw, the hint of moisture in his eyes, the old man doubted he would ever see his grandson again, and this was how he would say goodbye, with ruined eggs.

'You alright, Granddad?'

His granddad looked at him and smiled and said, 'I'm just upset about your mother.'

The boy reached a hand across the table and said, 'You still have us.'

Meant to be a comfort, this instead seemed to make things worse, his granddad's nose wrinkling as the words struck him. So the boy finished his orange juice in silence and pushed his chair back and went to stand beside his father.

'Thanks for everything,' his father said.

'You're already packed?'

'This morning. You want to say goodbye to Grandma, mate?'

His father gently pushed him in the back as though he were a small child and the boy reluctantly walked into his grandparents' room, a place he had seldom been before. It smelled of dust. His grandma, lying in darkness, was cloaked in a sheet. Just like his mother at her death. The blinds were drawn and there were wadded-up tissues littering the bed like leaves after a storm. Her body heaved with sobbing and the boy stood at a loss. 'Grandma?' he said.

She shooed him off with an impatient wave of her hand and didn't even turn to look. So he left. His father offered his sour expression a commiserating smile and a soft pat on the back.

TWO

1951

The young father squatted down in front of his son's book-case and looked over his shoulder as his son rushed in and clambered onto his back. With some effort he managed to wrangle the boy around and hold him to his chest, so they were both facing the small selection of books before them.

'Which one tonight, mate?'

'*Rabbits*,' his son said, and pulled the book from the shelf. 'Read Little Georgie.'

'Where he jumps over –' his voice shifted to menacing '– Dead Man's Brook?'

His son beamed. 'Uh-huh.'

'Dead Man's Brook?' More menacing, tickling the boy beneath the arms, each word louder than the one before.

His son laughed and squirmed. The boy's mother appeared at the doorway.

'What are you two up to?'

'Dad's reading *Rabbits*,' the boy said, holding up the book.

His father smiled. 'I sure am.'

'Do you two want a Milo?'

His father's face widened in mock surprise. 'A Milo?' Like he'd never heard of such a thing.

His boy's face followed his. 'Yes, Mummy.' Nodding theatrically

'Yes what, Mummy?'

'Yes, please.'

His mother, smiling, walked away. His father sat on the customary chair and patted his lap. The boy climbed up, struggling to hold the book while he did.

His father read the story about a small rabbit brave enough to jump a stream, chased by vicious dogs. He changed his voice to suit the characters – a higher pitch for the rabbits, a gruff timbre for the dog – which made his son laugh.

Soon the boy was in bed, upright, drinking the hot Milo brought in by his mother. She sat on the end of the bed; his father remained in the chair.

'You know your dad's heading back in a few days, sweetheart?' his mother said, one hand on his covered foot.

'To Tangalooma.'

'That's right. To Tangalooma.'

His father leaned forward. His son slurped the last of his Milo and his father took the cup and put it on the bedside table. 'But guess what? This time you and Mummy get to come and visit. And stay with me.'

'That's right,' his mother said. 'We're going to visit Daddy in a few weeks.'

'See the whales?'

'Yeah, mate,' his father said. 'You'll see the whales.'

'Mummy will come too?'

'Yeah, Mummy'll be there.'

'Will I go on the boat?'

'Yeah.'

His son smiled. 'And see Daddy?'

'That's right, mate. 'Cause you know I miss you when I'm away.'

A nod.

'Alright, now. Sleep time.'

'Water?'

'No, sweetheart,' his mother said. 'You just had a Milo.'

'Go to sleep, mate.'

His father turned off the bedside lamp and launched them all into darkness. The parents stood at the doorway a moment looking back on their son. His father's arm around his mother's middle. Then his father shut the door.

THREE

1961

Travelling north in their old car up Gympie Road the boy saw their turn-off coming up and was surprised when they passed it without slowing. His father gave him no sign to indicate his intention. They drove on, turned a corner. Soon there were odd trees the boy had never seen before flitting by the car with thin octopus arms sunk into the mud.

'We're not going home?' the boy asked.

His father's wrist rested on the steering wheel and he was slouched back in his seat. The radio off despite the boy's earlier pleas. His father staring hard at the road as it travelled beneath them. The boy had tried to mimic his father's gaze and conjure up something of interest, but failed. Instead the road blurred to a spinning black so dizzying he'd had to look away.

'We're not living in that house anymore, Sam,' his father said, his eyes boring holes in the road.

They turned another corner.

The use of the boy's name so strange from his father it rendered the boy momentarily speechless, but soon he asked, 'What do you mean?'

'I mean we're not living there anymore. I've sold it.'

He watched his father, waiting for more, but his father's face was still set upon that road, his eyes fierce in their focus.

At last the boy mustered the courage to ask, 'What do you mean?'

'Leave it, mate. We'll talk about it later.'

The boy sat back. He had no immediate emotional response to what his father had said, which aroused a faint curiosity regarding the state of his soul. If what his father had said was true, he should damn well bloody care, but there in the pit of him was nothing at all. Did it all mean nothing now? In light of her passing were all things now mute?

They drove. Soon, in desperate need of distraction, the boy wound his window down. The humid air whipped at his face and he leaned more fully from the window to better capture it. He squinted through the barrage of wind. The car climbed another incline and then turned right. Beside them now were green pastures dotted with cows. In the distance, up a long dirt driveway, squatted an abandoned house. Beside it, what once may have been a milking shed, buckled. The legs had long ago given way and the roof sat lopsided. A touch would bring it down.

A few minutes later they turned down a driveway that snaked around a hill on which a few sheep stood. The makings of small horns visible on their domes. The boy wound his window up.

On the other side of the hill there stood a house in better condition. It was timber and although one side of it was slightly tilted, the rest of it stood proud and white in the sun. There were potted plants dangling from the verandah's wrought iron lacework and as they approached the boy saw them sway in the breeze.

They pulled up on the gravel and the father, after clapping his hands on his knees and staring wildly at the boy, opened the car door and got out. The boy followed, intensely puzzled.

They walked to the house, the tangled mess of leaves and branches scratching at their faces. The giant fig tree had impressed itself upon the fence, some of the palings bulging in their middles. The boy pushed the leaves away from his face but his father ploughed through seemingly unaffected. The owner's laziness plain on closer inspection, cobwebs between the ferns that lined the path to the house, the white timber caked with mud. They clomped onto the wooden porch, the boy still wondering what they were doing here. His father knocked on the door.

A rumpled woman answered quickly. Short, overweight, hair up in a messy bun. The opposite of the boy's mother.

'You Walter?'

His father nodded. 'I called a few days ago?'

'Right on time. Come in, come in,' she said, and waved them through the door.

The inside of the house as dilapidated as its exterior. The beating heart beneath as grimy as the skin. The woman seemed most at home, navigating the clutter with precision. She led father and son to the living room, where she sat down on a laundry-strewn couch. Patting the seat beside her and grinning, she invited his father to join her.

The boy's father stood before her shifting his weight from foot to foot, awkward to watch. He smiled and said, 'If it's all the same, I'd rather just get the pup.'

'I need to talk to you, though, about what to do with him,' the woman said. She patted the cushion beside her again. 'Let me make you some tea.' She started to stand.

'If it's all the same, we've a ways to go.'

The woman became disgruntled. Her face squished in and her eyes grew dim. She lurched up and straightened her dress with angry hands and looked at the boy. 'You got the money?'

'Where's the dog?' his father said.

'Out back is where the litter is,' she said.

The boy, at the first mention of the dog, had been looking at the doorway. The woman smiled at this and said, 'Bit of a surprise for you then, is it?' She chuckled.

The boy turned to his father, feeling something slight in his gut. 'We're getting a dog?'

A nod. 'We need one.'

'Why?'

His father shook his head. An implied promise, maybe, to answer the boy's questions later. His father turned back to the woman and said, 'Can you show us the litter?'

'Follow me.'

She led them out to her spacious backyard. In the distance a barbed-wire fence and beyond only grass and horizon. A wire-mesh chicken coop stood to the left. Chickens busy being chickens. A kennel beside.

'Pups're in there,' she said, pointing.

'Well.' His father put a hand on the boy's neck.

The boy noticed how small he felt beside his father.

His father leaned down and said, 'Go and pick the one you want.'

'Except the dark brown one,' the woman said. 'She's getting picked up later. She's already sold.'

His father nodded at the boy and moved his eyebrows comically in the direction of the kennel.

The boy said, 'But how do I see in?'

'Just reach in there and feel around,' his father said.

'What if I get bit?'

'You won't get bit.'

The boy approached the kennel. Beside him a chicken pecked in its hay. The smell of excrement and farm. The kennel, the boy found as he neared it, had a panel on top he could lift to look inside. One fat dog within and three smaller ones asleep. The mother dog looked at him blearily and then thumped its head back onto the wood. The smallest pup closest to the bitch's rear legs. It had its head tucked in and looked ashamed. The boy levered this one out and cradled it to his chest. It was sucking at the air. It woke and yawned and stretched its limbs. No reaction from Mum, maybe thankful her child had been stolen. The boy stepped away from the kennel and lowered the pup to the ground.

In the grass it looked smaller than he'd expected. A scruffy ball with teeth and unsure legs. Fat as it walked. It sprang at the boy's feet in an attempt to be ferocious and gnawed at his leather shoe. One of his laces was longer than the other, and the puppy seized it and pulled.

The boy crouched and studied its movements. An innocent creature this, not yet ready for the world, to be taken from its mother and thrust into life. Rust-coloured fur. As it trotted towards the boy he noticed its two rear legs were socked with white. It had black eyes and its ears were small and tipped like peaks of pavlova. He tried to pat it. It darted away and bared its teeth once more.

The boy, still on his haunches, crab-walked closer and reached out his hand again, slower this time. The puppy nipped at first and then licked. The boy withdrew his offer and the puppy darted in and the boy got to his feet and took a step away.

His father, nearer to the house, yelled, 'He's only playing, mate.'

The boy, though nervous, reached out again and allowed the puppy its play. Its tongue was warm and its teeth were friendly. It licked and then bit too hard and the boy withdrew his hand and sucked on his finger.

His father yelled, 'He bite you?'

'Yes,' the boy yelled. He turned to look at his father, who said something direct to the lady who grew upset, judging by her crossed arms. She shrugged and sucked her teeth.

'Give him a smack,' his father yelled.

'What?'

'Smack him on the snout so he knows not to do it again.'

The boy tentatively tapped the pup on its wet nose. The puppy did not take this disciplinary measure as it had been intended. Undaunted, it waddled towards the house.

'Mate, nothing'd learn from that,' said his father, who had walked over to join him. 'Here, I'll show you.'

'But he won't remember what he did wrong,' the boy said.

'He does.' The father approached the dog, bent down and whacked it in the side. The sound of an open palm striking another. The pup keeled over and yelped loudly. It looked stunned as it lifted its head. His father said, 'No,' sternly, and pointed a finger. The pup scurried away from them both, crying for its mother. A few metres from them it stopped and peed on the grass, its legs trembling.

'He won't like us now,' the boy said.

'Doesn't matter if he likes us or not.'

The boy watched as the pup dashed back into its kennel, its crying loud enough to carry through the wood. The boy wondered what its mother might think.

'You teach 'em young and they'll grow up respecting you. Harder to teach an old dog. You heard that saying before?'

'Yes.'

'Well. That, then.'

The boy said nothing to this and his father, smiling, crossed his arms and nodded as though satisfied with this clay he'd sculpted.

'Can I go see if he's alright?'

'He's fine,' his father said, his arms still crossed. A statue the boy knew he would never shift with argument.

FOUR

Back in the car, the pup rested on the boy's lap in a cardboard box with holes cut in, an old shirt in the bottom. The pup whined softly, maybe for its mother. The boy watched as it nestled into the shirt and then fell silent, regarding its confines with canine apathy.

'What're you gonna name him?' his father asked. His smile seemed genuine.

The boy said, 'I get to name it?'

'Sure.'

The boy thought for a moment. 'It's a boy?'

'Yep.'

'How can you tell?'

'His balls. There.' His father pushed the almost-asleep pup over in the box and pointed at the dog's scrotum as it did its best to twist back onto its front, little legs churning.

The boy thought and after a moment said, 'Albert.'

'Why Albert?'

'Sounds like a dog's name.'

The boy watched Albert fall asleep and reached in to softly stroke the fur on his head. The car jolted, which stirred the dog. He got to his feet and scratched at the side of the box, regarding the boy with imploring eyes.

The boy looked up. They'd hit a dirt road that sloped downwards, dotted with dark blue rocks. The car moved slowly and his father grimaced as he drove. Beside them, the trees had tentacles again and were clustered more densely now, some of them even clawing the edge of the road. The old Ford scraped against them. The sound of squeaking metal. The smaller twigs and branches were snapped clean off and the boy watched them scatter across the stones. The father didn't notice, or didn't care, and ploughed doggedly forward.

The road levelled out shortly and became less rocky. More dirt, soon combined with sand. They drove a little further and then the car slowed. Before them stood a pile of new timber at the side of the road and, stretched out behind it, a muddy slop. An old-looking cement mixer too, caked in rust. Next to it an old wheelbarrow. Bags of cement stacked neatly beside the timber. The top few packets darkened, damp. The car crawled to a stop and his father sat behind the wheel, only staring. He looked down, breathed. Finally he lifted his head again, slammed it against the steering wheel.

'Damn it! Damn you, Gus, you mongrel!'

The whole dashboard vibrated with his rage. A red mark across his forehead from the steering wheel. Both fists crashed down again and again, the ruined one devoid of power.

The boy lurched out of the car, landing on his back in the muck, then realised he'd abandoned Albert in his box. He reached back into the car to grab the box.

The veins in his father's neck were pulsing, his eyes possessed by some foul demon, and the boy slammed the door to confine him. The boy huddled against a tyre, cradling the dog.

Soon he heard his father open the door on the other side of the car and slam it shut again. Then the sound of trees snapping and ripping nearby.

His father's fits of rage had usually been witnessed from a distance. Once, the boy had watched from the verandah as his father drove his fist into a fence post he'd been mending and swore. Carrying on like a pork chop, the boy's mother had said, safely out of earshot. The boy had never been this close to such wild aggression. The eyes. No telling what control the rage within him exerted over his father's body, if any, as he lost his temper.

The boy didn't move, his breathing shallow as he waited until eventually the sound of his father's fury grew fainter. No telling if the man had simply calmed down and now stood nearby, or if he had walked further away.

The boy got to his feet and, holding the box to his chest, risked a look.

His father was seated on the ground behind some trees, cross-legged, head down, with his back to the boy. The boy's heart was racing from what energy he'd expended and what fear still filled him, yet his father's body seemed composed now, capable of more, as though his rage had never existed. Behind the trees he was a spectre of unknowable intent. The boy continued to watch, but did not dare approach.

When he was feeling calmer, he took Albert out of the box and set him down, and watched as the pup struggled to stand and stretched his limbs one by one. The dog soon found his feet and dashed away. The puppy was a welcome distraction from his demonic father. He led the boy away from the car, further into the bush. As he waded through the overgrown thick of it and the puppy skittered between trees ahead of him, he was struck by the sound of waves. A seagull overhead. He had no idea they had travelled so far from the city and come so close to the water.

The distance from his father allowed the boy a moment of respite and he sat on a tree lopsided from the bog to think things through and watch the puppy at play. He had never before questioned a decision made by a parent. Until this day they had seemed to him incapable of error. Who was he, the boy, to question them? After a chase he managed to recapture the pup. He walked back to the car holding the dog, nervous about what he would find.

His father was now leaning up against the car smoking, a habit the boy thought his mother had expunged. His father's left foot was up against the door and his lips were relaxed, the cigarette dangling from them. The boy had never been more afraid and he stood immobile at the edge of the clearing and watched his father for signs of further violence.

'It's alright, mate.' His father rubbed the back of his head. 'I'm sorry, okay? I just lost my cool a bit. A bloke's allowed to lose his temper, yeah?'

'You scared me,' the boy said, still not coming closer.

'I know I did. I didn't mean to. It's just –' his father glanced at the trees '– bloody Gus has buggered this whole thing up.'

'Buggered what up?'

His father grinned. 'You've never used that word before.'

'Not in front of you.' The boy looked down, a little ashamed, the pup still in his arms.

His father stepped towards him and the boy, wary, almost fled, but instead he stood his ground.

The father held out his hands as though to calm a startled animal. 'Mate, come on.'

The boy did not move.

His father said, 'Come closer.'

'You won't get angry?'

'I've calmed down, mate. Bloody hell.' Another rub of the back of his head. 'I just lost my temper, alright? Blokes do that.'

The boy did not approach but when his father took another step towards him he did not back away. His father kept coming until he was beside the boy, and then he reached out a hand to stroke the puppy. He said to the boy, 'We're going to build ourselves a new home.'

'We're not going home?'

'I told you, mate,' his father said and looked down. 'It's gone. I sold it. All the furniture, the rest of our clothes –' a breath '– your mother's things. All of it.'

Now his father had said it again he knew his feelings were no longer dormant, that his mother's death had not rendered him permanently numb, because now he felt sick, like throwing up. Somebody else was walking around in their home, using their things. Wearing his mother's clothes. Asleep in the bed where she'd died. The life he had lived up until this point, he realised now, was truly gone, more of it than he'd imagined, stolen by a stranger. Some other kid wearing his things, being friends with his friends.

All that remained for him, his entire world, was this: this dangerous man and this dog. This wet, dirty landscape. He swiped at his eyes. 'But why?' he said, a crack in his voice.

His father looked away.

The boy released Albert and the puppy, oblivious to the boy's despair, trotted over to the car and sniffed the tyre.

'Because, alright?' his father said. He sighed. 'Because I didn't want to live there anymore. And I thought we'd do this. This . . .' he said, and waved his arms about. 'This adventure. You and me, together.'

The boy walked to the car and stood beside it and watched the puppy scamper beneath. 'Who's Gus?' he said finally.

'A mongrel. A mate,' his father said. He looked down and back up and maybe there was a softness in his eyes. 'Come here.' He held out an arm.

'Why?'

'Just come here, mate,' his father said. His crippled hand outstretched.

The boy walked forward and his father wrapped an arm around his shoulders and clapped him a few times on the arm. An awkward hug, both of them facing the car. 'He was an old mate,' his father said softly. 'Gave him a call and asked him to bring some timber up here for us. And the cement mixer. Paid him, too. But they're in the wrong spot.' The boy still held, uncomfortable. 'Our place is down there a bit.' He pointed down the road and the boy saw a clearing that at first glance appeared less muddy. 'So we, you and me, are gonna have to lug this damn wood and cement down the road by hand.'

The boy was released. He went back to the Ford and scooped the puppy up. He said, turning back to his father, 'Can't we put the timber in the car?'

The father shook his head. 'We can carry the cement down in the boot but the timber won't fit inside.'

'We could tie it to the roof.'

His father sighed, sucked his cheeks in. 'Yeah, maybe. It might damage the paint, but yeah. It'll be a bloody pain otherwise.'

He tousled the boy's hair. The boy shrugged off his father's hand and stepped aside and said, 'You can't do that.'

'What?'

'Lose your temper like that and act like it didn't happen.'

His father looked as though he might say something in his defence but instead he stopped and said, 'Alright.' The weight of this agreement seemed to strike him, but the boy remained unhopeful.

They spent what remained of the afternoon loading the car with cement bags and driving them down the road to their actual home. The bags were heavy and the boy struggled with them mightily until he learned to drag them backwards and use his heels as leverage. In a possible act of atonement, his father helped him lift and did most of the work himself, not mentioning the boy's lack of strength.

The pile of timber was substantial and the boy realised, as he gazed upon it with the sun heading down over the trees, just how long it would take them to rectify Gus's mistake. He felt an echo of anger similar to his father's and shook his head in an effort to disperse it.

The boy watched his father as he loaded wood onto the top of the car. His father turned and said, 'Walk down, mate,' and nodded his head. The boy picked up Albert and his box and the bag of pellets the lady had given them and walked to their new home. There he fed Albert some of the pellets, opening and shutting his fist on them as Albert dashed in and sat on his haunches and growled. The boy was used to the dog's sharp teeth now and refused to strike him, even when he bit too hard. Then the boy sat down near the cement and turned and regarded his father from a distance.

It was clear to him from his father's movements that the man loathed his crippled hand. It had no power of its own and when his father had to manage a heavy load he would use his left hand to grip and his right hand would dangle strangely beneath, his forearm taking the brunt. Sometimes it would seem his father forgot he had fewer digits and the poor hand, the thumb and middle finger, the stump of the forefinger, would struggle to grasp until his father remembered and changed hands. The boy had never known his father without this injury. He carried the weight of it to himself as though it were an indictment on his character and his son wanted to tell him to relax, for goodness' sake, nobody was watching, but knew that if he did he would hurt his father's sense of himself and the insecurity wrapped up in that hand would only further tighten its hold.

The father got into the car and, while securing the wood on the roof with his poor hand out the window, started it, put it in gear and rolled towards the boy. The wood swerved beneath the father's useless grip. The car slowly drew to a stop by the boy and his father climbed out and the two of them lifted the planks of wood off the car roof and settled them in a new pile, next to the cement.

The boy stood and surveyed their work and felt deep pride. Wiping his brow he said, 'Where are we sleeping?'

'In the car,' his father said. He was breathing hard and held his poor hand with his other, massaging between the knuckles.

The sun, almost down behind the trees, was losing its bright hold on the grey clouds above them.

'Where's the dog?'

The boy pointed at the box at the side of the road.

'I wouldn't leave him out like that, mate,' his father said. 'He's liable to run off. Puppies can jump, yeah? There's no lid on that thing. You been checking on him?'

The boy had not thought of this and grew afraid and ran to the box. Albert was still inside, asleep. 'He's fine,' he said. 'He's sleeping.'

'Good. Now. You want some dinner?'

They opened the back door of the car. Inside, milk crates full of supplies were wedged between the front and back seats. The boy had not noticed them the length of their drive and as the crates were unpacked from the car he wondered what other secrets his father had hidden from him. There were cans of baked beans and spaghetti and glass jars of Vegemite. There was one loaf of bread and his father said as he regarded it, 'We better eat this now, before it goes bad.'

'Where's the nearest store?'

His father threw a can of baked beans in the air and stretched out his weaker hand to catch it. He missed, and it rolled beneath the car. He dropped to his belly and reached for it under the chassis, cursing. As he got to his feet and dusted off the can, he said, 'Far enough away that I don't want to drive there unless I have to.'

His father found matches and newspaper at the bottom of a crate and, in the now almost perfect black, the two went hunting in the bushland for twigs and dry leaves to start a fire. Most of the stuff he found was wet or at the very least damp.

'It's no good, mate,' his father said after a while, and spat. His hand rested on the hood of the car.

'We can just eat the beans,' the boy said.

'I don't want to have to pay for bloody firewood.'

'There'll be more in the day.'

His father bit his lip and nodded. He bent down and rummaged through a milk crate and found a Stanley knife. He jabbed the knife blade into the lid of baked beans, stabbing it repeatedly around the rim until the can was opened. It reminded the boy of gutting an animal.

'Come grab some bread,' his father said.

They dipped their bread into the mushy cold beans like biscuits into tea. They ate in silence, the soggy bread unpleasant, but the boy did not comment.

When they'd finished eating, they changed into their pyjamas. It was difficult to find the button holes in the dark.

His father hauled the food crates out of the car and stowed them in the boot, then lined the front and back seats with sheets. No pillows. His father scrunched up jackets on which they were to rest their heads. Then he lay down across the back seat and the boy across the front, Albert in his box near the brake pedal. The boy looked over and saw his father's legs jutted up against the car window. As he watched, his father rolled onto his side and curled his legs up. The dirt on the boy's skin made him doubt he would be able to find comfort, despite his father's earnest attempt at bed-making. He thought of his old home, and struggled not to resent his father.

FIVE

1955

The boy walked faster, anxious to get home. School had let out only minutes before. With his quickened step he'd halved his normal time, he was sure. His bag whumped against his lower back as he walked. He hiked the straps up with his thumbs, so it would sit a bit nicer. He rounded the corner to his home, the asphalt beside him stopping abruptly, turning into gravel. The cement footpath ended too. He didn't mind. The dirt felt better beneath his shoes anyway.

As he neared their home he saw his mother's sunhat bobbing behind the kangaroo paws. She on her hands and knees, busy with the dirt. The boy could hear her soft, happy grunting.

He opened the gate. At this she turned and smiled.

'Guess who's home?' she asked.

'Dad?'

'Go and see.'

The boy looked at the doorway and did not move. 'Won't he be asleep, but?'

'That's alright. He won't mind. Go on,' she said, and waved her hand at him.

As he approached the front door she added, 'Bring him back out with you soon, though. I have a surprise for you two and we need the daylight.'

The boy nodded.

At the front door, he took off his shoes so as to not muddy the carpet. The snoring from his parents' bedroom distant and muffled. He placed his bag down carefully near the vestibule and took a few steps, then stopped and looked back at his mother, still outside, still gardening. He had to catch his breath.

He opened the bedroom door. His father draped in sheets, one arm dangling from the bed, his lips pursed up inside his beard, probably drooling. As the boy watched he hefted in a breath; it sounded like a lawnmower turning over. The boy stepped forward and regarded the man. It had been so long since he had seen him. His face seemed different. More tanned and heavier.

'Dad?' the boy said, his voice barely above a whisper.

The man in the bed didn't move. He snored in again and coughed a bit, then opened his eyes and rolled over onto his back.

'Dad?'

'Sam?' his father said. He sat up, tried to compose a smile, yawned instead. 'Sorry, mate. Let me look at you. You alright?'

'You're home?' the boy asked.

'Yeah. Hopefully for a bit this time, eh?' the man said. He was shirtless and the dark hair matting his chest made his tan seem darker. The boy looked at the stark white of his own arms in comparison. 'You're getting big, mate.'

'Yeah?'

'You playing footy?'

The boy had stopped playing half a year ago. He had always been too anxious about not getting the ball, and more anxious about what he would do were he to get it. He hadn't told his father.

'Not really.'

'What do you mean, not really? You're big enough for it.'

The boy looked at his feet and then at the lamp beside the bed.

His father leaned forward and said, 'Never mind, mate. Your mother tell you she has a surprise for us?'

The boy nodded. 'Yeah.'

'You doing alright at school?'

The boy brightened. 'I've been doing real good.'

'Yeah?'

'Yeah. I've been doing good at spelling. You have to get up in front of the class and the teacher says a word and you have to spell it the fastest. And I'm really fast.'

His father laughed and sat up so he could scuff the boy's hair. The boy felt warmed by the touch, proud of himself for having impressed his father.

'Let's go outside, mate. See what craziness your mother has planned.'

His father groaned up from the bed. From the floor he scooped up an old blue singlet with holes in it. As the two of them walked to the front door he pulled it on.

The boy's mother was still busy in the garden but she stopped when she heard the front door swing open.

'You two ready?'

'What've you got for us?' his father asked.

The boy stood in front of his father, his head up to the man's belly. He felt both powerful and capable with his father at his back.

His mother smiled. She had both hands on her hips. 'Just you wait.'

They drove. He sat in the back seat and listened to his mother and father talk. There was an aimlessness to their conversation he didn't understand. His mother would bring up subjects and his father would nod and grunt and sometimes ask simple questions, but he never really responded, not really. Then, when there was a silence, his father would begin to speak about his own world, Tangalooma, about how well he was doing. The boy heard the word promotion and asked, 'Does promotion mean you'll be away more?'

His father didn't turn, but said, 'No, mate. It means we'll make more money. And it means I'm good at my job, which is important.'

His mother added, 'It means he'll be the boss of a team of flensers. You know the principal at school? How he's in charge of all the other teachers?'

The boy nodded and said, 'Promotion. Does it have an *s* and a *h* in it?'

His father laughed. 'Bright kid, this one, isn't he love?'

His mother nodded and laughed as well. In their laughter acceptance and validation. When he had played footy the other fathers had lined the sides of the field and shouted encouragement or abuse towards their own sons. That he had received neither had left him aimless. Now, with this deep acceptance, he knew he could do no wrong.

'Just up here,' his mother said, indicating.

The father slowed the car to a stop by the side of the road. Next to them, beyond a barbed-wire fence, was a small hill.

'What're we stopping here for, Liz?' his father asked.

'Pop the boot.'

'Why?'

His mother was already climbing out. 'Just pop the boot.'

They climbed out, his father's face a mixture of anxiety and amusement.

In the boot, the boy saw two large objects draped in a blanket.

'What're those?' he asked.

'Pull the blanket off.'

'What're you up to, Liz?'

The boy leaned in and pulled the blanket off. Beneath were two steel barrels lying on their sides, the remains of blue paint flaking from both.

'What're you up to?' his father repeated. 'What are those for?'

'Right,' his mother said. 'Help me with them.'

'What're we doing?'

'Just help me get 'em out.'

They did so, his father hefting the main weight of them. He stood them next to the car and arched his back.

'So,' his mother said, 'we're going to put these over the fence and then you two are going to roll down this hill in 'em.'

'We're going to do what?' his father said, and laughed.

'Shut up,' his mother said, smiling. 'My dad did this with me when I was little. So now you're each going to climb in one of these and roll down the hill here.'

'Why in God's name would we do that?' his father asked.

His mother looked down at the boy then, and met his eyes. Without turning to the boy's father, she said to him, 'Sam misses you when you're away and I want you two to have something together.'

'We'll have bloody broken necks together,' his father said.

'Come off it,' she said, turning finally. 'It's a short hill.'

He looked up at his father, the underside of his beard. He felt braver than he ever remembered being. 'It'll be fun,' he said. 'Come on, Dad.'

Together the three of them lifted the barrels over the barbed wire. Then his father jumped over awkwardly, his fingers resting atop a wooden post. He levered open the barbed wire with his hands and feet so that the boy's mother could climb through. He let them go, though, before the boy could follow suit. The boy stood on the wrong side of the fence and looked at his father, feeling rejected.

'You climb over, mate. You're not a bloody girl.'

He looked at his mother, who only smiled and nodded at him. 'Go on, Sam. You can do it.'

The boy wobbled over the barbed wire, afraid he'd fall at the top. He managed to land clumsily on the grass, his elbow slapping into earth. He hurried after his parents, who had both walked on, rolling the barrels beside them.

They came to the top of the hill. From here the descent seemed to the boy quite steep. Impulsively, he latched onto his father's arm.

His father said, with raised eyebrows, 'You want us to roll down that?'

His mother laughed. 'It's a bit higher than I'd thought it was.'

'You're kidding.'

'It'll be right.'

His father bent down then and regarded his son. 'What do you reckon, mate?'

Buoyed by the new courage his family had instilled in him, he said, 'It'll be good.'

His father sighed, eyed the barrels. 'Right. Alright.'

His mother had in her hand a screwdriver, he saw now. She levered off the lids of the barrels with it, like they were giant tins of paint. They bounced onto the wet grass.

'Are we going down together?'

His mother nodded. 'Yeah. You'll be fine.'

They pushed the barrels onto their sides and climbed in. The boy fit comfortably but his father's upper body could not be squished in, despite his mother's boots on his shoulders and his swearing. He waved her off eventually. There they were, the father and son, on top of the hill, enshrouded by metal.

His father looked at him. 'Just make sure you stay pressed into the sides.'

'You won't hit your face?'

His father smiled. 'I'll see you at the bottom.'

'You ready?' his mother asked, her voice muffled through the metal.

His father nodded. The boy copied him. He felt the urge to scurry from the drum but then they were rolling. He wedged his body against the metal and felt the earth beneath him fall and rise and all he had known washed away in the chaos of it. He just held on and prayed for relief. No way of seeing what was to come. He felt the drum hit something hard, maybe a rock. It bounced and he wedged his elbows and wrists into the steel until he felt he was a part of it.

Soon the barrel slowed, then stopped. He crawled from its confines quickly, ears throbbing, head wobbly. He got to his feet then went down again, slopping into something wet, probably a cow pat. The world still spinning.

The other drum was nearby and from it dangled his father's body. The boy thought his father was probably dead, the way his form slumped against the earth, but, as his hearing returned, he realised his father was laughing. It was unstoppable, this laughter. The man was pushing against the barrel and laughing. 'Mate,' he said, 'give your old man a hand here.'

The boy wobbled over and fell again.

'Go easy, mate. You alright?'

Nodding, the boy found his way over. As he knelt down by his father he saw the man's face was coated in muck. 'What happened?'

His father laughed, brown dribbling over his lips. He spat. 'Soon as we started I went right over bloody cow crap. Landed face first in it.' He laughed again and spat once more. It hit the earth murky. 'Tastes like I used my face to wipe my arse.'

The boy started laughing too. Their two voices, young and old, father and son, each an echo of the other.

His mother, coming down the hill, yelling something. The boy tried to pry his father from the barrel, a hand beneath each armpit. An almighty struggle. Soon his mother's hands joined his own and they managed it together. The family then sitting on the ground, laughing. His mother put her hand on his back. The boy would always remember how it made him feel.

SIX

1961

The boy woke aching. The back door of the car was wide open and his father already absent. A cold breeze had raised goosebumps on his arms. He pulled the blanket higher, tighter around himself.

'You awake in there yet or what?' came his father's voice from outside.

'Yeah,' the boy said.

'Well come on out then.'

The boy struggled from the front, almost collapsing onto the dirt and mud. The surrounds were mostly wet with dew, the sun barely over the horizon.

'What time is it?' the boy asked. He blinked his eyes, trying to rid them of their weariness.

'I have to get going, mate. I left you some beans in the fire there.'

The boy looked, saw the smouldering can. His father already dressed and jumpy.

'You got the fire started?'

His father's smile bespoke deep pride. 'Sure did. Got up early to get it going for you.'

The boy blinked his sleep away. 'Get going where?'

His father looked back up the trail. 'There's something I need to do, that's all.'

'You're just leaving me here?'

'I won't be long, mate.'

'Can't I come with you?' the boy asked.

'I need the room in the car, mate.'

'What for?'

'Look,' his father said, and bent over. His ruined hand gripped the boy's shoulder. 'I won't be long, alright? I'll be back before lunch.'

He started for the car.

The boy realised he hadn't checked on Albert yet and hurried over.

The puppy was asleep in its box, one paw up near its eyes. As the boy shook the cardboard Albert was instantly awake and licking at his fingertips. He took the box from the car and put it beside the fire.

As his father got into the car, the boy's fear increased. 'You'll be back?'

'Of course I'll be back,' his father said. He looked out at his son still in his pyjamas. 'Your clothes are over there.' He nodded towards a tree. The boy saw his suitcase beneath it. 'You'll be right, won't you? You're big enough.'

The boy had no answer for this. His father didn't seem to understand the boy needed comfort, assurance, and pleading only seemed to irritate him further. The boy felt anger, deep in his stomach, at the realisation that he had no say.

He said, 'I guess.'

'Alright then,' his father said. He turned the key and fired up the engine. 'That's my boy.'

The car reversed. His granddad's implication from the previous day – that his father was not fit to be a parent – made his fists clench in fear. This man might not return. This might be all there was. It took all the courage the boy could muster for him to remain still as the car, and his father, moved off, leaving him behind in this strange place.

He sat by the fire and stuck a stick inside it, prying at the ash beneath, feeling his hands warm. Albert still in his box with his paws beneath his chin. The boy petted him absently and thought of his mother. He said, 'Sorry,' to her, and didn't know why he was.

Her death had not been easy on her. She had been confined to bed, always shaking with cold beneath the covers despite the humidity. At first he'd talked to her as though everything was normal; about friends, school, small things that hardly mattered. He looked at the puppy now and wanted to show her his dog. He imagined lifting the box to show her more clearly as she sat up there in heaven, and chided himself for being so foolish. She'd often coughed while she listened, and when she did she'd hold a small white handkerchief to her mouth. This had interrupted him sometimes mid-sentence as her body had sucked upwards and her back had arched and her hand had reached to her mouth and she had barked and barked. It had been difficult to not feel slighted. When she'd finished and turned away from him it was awful to try to work out if he should continue speaking or stop. Stopping was easier, so normally he'd just watched in silence as she drew ragged breaths, her body swelling up and down beneath the blankets like waves.

Towards the end he no longer pretended things were normal. He'd sit in the chair beside her bed without talking. In the last few days she'd forgotten who he was. He'd still gripped her hand. Her skin had caught on his fingertips.

His father was with her when she died. The boy was outside on the verandah trying to read, but really he was watching the tyre swing his father had hung from a tree years before sway in the slight breeze. There was no telling how long his father had sat by her side and watched her motionless body. Or what her final words had been. Had they been for him? No telling whether or not his father had kissed her goodbye, said something. If he had cried at all, the tears were gone by the time he walked outside and told the boy his mother had passed and that he'd better come in and say farewell. Maybe he hadn't cried but had simply sat, watching, gripping her hand with his half-imaginary one.

And this was clearly his father's way. To hold things back and get on with it and that was all. The boy knew he wasn't the same as his father and grew afraid that his father would draw from him this part of his mother's character, this softness. He determined then, with growing resentment, that there was no way in hell he'd let him. No way in hell.

When his father returned the boy was playing with Albert. He made a choice not to look at the car as it slowed and stopped. He heard the car door open and his father's footsteps. The sound of the rear door being opened made him turn.

'Come give us a hand, mate,' his father said. He was bent over inside the car, having a hard time retrieving something. The boy didn't want to heed his father's instruction but found himself curious enough that he came closer anyway.

His father grunted and heaved and from the car he yanked one of the old oil barrels. He stood it next to the car with his bad hand resting on it and looked proud of himself.

The boy said, 'You went home?'

The father seemed affronted by this, as though he had not expected the question. 'I just went to get the barrels, yeah.'

'You went back to our house?' the boy asked. When his father didn't reply he added, 'Without me?'

'I needed the room in the car for the barrels.'

The boy shook his head and almost laughed. There were tears in his eyes as he said, 'You should've taken me. You should've let me say goodbye to it.'

His father said quickly, 'Mate, it's just a bloody house, isn't it? Your mum's dead. She's not there anymore.' His father rubbed the back of his neck, his other hand still resting on the barrel. The boy saw in him deep regret and felt only his own brewing anger in response.

The father soon looked up at his son and said, 'I didn't think, alright? I didn't think you'd care about it. It's just a bloody house anyway.' He turned back to the car, shuffled the still-embedded barrel. He added, almost to himself, 'Thought these'd be useful for storing water. The new owners let me have 'em.' He tugged at it, then stopped. 'Can you get around the other side and shove it through?'

The boy hesitated, still angry, still upset. Before him now a decision. He would either have to relinquish all he felt and buckle under his father's rule, or stand up for himself and make everything harder.

The barrel beside him, in all its rusted blue, was a symbol for him of a better time, when his family had been whole. He remembered his mother's hand on the small of his back. So, wiping a hand over his eyes, without further word he rounded the car and helped his father dislodge the second steel drum. They rolled them beneath a tree and stood them upright. The sun high above them diminished by the canopy of leaves overhead. The boy wanted to ask if there was anything else they might proceed with in the making of their new home, but he didn't. Instead he played with the fire, keeping it going with fresh twigs and brush he found nearby. This was his task for the remainder of the day. He didn't watch what task his father took upon himself.

At night, after they'd eaten, they again scrunched themselves into the car to sleep. The boy found it strangely comfortable the second night. The box beside him, the puppy within. He dangled his hand over the cardboard lip and occasionally felt the puppy's tongue. The boy thought about his mother and the way she had with animals. This started him thinking about the life he had spent with her and so he asked quietly, as his father shifted again, the leather groaning as he moved, 'When do you have to go back to work?'

'Why?'

'Because.'

A sigh. 'June fifth. Ship out on the Monday. So I guess I gotta leave here the day before. Or early that morning. Why?'

'So that's about a month away?'

'Yes.'

'What do you normally do, to leave?'

'You know what I normally do.'

'It changes. Sometimes you go the night before and sometimes you go in the morning. What are you going to do this time?'

'I don't know yet, mate. Does it matter?'

Silence. The boy breathed and flicked his fingers against the cardboard box. Albert's head showed, tongue lolling, grey in the dark. The boy shoved the puppy's head back into the box. He said, 'What's going to happen to me?'

'Well you can't stay here.'

'I know. I gotta go to school.'

His father sighed and drew in a breath. 'You might not go back right away, mate. Year's half over anyway. And I was thinking –' his father coughed once, muffled by his hand '– it might be time I take you with me. You're old enough to learn what I do. You could make some extra coin for us, help us build the house. Eventually, anyway. You'd start off just shadowing me a bit, so there'd be no actual pay, but it'd set you up for later, which is important. Good to have options. What do you say to that, hey? Take after your old man?' The boy could tell, without looking, that his father was grinning. 'I gotta ask Melsom, of course. But it will be good for you. Get you used to working, being one of the blokes, you know?'

The boy was immediately struck with the fear of it. The thought of whaling, of flensing, of all his father had described to him. In this almost perfect black of the bush the boy sat up and regarded his father. Hard to make out his expression and hard to tell if he even noticed the boy. He was looking at the roof of the car with his arms behind his head. In his rushed voice had been a strange sadness, as though he had risked rejection. So the boy, despite his misgivings, murmured a half-hearted assent and laid back down, breathing terror.

The father seemed to take this for enthusiasm and added, 'You could end up liking it, you know? I know you don't like hurting animals, but they're already dead by the time they get to us. And, you know, there's not much to it. Good, simple work. Never have to go back to school at all, if you don't want.'

The two were silent after that and soon the boy heard his father's snoring. He pictured himself atop a whale carcass, slipping on the blubber and the blood. Pictured himself with a knife, violently stabbing the way his father had stabbed at the can of beans, and blood gushing from the wound he caused, covering him and the knife. And the smell. It had travelled back with his father at the end of every season embedded in his clothing. Despite weeks and weeks of bathing and heavy soaping, the stink would remain, and his mother, the boy remembered, had complained loudly and often.

One year she'd stormed out from the laundry, where she'd been cleaning his clothes, and onto the verandah. The father had been sitting drinking a beer and the boy had been reading and both had been silent, as was their custom. She had thrown the clothes at him and he, laughing, had chased her inside. She had squealed. The boy followed and had watched as the two of them collapsed onto the couch and the boy thought he was looking at the truest form of love. His father ruined this by forcing his mother to smell the clothes, wadding them up beneath her nose. She had resisted, playfully at first but then more forcefully, and screamed and pushed at him until he released her. He had fallen back, stunned, and she had stormed from the room, sobbing. His father noticed him staring. Shrugged and said, 'Women, mate.'

These memories, of course, made the boy miss his mother, compounded by the barrels sitting under a tree outside their car. As he tried to sleep, matching his father's breathing pattern, he forced himself to keep thinking of her and all the ways she had offered him goodness and life.

The last remnants of what he'd had with her – their home, his school – had been taken from him now. He'd clung to some hope that he'd return one day. Now he knew better. He cried silently, draped over the front seat with the puppy licking his palm, mourning this new loss.

In the dark of night, the boy was woken by the sound of the puppy crying. The boy rolled over to comfort the dog, but the puppy would not be subdued with pats or soft cooing. So the boy, as quietly as he could manage, opened the car door and clambered out with the dog. Leaving the door ajar, he carried the pup away from his father, still sleeping noisily on the rear seat. No telling what his father might do were he to be startled from his slumber.

He put Albert down his pyjama shirt and let the dog scratch at his unprotected belly. The puppy's high-pitched whining carried to the trees. The moon was full and silent and there were few bats flying now and the trees shook only slightly in the breeze. The ocean sound was full and rich and more present once Albert ceased his noise. The gentle sound of the waves was somehow warm, steady as a heartbeat. The puppy soon fell asleep and the boy debated whether to take him back to the car or instead remain awake until the sun came up. He wondered what the time might be and looked at the moon, but couldn't tell.

He stood a while and regarded the moon, then decided to try his luck. He slowly eased the car door open and climbed in and lay down across the seat. Starting to sweat. The boy unbuttoned his pyjama shirt to release the sleeping puppy and brought him up to cradle him in the crook of his arm. Albert didn't stir. Nor did the father. The boy was pleased he had been so brave. His mother would have been proud. He shut his eyes and quickly fell asleep.

SEVEN

They woke, sweaty and baked in sun. His father groaned and the boy could see his feet jab against the window and his knees straighten. His head popped over the seat and he looked down at his son with a grim expression.

'You sleep all night with that puppy?' he asked.

The boy rubbed sleep from his eyes. 'Yes.' He looked down at the sleeping mutt, so peaceful.

'You know, you mollycoddle him and he won't ever sleep on his own.'

'What?'

'He has to learn to go to sleep by himself,' his father said. He reached down and scratched the dog behind the ears.

The boy almost snatched the dog away before his father's hand could touch it. 'If you answer his cries at night, he'll learn that's how he gets attention. And for the rest of our lives he'll be whining at night to get into bed next to you. It might be cute one night, but you'll soon hate it, believe me. We did the same thing to you. You would cry at night. We had to leave you in your room so you learned to go to sleep by yourself. Your mother hated it, but it was good for you.'

The boy looked at the pup and imagined a baby's face there and wondered what he would do if his own son cried. The rust-coloured fur of the puppy was dull and dusty and the tip of its nose was somehow always moist. He scratched behind Albert's ears.

'I like having him here,' the boy said.

'Yeah, well, he's not going to be able to do what we need him to do if he's crying for you every night, is he?'

'What do we need him to do?'

His father opened the car door without answering and more sunlight streamed in, low over the horizon of swishing leaves. The boy, holding the dog, opened his door and let Albert down. The pup shook himself and scampered off. The boy gave chase and quickly caught him up in his arms and put him safely back in the box in the car. He lowered a window and shut the door, the puppy already whining.

They ate more of the bread, butter and Vegemite. His father spread the tar-like paste too thick but the boy pretended to enjoy it. He got up from his milk-crate seat and offered some to Albert through the window.

The father eventually stood and opened the rear car door and got in, sat with his legs swinging out the side. The puppy's crying was silenced with a stern 'no'.

'What are we doing today?' the boy asked from his seat on the milk crate.

'Well,' his father said, and his legs stopped, 'we gotta shift the rest of the wood, I guess. And the mixer.'

They changed into clothes that still smelled like sweat. As he put his shirt on, the boy wondered how they might wash their dirty clothes in this, their new home. He stuffed his pyjamas back into his suitcase and then walked into the forest and urinated against a tree, the sound of the ocean duller in the light of day.

Moving the wood took until past midday. Albert cried, but the boy had no leash for him and no way to keep an eye on him were he to let the pup roam free, so he stayed confined within the box next to the pile of cement bags. When they were done the boy stood back to survey the pile of timber and found there was less of it than he'd expected. Nowhere near enough to build an entire house. He told his father so as the man approached and dangled a bottled orange juice over the boy's shoulder. The boy opened it and drank the warm liquid.

'We're not building the house straight away, mate,' his father said. 'I don't even have plans. We're just going to build a temporary shelter for the two of us. Just for now. Then, after the whaling season, we'll start the house. You remember Phil? He's got plans. We'll look at them to get an idea for what we'll need to buy, including the wood. Does that make sense?'

The boy thought for a moment. Then he asked, 'Where are we going to go to the toilet?'

'You mean, where are we going to take a shit?'

The boy blanched but said nothing.

'There's no women around, mate,' his father said, laughing. 'We can talk like men out here.'

The boy nodded, but was secretly frightened by this idea.

'I don't know,' his father continued. 'In the bush. Just make sure you walk far away and bloody bury it when you're done.'

'But we'll get a toilet eventually?'

'Yeah. We'll get plumbing.'

A pause. The boy said, 'Why are we doing this?'

His father finished a sip. 'Why?' The boy nodded and his father sighed, then laughed, an angry snort. 'I don't know. Your mother always wanted to live out bush. I couldn't stand being in that house anymore with all her things. And that hospital smell of it all. Just a fresh start. I don't know.'

The boy swigged the last of the orange juice and his father did likewise, then clenched the bottle with his poor hand. 'Come on. Let's get the cement mixer and the barrow.'

They did so. Heading down the road, the small plastic wheels on the mixer almost cavorted off. Albert the puppy sat inside and looked as though he was enjoying the adventure, his tongue hanging out. The boy struggled with the last of the trek with the wheelbarrow. It sank in the dirt and he struggled to push it through. When he was done he fell on the ground, spreadeagled, soaking in the sky. His father with sweat-stained brow. 'Harder work out at Tangalooma,' he said. 'We better get you ready. Get you working hard.'

The boy breathed. He slowly flapped his arms, letting them brush against the dirt. They had less than a month before they'd be on Moreton Island and he was deeply afraid. He didn't want to count the exact number of days for fear their number would already be too small. So he tried, with some difficulty, to forget his troubles for that moment and instead regarded the sky with new eyes. The sound of the ocean not so far away. 'Can we go to the beach?'

'Now?'

'To swim?'

He sat up and his father was looking at the watch on his wrist and scratching his beard.

'I really wanted to start on the shelter,' he said. He looked at the pile of timber. 'It's bloody uncomfortable in that car. Want to spend as few nights in there as possible.'

'It won't take long.'

Eventually, his father nodded and smiled. The two quickly changed into their swimming clothes. Ill-fitting shorts for the boy. Now he understood his father's strange insistence that he pack them for the funeral. With the boy carrying Albert under one arm, they headed towards the sound of waves.

The beach was rough and strewn with sticks and ropy weed, like thousands of flat brown snakes, dead and frying on the sand. The sand itself was muddy and gelatinous and the boy could see small sticks jutting up beneath the water. The water, though, was bright and inviting. A perfect turquoise glinting in the sun. He let Albert loose and the puppy scampered off, but because the boy could see him he didn't bother giving chase. Instead, with hands on hips, he squinted into the water and shielded his eyes to better see through the sun's glare.

Beside him, his father was already removing his shirt and shoes. He soon dashed towards the water. Before he reached the blue he turned and gestured to the boy. In his eyes a freedom the boy had not expected. His father waded into the small waves and, without looking at the boy again, turned onto his back and swept his arms through the water, face tilted towards the sun. All thought of his situation and his son apparently absent.

The boy, still shielding his eyes, watched his father at ease. His father was not just his father. Seen from a different perspective, the boy knew he would see a simple man, a small man, a man who'd lost his wife recently, a man possibly doing his best. Long ago he'd lost his fingers. Was this pity? The boy wondered what it might feel like to have the salt water swish past the ancient nubs, whether there was any dormant memory of how they used to be.

The puppy, further up the beach, was creeping towards the water with his nose lowered. He stood motionless as the tide receded, then dashed away as it returned to lap at his paws. The boy laughed. The sound startled him.

Soon he entered the cool water. Up close it was murky and impenetrable. His feet squished into soft mud. The waves were gentler than their sound had implied.

'Good bream country,' his father said. 'And maybe flathead. Maybe out a bit further.' He motioned with his head in some direction. The boy grew afraid he might step on one of the ugly brown fish buried in the sand with its eyes glazed and its spiny ridge ready to transmit toxins. In pain for maybe days. He began to move his arms more vigorously to keep his feet from touching the bottom, trying not to let his father see he was scared.

'Too bad you didn't bring any fishing rods,' the boy said, breathing heavily.

He hadn't meant anything by this comment, but his father's face darkened and the freedom the boy had witnessed in his eyes abruptly faded. He said, 'Couldn't bloody think of everything,' and swam away. He called back, 'Like your bloody mother.'

Bewildered, the boy watched him go and then looked at the murky bottom and replanted his feet and squished the mud between his toes.

Later they sat on the beach, hugging their knees to their chests, and watched the sun go down, all thought of work forgotten. His father, seemingly having forgotten the boy's earlier words, tousled his hair.

'You see that island out there?' his father asked and pointed.

'Yeah.'

'That's Moreton Island,' his father said, and lowered his hand. He looked serene. 'That's where we're going. That's where Tangalooma is.'

The boy looked. In the oranges and pinks of the sunset it floated on the water's surface like some giant turd. He squinted. In the distance he saw some lights flicking on near the beach. Impossible to make out structures.

'You excited?' his father asked.

'I think so.'

'Yeah?'

'I'm scared I won't do good.' The boy looked down.

His father said, 'You'll be fine, mate. I'll look out for you.'

The boy nodded slowly. He stood and walked over to fetch Albert and had to race down the beach when the puppy refused to heed his call. Eventually he caught him and bundled him up. The puppy licked dried salt water from his skin as he walked back to his waiting father.

EIGHT

The next day they went into town. The boy did his best to note the direction in which they travelled, but lost his bearings when he lost the sea. In half an hour they were there. They pulled up at a petrol station and the attendant came out and looked wearily at their car and his father smiled and walked inside with his son. The two sat at a round table that reminded the boy of the one in his grandparents' kitchen. They ate bacon and egg rolls and the yolk almost dripped on his shirt but he slurped it up and smiled at his father, who did not return it. His father went to order a coffee from the petrol attendant at the counter. He turned to the boy and raised his eyebrows. The boy answered with a shake of his head.

As they were leaving the store the father saw a stack of firewood outside. The boy was at the doorway as his father returned to talk to the attendant, who told him a price. His father moved his hands as though summoning angry magic and then he took a wadded note from his pocket, threw it on the counter and stormed out. They loaded wood into a milk crate then put it into the boot of their car. The boy looked at his father as he slammed the lid. They drove the car to a side street and left Albert inside with one of the windows rolled down.

They walked along the footpath of the main street and in the eyes of the locals the boy saw recognition and judgement, as if they were all aware somehow of the father and son's strange relationship, of where they slept. The boy avoided all eye contact and stayed close to his father. They entered a general store. The boy held his arms out and was loaded up with cheap fishing rods, thin rolled-up mattresses and sleeping bags, pillows, some food. Despite their old barrels – one of which they'd brought with them in the car – the father also bought a jerry can. They paid for the items and lugged them to the car. Nearby, his father found a tap behind a pub and retrieved the barrel. He made the boy keep watch while he filled the barrel from the tap. The boy felt shifty. The water slapping into the metal loud and unrestrained. The boy wanted to leave the town as soon as they were finished. Instead they went back to the car, rolling the steel drum along the footpath, and put it inside. The boy patted Albert, who started to whine before he shut the door once more.

As they walked away again the boy said, 'Where are we going now?'

'Hardware store,' his father said.

'Can we get a leash for Albert?'

His father nodded. 'Good idea.'

In the hardware store, the boy found a leash and a metal bowl, while his father sat on his haunches and studied pieces of corrugated tin. He lifted a corner and saw the small yellow price tag and scoffed aloud. He brushed his hands together, an awkward gesture, and stood.

'What do you think of these?' He indicated the sheets of tin.

The boy looked. 'For what?'

'For the walls.'

'Won't they make a lot of noise?'

'In the wind, you mean? I don't think so. Not if we nail 'em.'

The boy thought, then said, 'You know more about this sort of thing.'

'I know I do. Doesn't mean I don't want your input.'

Soon his father decided and hefted up at least ten, maybe twenty, of the sheets and awkwardly carried them to the front counter. They wobbled and warped with each step.

The attendant watched this enterprise gruffly and then looked around his father at the boy who, realising he was still holding the leash and bowl, took them to the counter. Reminded of the dog, he pictured him roasting inside the hot car. 'Can I go check on Albert?'

'I need your help with this, mate.'

'He might be thirsty.'

His father grumbled and dismissed the boy with a wave of the hand.

Albert, when the boy reached him, seemed unaffected by the warmth of the car. The boy's arms stuck to the vinyl as he slid across the seats and he greeted the dog with a scratch behind the ears. He filled a cup he'd brought with him with water from the steel drum, which he had to angle over the seat. The dog immediately lapped it up.

His father returned not long after with his arms full and his face strained.

'I needed your bloody help with this,' he said and slammed the tin down into the car, his brow heavy with sweat.

'Sorry,' the boy mumbled.

His father put the sheets of tin and leash and bowl on the back seat, the tin bent in the middle. Then he got in, started the car, and drove them back to their new home. They didn't speak once on the drive.

NINE

They carried the new things they'd bought out of the car and heaved out the old barrel – a mighty task now that the barrel was full – and stacked it all in neat piles. The boy's father rubbed his hands together as he looked from the piles to the boy, who did his best to mimic his father's enthusiasm.

After Albert was watered and fed and tied to a tree with his new leash, his box beside him on its side a make-shift kennel, the father instructed the boy to collect some sand from the beach in the wheelbarrow. The boy looked in the direction his father pointed and saw there was no clear path. He would have to hew it himself. He pushed the wheelbarrow before him across dirty sand and roots and past overgrown trees whose branches prodded at his face, claws from another world. The wheel got caught and after some stubborn shoving the boy walked to the front and lifted the whole thing up and carried it. Cuts up his arms and across his bare legs marked his efforts. After a while he stopped and sat on the ground and wiped his brow. The beach through the trees, the mighty blue of it. Some small breeze now he was closer to the shore.

He looked at the sand on the ground beside him. It was dirtier than the sand of the beach and there were twigs and leaves and bits of bark buried in it. It was clearly no good. Still, he took the shovel from the barrow and scooped in the dirty sand, knowing as he did that it was a poor decision and stemmed only from his laziness. With the sound of the ocean behind him, he forced the wheelbarrow back along the path to the clearing, spilling much of the sand as the barrow wobbled over obstructions.

His father was measuring something when the boy emerged. Then he placed one plank across another, like a cross, and tried to hold it steady with his poor hand. He picked up a saw and held it to the place he'd marked but instead of sawing he threw the tool down in frustration and kicked at it. The look on his face would have been comical if not for the ferocity beneath it. So the boy approached the mixer quickly and, before the father could assess the quality of the sand with all its leaves and twigs, shovelled it in, added half a jerry full of water and then spun the handle until the sand was sloppy. He could sense his father's eyes on him.

He dragged a bag of cement to the mixer, tore it open and had lifted it up to tip it in when behind him his father shouted, 'Wear a damn mask, mate! That stuff is toxic.'

The boy turned to look at his father. 'Where are the masks, then?'

'In the toolbox, where do you think?'

The boy retrieved a mask and fitted it to his face, grumbling quietly to himself about his father's lack of directions.

The wooden frame his father had constructed was around the size of two cars. As the boy emptied the bag of cement, his father stood the frame up and inspected it. It wobbled even as he held it.

The cement smelled of cold moss. The boy struggled to breathe and turned his head aside. He added more water once it was all in and started the rusty cylinder spinning once more. It reminded the boy of his grandmother's cooking. The dry cement powder and dirt mud blended into one another. Flour beaten into milk.

His father was starting to struggle with his square frame. Parts were falling off and the old man was cursing and spitting. As the boy mixed, he watched his father place his frame atop the dirt and do his best to make it flat with the orange leveller. He hammered at the corners and checked again until he was satisfied. It looked flat to the boy. His father glanced over at him and said, 'Keep your eye on what you're doing, mate.'

Out of the corner of his eye he watched his father's progress. The man took another piece of timber and, without much care, sawed it into eight sections. With a small hatchet he chipped at the base of each piece until it had a pointed tip. Once finished, he drove each stake into the ground at the corners of the frame in order to secure it. The boy added more water while his father secured the stakes to the frame with nails. He swung the hammer at an awkward angle and most of the nails bent as they went in, but his father seemed happy.

He moved around the structure, putting a foot on each corner of the frame, testing its stability. It moved slightly but the stakes held and his father smiled. He walked to the car and retrieved two more bottles of warm orange juice. He offered one to his son as he inspected the churning muck within.

'How's it looking?'

'How's it supposed to look?' the boy said.

His father scratched his head. Had another sip. 'Like it is, I guess. Why's it so lumpy?'

'What?'

'It's too lumpy.' He motioned for the boy to stop spinning. He put his right hand in and ran his two and a half fingers through the muck. It dripped from his hand like curdled milk. 'It's not supposed to be like this. What sort've sand did you get?'

'Just sand.'

'Did you sift it?'

The boy said nothing. Then, 'I didn't know I was supposed to do that. You didn't tell me.'

'You should know to do that, mate.'

'How?'

'It's common bloody sense.'

'I mean, how would I sift it?'

His father stood back and folded his arms. He looked at the car. Then he grinned without humour. 'Guess I forgot. Anyway. Get better sand next time, yeah?'

The boy thought he had accomplished some small victory but underneath his father's voice was steel and bone so cold the boy did not dare meet his eyes, for fear the enraged demon had awoken once more. So instead he focused on the mixer. He turned the crank steadily and the mixture inside swirled. The sound was chunky, full of dirt. Something satisfying about the sounds and smells. An honesty. The work soothed him and soon he had forgotten the man working beside him.

When they were both satisfied with their cement mixture, they filled the wheelbarrow and then tipped it messily into one corner of the frame. His father started to spread it with a shovel, patting it down. 'Go get sand,' he said. 'Make some more.'

The boy took the wheelbarrow and wheeled it back towards the path he had worn, stopping on the way to check on Albert, still tied to the tree. He crouched down and the pup licked his fingers and did his best to climb onto the boy's lap. When the boy left again, the dog started whining.

The entire slab took five wheelbarrow loads of clean sand and the remaining day to fill. It was almost dark when the last load was tipped into the mixer. The car was parked facing them and the headlights were on, and his father was light and dark both as he moved in and out of shadow. He spooned the mixture into the corners with a trowel, then patted it down with the back of his shovel. He levelled the slab off with another length of wood slid across the top. He had to reposition his mangled hand many times before he was finished. Then he walked to the car and found his good leather shoe, one of those he'd worn to his wife's funeral, and returned. The light behind him streamed into the trees. He smoothed the cement further with the shoe's sole.

The two stood and surveyed what they had wrought, the boy's arms aching. The father smiled and rummaged in one of the milk crates for a can of beer. He opened it, then tipped his head back and chugged some down.

He held the can out to the boy. 'You want some?'

It smelled stale and sour but the boy wanted to impress his father, so he took the warm steel and swigged. It tasted bad and smelled worse up close. The boy tried to smile but failed.

The father didn't notice. He took the can back and downed the rest. 'We better get some dinner, hey?'

The boy nodded.

His father found another beer and cracked it open. 'What do you want?'

'I don't know.'

They settled on spam sandwiches and a warm bottle of Fanta each to follow the beer, and the father decided to warm the spam next to the fire they were yet to build. The headlights of the car illuminated them both while Albert, who was now curled up in his box, looked as though he had been swallowed up by shadow. They built a wobbly pyramid of kindling over scrunched-up newspaper and lit it. It caught quickly and the father grinned in the firelight, a face-wide chasm that spooked the boy.

'This is fun, right?' his father said, spreading his hands before the warmth, the ruined hand crab-like with its missing fingers. His smile invited a response but the boy refused and instead spread his own hands.

They boiled water scooped from the oil drum, resting the billy can in the embers. While they waited they spread the lukewarm spam on bread. It stuck like gum to the knife and the boy grimaced. He chewed quickly and offered some to Albert, who munched happily in the shadows.

After they'd eaten, they fetched a washcloth, towels and fresh clothes from their suitcases. Once the water in the billy had boiled the boy's father added some cold water, then he took the billy in one hand and draped a towel and his fresh clothes over his shoulder and walked off a short distance. There he stripped naked. The boy noted the way the hair on his chest was matted and how the muscles in his calves roped together. Then, embarrassed, he turned to study the fire.

His father soon returned and plonked down on the milk crate opposite the boy, still towelling dry his hair.

'I left you the billy.'

The boy stood up. 'Is the water still warm?'

'If you hurry up it will be.'

The boy picked up his own towel and walked into the darkness, starting at every noise.

The water in the billy was tepid. He stripped off quickly and began to shiver. He draped his clothes over a tree and pulled the washcloth from the billy.

When he was done, he dried himself and dressed. He returned to the fire with the billy and his dirty clothes.

His father had started brewing tea in another billy which the boy did not know they had. They could have used it to boil more water so that the boy could have had a warm wash too, if only the father had thought about it. A sad realisation: his father often forgot about him. The more he thought about it, the more his resentment deepened. He couldn't let it go, and wouldn't if he could. It made him even more nervous about going to the whaling station. What if his father forgot about him out there, on the island? He was on the verge of asking his father to place him in the care of his grandparents, when his father said, 'I'll get you a cuppa.'

Instead of telling his father that he did not like tea, he decided instead to give the old man a break.

His father poured the brown liquid into a cup, added a dash of milk, then brought the cup of tea around the fire and put it in the boy's hands. It tasted like a tree. He looked up at the stars and his father clapped him on the shoulder and returned to his seat and took a sip from his own cup. Then he said, 'Good work today.'

The boy said, 'Thanks.'

'It must have been hard going through the bush with that barrow.'

'Yeah.'

'Not much of a path?'

'Not really.'

A pause as they both sipped at their tea. The fire between them danced around the remains of some paper his father had screwed up and put in.

'How you doing?' his father said.

'With what?'

'With anything. I don't know.'

'Alright.'

'Yeah?'

'Yeah.'

'I mean with your mum dying,' his father said. 'I mean, how are you?'

'I'm alright.'

'You don't want to talk about it?'

'Not really,' the boy said. 'Not now.'

His father smiled. 'You sound like me.' He shifted forward and then stood quickly. He put down his cup and brushed his hands on his pants and said, 'I almost forgot!'

'What?'

'I've been wanting to teach you this.' He moved around the fire to where the boy sat. 'Stand up.'

'Why?'

'Just stand.'

The boy stood and then his father extended his good hand and smiled at the boy. 'Shake it.'

The boy shook his father's calloused hand. 'Why?'

'I gotta teach you to shake a man's hand right. I saw the grip you gave the minister and your uncles at the funeral. See this?' He raised their hands coupled together skywards and wobbled the boy's arm. It flopped about. 'You got no strength behind it. You gotta really grip the other bloke's fingers.' His father's grip tightened. The boy clenched his fingers and his father grimaced then released his hand. He said, 'Go easy.'

'Like that?'

'No. Don't do that. You gotta be firm without shouting about it. A bloke who knows who he is won't crush the other bloke's hand 'cause he doesn't have to. He's just firm about it. Do it again.'

They clasped hands once more and the boy felt his father's assured grip. They shook up and down three times and released. 'Like that,' the father said.

'Why?'

'You can tell a lot about a man by his handshake. We don't want you shaking hands looking weak. You gotta present a strong front for other blokes, mate, or they'll walk all over you.'

It seemed to be this way with his father; in the midst of a lesson the boy would feel both forgotten and loved all at once. As though his father's aim was off. His father teaching him to shake hands wasn't what the boy really needed. He needed a home, a bed. It was the same with the barrels.

The boy had not cared about the water his father had been so intent on providing, but about seeing his old home, his mother's old bed. His father had provided for him, sure, but didn't really seem to listen. Like he cared about some version of the boy that wasn't real. The boy his father hoped he was.

They left Albert outside the car when they went to sleep. Through the night the boy woke several times to hear the pup whimpering outside and wanted desperately to comfort him. He found himself reluctant to sleep while Albert was in distress. If he must endure, he thought, then so must I.

TEN

The next morning, after they'd eaten their eggs and bread and rinsed their plates with water, the boy's father stood and brushed his legs and knees free of crumbs. He said, 'Now, I want to show you why we got the dog.'

'I thought we just got him as a pet.'

'No, mate,' his father said. 'He has a job.'

'What do you mean?'

'Come here.'

They trudged back up the road they'd driven in on, Albert cradled in the boy's arms like a newborn. When they finally reached the top of the hill, they could see spread before them their home and the mud that surrounded it. His father grabbed the puppy roughly and chucked him on the ground. Albert pranced away happily and then stopped and scratched at his ears.

'What I want you to do every morning from now on is train the dog to watch out for intruders,' his father said. He crouched beside the pup. 'If we're both going out to Tanga-looma, it means leaving all our stuff here. Everything that won't fit in the car. And it's not like at home. Anybody could take whatever they wanted. Any old mongrel who happened along. So we need this guy –' he patted the dog '– to guard our stuff.'

'We don't have that much stuff.'

'We will, though, mate. We gotta think into the future a bit. Be prepared.'

The boy nodded but doubted his father was telling him all of it. His father wouldn't even look at Albert. He said, 'What do I do?'

'You gotta start with basic stuff, like *sit* and *stay*. Then you gotta get him to bark when he sees other people. And jump them a bit. Should startle any bloke come to rob us.'

The boy looked at his small puppy. In that moment the boy felt nothing for his father, whose aim it was to destroy this beautiful thing which had been such a comfort. The boy adored the gentle nature of the pup; he didn't want a vicious brute. He looked at his father patting the dog, plainly delighted with his plan. All the pieces of the puzzle his father had devised were falling into place. There was no way the boy would convince him to leave the puppy be.

'We can't just leave him here when we go,' the boy said. 'Who'll feed him?'

His father stood, without responding, and walked away.

The boy watched the pup frolic. He said, 'Sit,' in the most commanding voice he could muster.

The pup paid him no mind, so he bent down and forced the dog's rear into the dirt. The puppy squirmed beneath his grip but the boy was unrelenting. 'Sit. This is sit,' the boy said.

The pup just looked up with its tongue out and love in its eyes.

The boy let him go and then tried the command again. The pup stopped and looked and then kept trotting. The boy knew then that he would not follow his father's orders. He would not turn his friend into a ferocious brute. That would be the last time he tried to train the dog.

Down the slope, he watched his father take a shovel from the car and begin tapping the concrete with it, the metallic clang reaching the boy clearly. It had set well. His father's pride plain in the way he held himself, his hands on his hips. The boy crouched down and stroked Albert. From the bottom of the hill his father shouted, 'Come take a look, mate.'

'In a minute,' the boy shouted back. He pretended then to train the dog but instead played with him and soon enough his father had forgotten his request. The boy did not want to go near his father. As he played with Albert some of the rocks at his feet scurried down the slight hill and then in the distance the boy saw the oil barrels, still situated beneath their tree, and was struck with an idea.

He approached his father, Albert at his heels. 'Dad?'

'You see the concrete, mate?' his father asked. 'It's set a beaut.'

'You want to roll down the hill with me?'

His father turned and looked at the slope. His face tightened. 'In the barrels?'

The boy nodded.

'Like what your mother made us do?'

'It's not that steep.'

His father laughed. 'That's what she said. No, mate. I'm going to finish here today. One of 'em is full, anyway.'

The boy said, 'Finish what?'

'Finish pegging in these uprights.'

The boy looked at the slope, at the barrel. He knew it would only take a few minutes, but did not press the matter further. His father clearly did not want to spend his time that way.

Albert darted off into the bushes and the boy ran after him. Scooping up the pup, he looked at the barrel, then at the squirming dog.

It took him a few minutes to roll the empty barrel to the top of the hill. He put the barrel on its side, flaking rust coming away on his hands. He picked up Albert and moved him towards the opening. The puppy, maybe sensing what was to come, started to struggle. The boy had to shove him in.

'You ready?' the boy asked.

The pup showed no sign of having understood the question.

The boy pushed and the barrel was soon racing down the slope. The instant the boy heard the puppy yelping he was struck by how small the puppy was, what might happen to his body as he slammed into the rocks. The boy chased after the barrel as it hurtled down the hill, each smack into the earth a slap to his heart. The dog barking now.

The barrel rolled to a stop. Before the boy could reach it, he was already telling Albert how sorry he was.

Albert stepped blearily from the barrel's dark interior. He tottered on his feet then fell face first into some mud. The boy looked at his friend and saw his fur matted with yellow-brown vomit. The puppy didn't move from where he'd fallen. The stink of it. The boy rushed to his side and lifted him up.

His father looked up from his work. 'What're you doing?' he asked.

The boy turned with his friend in his arms and said, 'Nothing.'

'You roll that puppy down the hill in that barrel?'

The boy said nothing.

His father stepped closer. 'Did he vomit in there?'

'I'll clean him up.'

His father laughed bitterly. 'I don't care about the dog, mate. He'll be right. But clean that vomit out of the barrel, yeah? Use the soap.' There was something in his father's eyes, the way he didn't turn from the boy for a moment. Maybe remembering. But then he turned.

As his father focussed on his task the boy took the soap from the front of the car and trudged through the jungle, holding the dog to his chest. The pup seemed fine now, but the boy felt awful. He emerged onto the beach and waded into the water knee deep and plunged the puppy into the briny muck. The puppy came up kicking. The boy used the soap to wash off all the vomit, getting his fingers entwined in the fur. He scrubbed with care and made sure not to get any soap in the puppy's eyes. He kept saying he was sorry. His carelessness had hurt his friend. He resolved never to be so thoughtless again.

ELEVEN

A week later, the boy and his father sat side by side on the beach with the fishing poles between their legs, the tide licking at their toes. Albert, fully recovered from his trip down the hill, was slightly larger and more sure of the two of them now. He had taken to chasing the tide, getting his white-socked paws wet before dashing back and yipping. The boy watched the puppy while the little finger on his right hand held the line taut so he would notice the striking of a fish.

On the horizon, clouds gathered, grey and daunting. To his right sat Moreton Island. In two weeks the boy would be there. He'd been reluctantly counting the days with trepidation. He tried to avoid looking in its direction, but found himself without conscious decision risking the occasional glance, and now he dared a long one. In the middle of its mass some golden sand, but beyond that there was foliage and little more. What would he do there? The whales in his mind were big mountains of black, gleaming wet in the sun. The knife sinking into their skin, slicing slowly, methodically. He shuddered. He didn't even want to cut or scale the fish he might catch now. Hammering the knife in behind its head, like he'd seen his father do. He didn't really want to catch a fish. If he was reluctant here he was sure he'd be reluctant out there, facing that giant animal, seeing its skin tear open. He had not felt a nibble for some time though, thankfully, and found himself focussing instead on his father's mostly silent company.

His father stirred and said, 'You been training that dog?'

The boy nodded, though it was a lie.

'What can he do?'

The boy looked at the dog. 'Sit!' he called.

The pup stopped what he was doing and looked at the boy in bewilderment but did not sit. The boy said the word again, and again, sterner each time. He put down the rod and stood, and as he did the dog sat. The boy picked up his rod again. He doubted his command had had any effect, but he decided to act as if it had. He turned to his father and smiled. His father only nodded and stared back out to sea. He said, 'Good start.'

They caught no fish and returned to their shelter. They had crafted the walls of tin and ill-cut lengths of timber. The roof above, made out of the same tin as the walls, walloped with each gust of breeze. The boy winced every time, afraid it might collapse.

His father stood in the doorway as the boy sat on his bed and looked at the grey clouds, which were closer now. He held his hand to his forehead like a visor despite the lack of sun. Then he dashed outside in a seeming panic, returning with an armful of the leftover timber. He dropped it onto the concrete between their makeshift beds. From his pocket he took nails, from his belt he unhooked his hammer, and raised a piece of timber to a corner post and nailed it in. He lifted the other end and, even though it was nowhere close to horizontal, nailed that in too. Like a spider's web, this strange mess took shape. The boy watched and waited to be instructed, glancing fearfully at the roof as it whomped again. He knew it would leak, was amazed it hadn't already after the light rains they'd been experiencing.

Albert was outside, tied to his tree. The boy listened for his whimpering but didn't hear it and assumed the puppy was learning to keep quiet about its feelings.

'Give me a hand,' his father said. 'Don't just bloody sit there.'

As the boy stood up from his mattress, a bat flapped by their doorway. He knew it wasn't a vampire bat, but it frightened him all the same. When he had been frightened by a bat as a child it was his mother who had comforted him. She had returned with him to his bedroom to stare at the bat that dangled from the branch outside his window and stared at him with its sightless eyes. It had stretched its wings and swung. She had explained, whispering in his ear, her soft hands on his shoulders, that vampire bats lived only in Africa, and Australian bats were just after fruit. He remembered the trust he had placed in her words.

'Quit daydreaming, Sam,' his father said.

He looked over and saw his father was holding two pieces of timber positioned crossways between two uprights. With his crippled hand, he proffered nails and the hammer.

'You want me to nail them in?' the boy asked.

'No, mate,' his father said. 'I want to stand here just like this the rest of the night.'

The boy took the nails and hammer. Thunder rolled in the distance. The boy hammered a nail into the wood his father held. It bent and stopped sinking, despite a few more whacks. The head sloped over and made a divot in the pine.

'Pull it out,' his father said.

'How?'

'Just pull it out with the back of the hammer –' he pointed 'and get a new nail. Come on, mate. I can't hold it all day.' His father tried out a smile that seemed fake before it started.

'Let me hold it up then.'

'Just hammer the damn thing.'

The boy yanked the nail out with a mighty struggle. It squeaked against the wood as it exited. He found another nail and hammered it in. Same result. Thunder nearby. He kept hitting this bent nail and finally, near the end, it righted itself a little. His father carefully released the wood; the nail held.

They continued in this haphazard way around the whole shack. The boy unsure how it helped, if it did at all.

The rain did not come on slowly but instead hit the roof and the side of the house in a torrent. The first tropical storm they'd experienced since his mother died. It pelted against the roof like movie-bullets into cars. It flew sideways through their open door and reached the foot of his father's bed.

'Bloody hell,' his father muttered. He grabbed their clothes and rolled them up like snakes and put them under the door to stop the water seeping in.

Outside, in the storm, Albert yelped. The boy flung the door open and dashed out, almost leaping over his father. He untied the puppy and cradled him to his chest in the harsh wind. He ran back in, blinking the rain from his eyes.

His father shook his head. 'Albert can't stay in here.'

The boy shook his head, sending drops of water flying. 'Why not?'

'He's soaking wet. He'll stink. Put him back out.'

'It's raining.'

'It know it's raining, mate. I can bloody see that. The dog'll be fine. Dogs live in the wild. You ever hear of a dingo? They just sit out there in the rain and they do alright. No trees or nothing, out in the outback anyway. Albert'll be okay.'

His father expected to be heeded.

The boy looked at the puppy licking water from his forearm. 'He's too little.'

'Mate, throw the dog outside before I throw him, yeah? And I don't give a good damn if he runs away or not. You understand me?' Pointing his finger.

'He won't be alright. He isn't like you say.'

'Well then he's useless, right?' his father said. 'We got him to guard our stuff and if he's too bloody soft for rain then he's too bloody soft for all of it.'

'I don't want him to be a guard dog.'

'Well then what's he good for?' A mean look in his eye. 'What bloody good is he? We'll take him back. We don't need another useless mouth to feed.'

His father turned away from the boy. A quality to his voice that demanded acquiescence. Something final and damning. The boy surprised at how little he felt his father's condemnation. Maybe this was the saddest thing. The boy tucked the puppy into his shirt, and set to helping his father.

TWELVE

They drove to Brisbane city a few days later and the boy sat with the car window down and watched the buildings as they changed shape with each new suburb they travelled through.

His father said, 'Hate the city.'

'Why?'

He coughed. 'Too dense.'

After a moment the boy said, 'You sure he'll be alright?'

'He's got water and food. He'll be fine.'

The boy watched new houses fly by, waterfront properties elaborate and expensive. Some of them had short jetties attached to their rears with large boats moored to them. The boy wondered if the humbleness of their current home bespoke a kind of pride just as the extravagance of these houses did.

They turned left away from the river and its murky waters, then turned left again. His father seemed to know the way without consulting a map. They pulled into a tree-shaded brick driveway and parked behind a car some way down. Outside the house was a shirtless bloke leaning against the verandah rail with a stubby in his hand. He laughed as they got out of the car and yelled, 'Walter!'

His father laughed too and looked up, shielding his eyes.

The shirtless man rushed down the stairs and the two men shook hands warmly. The boy wondered why he had no memory of this man his father knew so well.

The man turned to the boy.

'This your boy all grown up?'

'This is Sam, Phil.'

'Haven't seen you since you were this big, mate,' Phil said, and put his hand to his knee. He extended a hand to the boy and they shook, the boy doing his best to remember his father's advice. The man's hands were calloused and rough, his grip too strong. Phil said to the boy's father, 'Good handshake on him,' and his father smiled.

Phil added, turning back to look the boy in his eyes, 'I hear about you all the time, mate. He won't shut up about you. Sam did this and Sam did that. You got some sort of prize at school for spelling a while back, didn't you? It was spelling, right?'

The boy nodded.

They walked up the stairs. The boy had never suspected his father bragged about him and the idea did not settle in his heart as true.

Phil said, 'Sorry to hear about your mum. Yeah.' He scratched the back of his neck. 'I don't know what to say.'

'It's alright,' his father said.

Phil looked at the boy's father and nodded and the boy knew that this would be all the sympathy the two would exchange, all either of them would need. The boy, though, was not like his father. He didn't know what he wanted, but knew those few quick words might as well have not been spoken.

Phil asked them to remove their shoes, then they stepped inside, the boy's feet immediately swallowed up in shaggy brown carpet. Plants in terracotta pots sat on the kitchen counter, so many of them that it looked like a mini jungle, and there was no space for meal preparation.

His father plonked himself down on the couch and the boy sat beside him.

'Beer?'

'Yeah, mate. God, yes.'

'Sam?' Phil said, his head already in the fridge.

The boy looked at his father, who smiled. 'Yes, please.'

His father laughed. 'Had his first a few days ago. Didn't think you liked it.' He slapped his knee.

The boy was thrown a cold XXXX from the fridge and he copied his father's mannerisms as the man leaned back and put his feet on the coffee table in front of them. His father cracked the steel can open and swigged it back. The boy followed suit, did his best to appear accustomed, but choked on the foul taste and sat upright. Some went down the wrong pipe, which made him cough.

'Go easy,' his father said, and clapped him on the back and laughed. 'No rush.'

'How've you been?' Phil asked. He situated himself opposite them on the leather armchair, a television set beside him. 'I mean, with everything.'

'Okay. I don't know.'

Phil took a sip of beer. 'How's the place?'

'It's getting there.'

'Yeah?'

'Well,' his father said, and looked at the boy. 'We haven't really started the house yet. We've just made a bit of a shelter for ourselves, which should see us through till we start building.'

'Is it a couple of twigs nailed to a tree?' Phil said, grinning. 'Is it a tarp draped over a stick?' He turned his smile on the boy. 'Tell me it's more than a bloody tarp.'

The boy said nothing, tried to smile in return, drank his beer to hide his discomfort.

His father said, 'You still got the plans?'

Phil put his beer on the coffee table, lurching upright, and said, 'Still a bloody stupid idea if you ask me.'

'I already know what you think.'

Phil laughed. He went to the kitchen and rustled through a stack of paper on the counter. 'There's no way you'll do this by yourself. It'd take you twenty years.' He came back to the lounge holding the plans.

'I'm going to try. No harm in that, is there?'

'Now, now,' Phil said. 'Don't get bloody testy. I'm just saying. How much have you spent on it already?' He took a blue singlet that was draped over the back of the chair and slipped it on, pushed the long hair that fell to his shoulders in golden curls behind his ears. A different breed this man, though he swigged his beer the same way. He added, 'Don't get that look in your eye, mate. I've seen that look. A mate should be able to talk honestly with his friend, yeah?' He took a sip of beer. 'I'm only playing, anyway. I know you're a careful bloke.'

'It's none of your business,' his father said and snatched at the paper Phil proffered.

Phil raised his hands in mock alarm and laughed and looked at the boy. 'He always like this?'

The boy said nothing and Phil sat down opposite them once more. The boy shuffled closer to his father to take a look at the plans. Indecipherable diagrams covered with numbers and arrows drawn in barely legible script. On the side of the large sheet a colour photo of the finished house. It looked like his grandparents' house. There was a small concrete base and an overhanging gutter and small, vertical windows.

'This is it?' his father asked.

'That's them.'

'It says 1946 on the front here,' his father said, holding up the diagram and pointing.

'I know.'

'Well?'

'Well what? You wanted something classic. That's Edwardian architecture.'

'I don't give a damn about that.'

'That's it then,' Phil said, throwing his hands up. 'That's all I got. Why don't you go speak to somebody who actually knows what they're on about? Why don't you speak to a real estate bloke? Don't know why you asked if you're going to grizzle about it.'

'No,' his father said, and took another look. 'These'll be fine. We'll make it work.'

'You sure, mate? You sure you don't want me to run all over the bloody country?'

'All you did was talk to your dad, didn't you?' his father said, refusing to look up from the plans.

'You know I hate him,' Phil said, and looked at the boy. 'He's a bloody mongrel.' He smiled, which seemed to belie the seriousness of his words. The man clearly enjoyed teasing, something the boy had never been comfortable with. An uneasiness, it would seem, he and his father shared.

'Thanks,' his father muttered. 'I'm sure these'll do. We'll maybe change a bit of the façade . . .' He wafted his finger over the drawing, as though shooing a fly. 'But the structure's all there.'

'You sure now?'

'Yes. Thank you,' his father said.

Phil leaned back and drank in long swallows, and the boy could tell by the way he lowered his can he had downed the whole thing. 'You ready to go back, or what?'

'Feels like we were just there,' his father said. He didn't take his eyes from the plans. He traced the lines with his good hand.

'It was six months ago. And we were only there a few months.'

'I know,' his father said. He folded the plans carefully and laid them beside him, then clapped his son on the shoulder and added, 'It just seems when I'm not there I'm not really in my life, you know? You don't know.' A sigh. 'I'm taking Sam with me this time.'

Phil met this announcement with widened eyes. 'Yeah?'

'Thought it would be good for him.'

'How old is he? How old are you, mate?'

'I'm thirteen,' the boy said.

'Thirteen? And what's he gonna do?' Phil asked, turning back to the boy's father. He stood and switched on one of the ceiling fans and the boy noticed both men had started sweating. As he sat back down he said, 'He won't be flensing, surely?'

'He'll be helping. I don't expect he'll be paid this time out but I thought it could set him up for the future.'

'You check it was okay with the Norwegians?'

'No.'

'You're not going to?'

Silence for a moment. His father's clawed hand shifted slightly closer to his leg. Then, 'If they don't want him there he can just go back home.'

'By myself?' the boy said. It had sprung from him unbidden and his voice had sounded childish in contrast to the men.

Phil laughed. 'They won't want him there.'

'They'll have him. He's a good worker,' his father said.

The boy added, 'I'll work really hard.'

His eyes were down and so he didn't see Phil's expression as Phil said softly, 'I'm sure you will, mate. Your old man tell you how to flense the whale? Separate the blubber?' The boy looked up and Phil smiled. 'You know how the shifts work?'

'He won't need to know that. He'll shadow me for a while.'

'Alright.'

A pause before his father said, 'You doing anything for work?'

Phil grinned. 'What've you done?'

'Worked at the pub. You know. Then been looking after things a bit, and Sam here,' his father said, looking down. The boy knew how his father resented working at the pub, the rhythm of normal working men boring to him, the way they'd look at him if he mentioned whaling. He took another sip of beer.

'Wanna see what I've been doing?' Phil asked. Without waiting for a response, Phil stood and, grinning maniacally, rushed into the adjacent hall. He returned quickly with an acoustic guitar, frayed around the pick guard. 'I've been gigging a bit.'

'Yeah?'

'Yeah. Mostly covers, but I slip in a few originals every so often.'

'Pay better now?'

'Pay's still garbage,' Phil said, laughing. 'But I enjoy it, you know? Better doing something you enjoy.'

His father nodded, maybe in his countenance the sense of having been chastised.

The boy pointed to the guitar and said, 'Can you play?'

'What do you think gigging means, mate?' Phil said with his large grin. Without further prompting he strummed a chord then began to sing. Something about whaling. His playing so loud and his voice so strange it was difficult to decipher the lyrics. He was a passionate singer. He launched into a chorus wherein whaling, with all its difficulties and all its blood, was a task fit for poets and men. The boy doubted he would feel the same affection for it that Phil did.

THIRTEEN

The boy began work on a raft without his father's knowledge. He found himself contemplating travelling out to sea as far as the vessel would take him to avoid going to the island with his father. He would smile, knowing this for a flight of fancy, but kept on building regardless.

Over the course of several days, he stole four pieces of timber from their worksite, waking at sunrise while his father slept and going to the beach to hammer the timber into a wooden frame which he kept a little way down the sand from where he and his father normally fished.

Late one afternoon, he lashed twigs and sticks across the top of his square frame with an old shirt cut into ribbons.

It looked too flimsy to float. The twigs and sticks were too sparse and the timber looked ill-fitted beneath. The boy stood back, almost tripping on a tussock, and surveyed what he had accomplished. He turned then to study Moreton Island. At dusk, the whaling station's lights winked on. He was curious to know why the station was built facing inland across the bay. Surely it would make more sense to face the open ocean, where the whales migrated.

His father had explained about the annual migration. The whales grew plump in the Antarctic, which was important in the collection of their blubber, and then they travelled north as far up as Papua New Guinea and mated in August. Then they travelled back along the same route and got fat and so on. What made the boy sad was the effort the whales expended in the pursuit of their happiness – or for what fulfilled them, such as they were – only for a harpoon, a giant metal gun, to shoot two tiny explosive grenades into their bodies. Sometimes maybe, his father said, the whales were killed instantly because the grenades had embedded in their brains, but sometimes it only struck their bodies and the whales would slowly bleed out as they were dragged behind the chaser. Then they were dragged up a wooden ramp and dissected and used for various boring things like dog food and jewellery, and his father's voice had held no emotion while he spoke of such things, and remembering it now the boy grimaced. So much effort from the whales for such terrible reward. They would be better off staying put and not bothering.

His father, after his long explanation, had looked at the boy with tired eyes and then retreated to their shelter, as was his current custom. He had started to forget about the boy completely. Each day he sat in their tin shack and scratched his head and looked at his plans. Only days now before they left. The boy remained outside with Albert and rarely spoke to his father, leaving the old man to what the boy assumed was some type of mourning. They made no further progress on the construction of their new home. The father, two days before, had decided he would attempt to peg out the corners of the house with newly hewn stakes and did so, using his tape measure for accuracy, growing quickly irritated by how fiddly it was. But beyond that there had been nothing.

The boy, seated, watched the ocean as the sun sank. Bats flew over his head out to sea. He couldn't track them past a few metres as they were swallowed up in sky. Darkness soon settled about him wholly and so the boy returned to their camp to fetch Albert, who was tied to his tree. The puppy licked him as he was released and leaped around the boy's legs.

In the shelter, the father was just as the boy had pictured him, lying on his mattress with the plans in his hand and an oil lantern beside him licking him in honey, illuminating the pages.

The boy had noticed there was no fire for dinner outside and so he said, 'No fire?'

His father didn't turn. 'What's it look like?'

The boy set to it and built a fire, which was difficult in the dark, and boiled two billies full of water. They had finished the last of the water in the old oil barrel the day before so had taken to collecting water from a nearby river. They only drank it after they had boiled it well. He wrapped three potatoes in tin foil and threw them in the embers and on his knees chopped up some ham on an old plastic cutting board. He also cut some slices of cheese.

When he returned to the shack his father had not moved.

The boy served the baked potatoes to his father on a tin plate. His father barely acknowledged him at all and ate the crumbly spuds with his fingers.

'Only a few more days till we leave,' the boy observed. In the absence of conversation, he had started asking questions. They were rarely answered to his satisfaction.

A grunt. 'I know.'

'Is there anything else we need to do?'

His father sighed. Said, 'You sound like your mother when you talk like that. Bloody nag that woman, sometimes.' He seemed to catch himself then because he looked aside and said no more.

The comment brought tears to the boy's eyes. He blinked them away as he thought of her and said nothing in response, just concentrated on his baked potato. Once he was done he headed outside to play with Albert in the dark. He had been using a piece of old rope he had found in the boot to play tug-of-war. He picked up the rope now and immediately the hound was upon him, growling his puppy growl.

The boy kept looking back at the shack with its flickering internal glow and waited to see his father's shape materialise in the doorway. But it never did and inside all was silent save for the sputtering of the lamp and the occasional rustle of the paper.

Later, the boy on his knees looking after Albert, who had run off with the rope, he was startled to hear his father's voice behind him 'How's his training coming on?' There was a slur to his words and a wobble in his step and his clawed hand grasped at nothing as though to steady him. The boy knew he had downed too many beers.

The boy said, without looking at his father, 'It's okay.'

'Can he guard this place yet?'

'Not really.'

'Why not?'

'Well,' the boy said, measuring his words, unsure of what argument he was being drawn into, 'he's still a puppy. He doesn't know.'

'He can keep possums out, though, yeah? So the place isn't covered in their filth when we get back? That'd be good.' He wobbled forward then steadied himself. 'They'd get into all of it. He growls at possums at least, yeah?'

The boy walked over to the dog and picked him up. 'We can't leave him here. Who'll feed him?'

'He gets at the possums, doesn't he?'

'I don't think he's ever seen one.'

'We can fix that,' his father said, and snatched the puppy from the boy's arms and carried him to the nearest tree. So dark it was hard to see. The boy held a torch and aimed it at his father's eyes in an effort to distract him but it did nothing except lengthen his stride. As they neared the tree the father threw Albert towards it and said, 'Get to sitting there, dog.'

Albert's head cracked against the trunk and he whimpered then staggered off into the bush as though drunk like his abuser.

'Dad!' the boy said.

'Oh, he's fine,' the father said, lurching. He steadied himself against a tree trunk with his poor hand but slipped so that he was leaning against it for support.

'Go back inside, Dad.'

'Don't tell me what to do.'

They stared at each other. His father breathed heavily. His whole body shook with effort.

The boy peered after Albert, who was now engulfed in bush and darkness.

'You said you wouldn't do this anymore,' the boy said.

His father laughed. 'Do what?'

'Get angry. Get drunk.'

Another laugh, an angry one. 'You *are* your bloody mother! I'm not drunk, for God's sake. I've had a few, that's all.' He tried to push himself off the tree trunk. 'The dog'll be fine. He will. Toughen up, mate.'

His father stood with his head lowered for a moment, maybe an apology in his posture. Then he walked back to the shack.

The boy could still feel the thud of his heart as he set to finding the dog, shining his torch at the base of the trees. 'Albert?' the boy called. He remained motionless and listened to the sounds of the bush but there was no answering bark.

The boy walked in the direction the puppy had scampered, pushing through jungle and stumbling over roots, the torch beam the only illumination. He couldn't see the moon or the sky through the leaves overhead.

After around an hour of searching he found Albert near a tree, shivering with cold or fear. The puppy's heart beating through its skin. The boy held him tight to his chest and then tucked him inside his shirt and whispered to the pup that the world was alright. The pup clawed and scratched at his skin, clearly panicked. The boy tried to soothe him with further soft words but the puppy strained so hard against the shirt that the fabric began to tear, so the boy took him out and the puppy struggled out of the boy's grip and landed hard on the earth. The puppy cried and dashed away with his tail tucked in and his ears down, a slight limp in his stride. The boy crooned and cajoled, creeping forward with his hands out. Stroked him a little before scooping him up again.

They walked back to the shack, two hurt and bewildered souls. His father's snoring bounced through the thin tin of their shack and the boy sat down beside the fire and offered the puppy some discarded ham rinds, which he devoured quickly. The boy eyed the car, contemplating taking the keys which were on the seat and putting them in the ignition and gunning it, with Albert beside him, to his grandparents' house – though he'd have to learn how to drive first. His father was so drunk he would probably sleep through the noise. He would explain to his grandparents what his father had done and beg for sanctuary for himself and the puppy. Then they'd sit around the table and eat bad scrambled eggs and drink cups of tea. The boy could sleep in his mother's old bed and look at photos of her and forget about this father of his.

The boy sighed and tied Albert to the tree and put the rest of the baked potato beside him. He tiptoed into the shack, changed into his pyjamas and climbed into bed. The corrugated iron above him wobbled in the slight breeze.

FOURTEEN

A few days later they packed their things into the car in
the morning and ate breakfast. The boy dripped runny egg
onto his shirt and looked at his father. His father glared,
said nothing. The boy changed into a different shirt, which
caused them a short delay. His father fidgety as they finished
packing. The day before he had fashioned a type of door for
their shack. No hinges. More of a barricade. It just stood
in spot and shifted when you carried it or pushed it over.
He used chains to lash it to the structure. There was a lock
on the chain, though it looked weak and rusted through,
flaky dust coating the metal. As they drove away they both

looked back at their new home, the old barrels next to the tin, the wheelbarrow upside down in case it rained.

'What do you think?' his father asked.

'About what?'

'About our stuff being safe.'

They went up the pebbly incline down which Albert had barrelled. 'I don't know.'

'I think it'll be alright.'

'Alright,' the boy said.

'Shouldn't worry about it, anyway.' His father sounding insecure. 'Why I got the dog, you know? Hoping he'd do it. Take care of our things.'

The boy said nothing to this but resolved again in his heart to never let this be. They reached the dirt road and soon the dirt beneath them turned to blurred asphalt. His father sped. The boy kept a subtle eye on the odometer, worried that his father's nervousness would turn into reckless driving, and petted Albert, who was resting on his lap.

An hour and a half later they arrived at his grandparents' home. The boy was so excited to see them he jumped from the car before it had stopped moving. His granddad stood in the doorway with a large smile on his face.

He said, 'It's good to see you again, bud.' Shaking the boy's hand warmly.

His granddad's eyes flicked up to the man who approached behind the boy, carrying Albert under his arm.

The boy was quick to rescue the puppy and held him out for his granddad to see.

'Who do we have here?'

'Albert,' the boy said.

His granddad smiled. 'Why Albert?'

'Sounds like a dog's name.'

'You know my dad's name was Albert?'

The boy looked at his father and then back to his granddad. 'No, Granddad.'

His granddad gave the dog a firm pat and the dog's head bowed beneath it. His granddad looked up at the boy's father and said, 'We tried calling.'

'We're not living there anymore, Charles.'

'Then why did you say that was where you were heading?'

'You don't have to know everything we do.'

'He's our grandson.'

'I just wanted a bit of peace, mate,' his father said. Both men's voices had remained monotone and steady, but now his father raised his as he added, 'Alright? I didn't want to talk to anybody for a while.' He took a deep breath. 'I should've let you know, though. Not sure I'm making great decisions at the moment. Bit hard with Liz gone, you know?'

His granddad only nodded at this admission and patted the puppy again. Then he stood and allowed them entry into the house after they had removed their shoes. He stopped the boy, though, as he took a step.

'You'll have to tie Albert up outside, mate. Sorry. He can't come in. He'll make a mess,' his granddad said.

The boy carried Albert outside and tied him to an empty hose reel, telling him that he would only be a little while.

Inside, he found his father and grandparents seated at the round table in the kitchen. They weren't speaking. At the sight of the boy his grandmother beamed and rose from her chair. She walked over to him and cupped his cheeks in her weathered hands and kissed him on the forehead.

'Oh my boy,' she said, and it sounded as though she had been crying. She held him tight, shaking a little. The boy returned her hold. She stepped back and, looking into his eyes, said, 'I'm so sorry I didn't say goodbye to you properly when I saw you last, sweetheart. It's been weighing on me. I wasn't sure I'd see you again.' She enveloped him again in her squishy arms and he struggled for breath. She let him go, her hand resting awkwardly on his arm.

His father eyed them both without expression.

'You want a tea?' his grandmother asked, moving to the kettle, as the boy took his place at the table.

'No, thanks,' his father said. 'We have to keep moving. We're heading to Kangaroo Point.'

'Oh?' his grandmother said. 'Why's that?'

'We're staying with a mate,' his father said.

'And where are you two calling home now?' she asked. She was readying three cups of tea, despite his father's refusal.

'We're building a house up near the water.'

'Is that right?'

'Yes.'

'And why's that?'

His father looked down and leaned back on his chair, the two front legs airborne, something the boy knew his granddad hated. The vinyl squeaked. 'Just thought we needed a bit of a fresh start, you know?'

'Things at home remind you a bit too much of her, eh?' his granddad said. This was said without sarcasm, with a depth of feeling that told of the man's own sadness. He went on, 'I actually threw a few photos of her out before I realised what I was doing. Had to scoop 'em out of the bin.'

The orange kettle was placed on the stovetop and his grandmother fiddled with the burner for a bit before sitting down. She said, 'And why are you staying with this friend of yours?' Her tone was affable, but the boy could see that her mouth was tight.

His father said, 'Just for fun.'

'Just for fun?' his grandmother repeated.

His father shrugged. 'We'll go fishing or something. We're right near the water up there. Maybe we'll go out on Phil's boat, right, mate?'

The boy nodded and then remembered his manners. 'Maybe. Yeah.'

His grandmother cleared her throat. 'Why have you stopped by then?'

It sounded like an accusation. There was a strain between his mother's parents and his dad that the boy had never noticed before. Now he understood that this had always been the case, that what he had taken for affection had in fact been a façade.

'We just thought we'd pop in on our way,' his father said. He looked at the boy's granddad and said, 'Told you we'd visit.' He tipped the chair forward again. 'Plus we wanted to see if you wouldn't mind looking after the dog.'

'The dog?' his grandmother asked.

'They have a dog now,' his granddad explained.

'His name's Albert,' the boy added.

The kettle started to whistle and steam billowed from its spout. His grandmother removed it from the stovetop and filled the cups. 'For how long?'

'A few weeks.'

She carried the cups to the table, taking care to turn the handles towards the men. The third cup was for herself. As she sat she said, 'And why can't you keep him? You bought him.'

'You don't have to take him, yeah? We'll take him.' His father rubbed the back of his head and muttered, 'Bloody hell.'

'Mind your mouth,' his granddad said softly.

Silence for a bit. Then his father said, 'Sorry.'

His grandmother nodded at this but did not look appeased. She turned to the boy and smiled then looked back at his father. 'So why can't you keep him?' she repeated.

He sipped at the tea. 'We don't know how long we'll be staying with Phil. And he has no fence. Nowhere to keep him, unfortunately.'

'Isn't it whaling season shortly?' his grandmother asked.

'Not for a few more weeks this year.'

'And what are you going to do with Sam for those few weeks? Do you want us to mind him for a bit?'

'No thanks,' his father said curtly. 'He's staying with a school mate. He'll be alright. He needs to go to school.'

The boy wanted to tell his grandparents his father was lying, that his father was taking him to Tangalooma and that he was scared. But he knew if he did not go then he would forever feel a coward. So, ignoring the tightness in his gut, he said nothing.

There was a silence. Finally, his granddad said, 'We can mind the dog. But you better come back for him.'

'What else would we do? He's our dog.'

The boy said, 'We wouldn't leave Albert behind forever. Plus, I'm coming back to visit at Christmas.'

'I mean come get him before Christmas, yeah?' his granddad said. 'I didn't sign up for a dog. Don't know why you bought him, Walter, with you out whaling every season. Hard to keep a dog.'

'I bought him for Sam,' his father said softly. Though the boy knew this was another lie, he saw how his grand-dad's expression softened. His father added, 'And we'll have a place next time. The dog'll stay with people.'

Soon the four of them headed outside so the boy and his father might say goodbye to Albert. Albert seemed to understand they were leaving and whimpered and strained at his leash. The boy felt afraid for the dog's neck.

'It's okay, Albert,' the boy said. He felt overwhelmed by sadness. The puppy had been his one source of comfort during this whole ordeal; to be separated now was cruel. He wanted to cry, but he didn't want to look weak in front of his father and granddad.

His father walked over to the pup and sat down cross-legged on the concrete. The dog jumped eagerly into his lap and his father petted him gently. He said soothingly, 'It's alright, mate.' The boy wondered where this benevolence had been the last few weeks. Seeing his kindness to Albert now made him inclined to forgive his father for his lack of care, his violent temper, but then he remembered their shack in the wilderness, the sound of Albert's skull colliding with the tree.

His father petted the dog until he was calm and then stood to leave. The puppy whimpered as they walked away.

FIFTEEN

1956

His mother put her hand on his shoulder and shook him awake. He was instantly wide-eyed and terrified, staring at the formless shadow, fearing monsters and claws, until in the early light the shadow assumed the shape of his mother, and he was able to breathe normally again. He was fairly certain she was smiling.

'Gotta get up, matey,' she said.

'What?' he said. He blinked. 'Why?'

His mother had already moved to his wardrobe and found some clothes for him.

'We gotta go help Aunty Wendy with her new cow.'

'Why?'

She helped him dress, tugging on his pants, the ones he'd normally wear outside in the wet. Instead of taking off his pyjama shirt she put a woollen cardigan, knitted by his grandmother for Christmas, over the top.

'Because she asked,' she said.

'Why?'

'Just because, I guess. I don't know.' She kissed him on the forehead and rose, saying, 'Grab your boots.'

Outside, dawn was breaking through the trees. The boy followed his mother out to the old station wagon. She started the car and let it idle a bit, rubbing her hands together in front of her face and breathing into them for warmth. She was wearing a maroon woollen beanie.

As they were driving to Wendy's property, he noticed that his mother was shaking her head as though she were warding off bees.

'Mum,' he said, 'what are you doing?'

'Nothing, sweetheart.' She sighed. 'Just shaking away the bad memories.'

'What bad memories?'

'About something that happened when I was a kid.'

'What happened?'

'Well, Aunty Wendy's new cow is birthing now and she's struggling a bit. And one time, when I was a girl, we had a cow in trouble like that and your granddad had to shoot her. I keep remembering the way the cow looked at me, you know? Her face keeps popping into my mind – and I don't like thinking about it, that's all.'

'And shaking your head makes the thoughts go away?'

She smiled. 'Not really.'

'Why'd she call you?'

'Aunty Wendy?'

'Yeah.'

'I think she just wanted somebody to be with her. Maybe I told her once about what happened when I was a girl.'

'What are you going to do when we get there, Mum?'

His mother gripped the wheel. 'I don't know. Bit of an adventure, hey, sweetheart?'

'An adventure,' he repeated. 'Yeah, it is.'

He sat in silence and watched the township pass by outside the window until they were driving through rolling greenery, cordoned off by barbed-wire fences.

When they pulled into Wendy's gravel driveway she was standing waiting on the verandah. She said, 'Thanks so much,' then led them through a gate at the side of the house. The boy found himself struggling to keep pace with the two women as they hurried across the small backyard, went through another gate, and came to a large shed stacked to the spilling with hay. A cow lay in front of it and its legs weren't moving but as they drew closer the boy could hear it breathing heavily. It was swollen and its rear was sodden with something.

'Oh, Wendy,' his mother said. 'She looks bad, honey.' She shuffled to her knees near the head and looked into the cow's eyes. The boy didn't know what she thought she might see there.

'I know, I know,' Wendy said. 'I've been looking after her like Brett said, but I don't know what's gone wrong.'

'You call the vet?'

'He's coming.'

'When?'

'He said when he could.'

'Bloody hell,' his mother said. She shuffled on her knees to the rear of the cow and lifted the tail. She cupped her hand and reached down and grimaced. Aunty Wendy hugged the boy to her side as his mother inserted her hand into the cow. The boy wasn't sure what to think but knew he felt like his mother was doing something dirty, and also knew she really wasn't.

'Come look,' his mother said to Wendy, who released the boy and went to her.

He also crept forward to stare.

'She's good and stuck in there,' his mother said. Her hand went back into the cow and when she withdrew it the boy saw it was covered in a sticky white fluid like glue. 'She's stuck in there and she's not moving at all when

I'm grabbing her. She'd buck, or something normally, I think.'

Wendy seemed to be crying. She nodded once and said, 'You sure?'

'No, I'm not sure. I've barely got a clue what I'm doing here.'

'Is she suffering?'

'The cow? Or the calf?'

'Both.'

His mother drew a breath and squinted at the newly risen sun. 'I'd say the calf is dead, and the cow won't be long after it.' She stood, wiped her hand on her pants leg and looked at her son. 'You alright, sweetheart?'

The boy, who was feeling sick and ashamed without knowing why, nodded once. 'What's happening?'

'Aunty Wendy's cow has a baby inside her that she can't push out,' his mother explained gently.

'The baby's dead?'

'Yeah, I think so.'

The boy nodded and Wendy moved over to the head of the cow and stroked her snout. The cow groaned a bit and lifted her head. The boy looked into the eyes beneath the lashes and tried to imagine what his mother had seen.

'I think we should shoot her, Wendy.' His mother moved forward and put her clean hand on her friend's shoulder. 'I think we gotta stop her suffering.'

'We can't pull the calf out?'

'I think she's gone further than that, honey.'

Wendy stood, gave her friend a sad smile. 'I thought so. Didn't want to hear it, but that's what I'd guessed.'

'You want me to do it?' his mother asked.

Wendy looked at her cow, then nodded.

'Where's the gun?'

Wendy pointed at the shed full of hay.

'What's her name?'

'Daisy,' Wendy said, and wiped her nose on her sleeve. Tried another smile. 'Stupid name, really.'

'No. It's a good one. She's a good one. She tried, didn't she?'

'Yeah. She tried.'

His mother was speaking to her friend the way she spoke to the boy when he didn't understand something.

'Sweetheart?' his mother said, turning to him. 'Aunty Wendy's going to take you back to her place while I look after Daisy here.'

'What're you going to do?'

'I'm going to shoot her.'

'You're going to kill her?'

His mother nodded.

'Why?'

'Because she's in a great deal of pain, and I want to put a stop to it.'

'But then she'll be dead.'

'You understand what dead is?'

'Yeah. She won't be alive anymore.'

'No. She won't.'

'So. That's worse than pain. Isn't it?' He looked at Aunty Wendy desperately, but she refused to meet his eyes.

'Well, she'll be in heaven then. So she won't feel any more pain.'

The boy shook his head. 'I don't understand.'

'Honey, can you just go with Aunty Wendy, please? I'll explain it a bit better later.'

'But I don't understand, Mum.'

'I know, honey.'

His mother nodded at her friend, who put her hand between the boy's shoulders and walked him from the paddock. He thought Aunty Wendy might say goodbye to the cow she seemed to love so much but she just kept on walking.

She took the boy inside and they sat together in the living room, Aunty Wendy hugging her knees to her chest on the couch, the boy cross-legged in front of the fireplace. From outside there was the crack of a gunshot, louder than he'd expected, like some giant cannon. He pictured in his mind what the cow's face might look like now after the shotgun and then shook his head to clear it of the thoughts. Wendy was quietly sobbing, still hugging her knees.

When his mother returned from shooting the cow her face was grim and hard like he'd never seen it before. When she saw him, though, she forced a smile and bent down and spread her arms. The boy rushed into the hug and felt her warmth through her jacket and his itchy woollen cardigan. Wendy came to stand beside them, snuffling. His mother pulled her into the hug and Wendy bawled and said, 'Shouldn't've bloody bought the stupid thing.'

'No, no,' his mother said, one hand on the boy's back, the other on her friend's. 'No.'

'Did she suffer?'

'No, she went quick,' his mother said, and released the two of them. 'Let me go and wash my hands.' She walked into the laundry and the boy heard the sound of running water. His mother called out, 'You'll have to get that damn vet to take care of her body, yeah?'

'I suppose,' Wendy replied.

His mother came back into the living room and said firmly, 'I mean it, honey. You can't go back out there, alright? You don't want to look at her. Get the vet to do it.'

Wendy nodded and said, 'This how it was for you?'

'Well, I was a bit younger.' His mother smiled. 'You reckon you could fix us a cuppa?'

Wendy went obediently to the kitchen and a few moments later the boy heard the normal sounds of a kettle being filled and a burner being lit.

His mother fixed her eyes on his and said, 'You understand about heaven?'

The boy shook his head. 'Not really.'

'Well, when somebody dies they go to heaven to be with Jesus.'

'Why?'

'That's just the way it is, I guess.'

'What's heaven?'

'You haven't heard about it at Sunday school?'

The boy thought, then nodded slowly. 'Yeah, but I didn't understand.'

'Well,' his mother said, 'heaven is just the best place ever. Everybody is always happy in heaven.'

The boy considered this for a moment. 'So when you die you'll go to heaven?'

'Yes.'

'And me too?'

'Yes.'

'And Dad?'

'We'll all be there, sweetheart.'

'But what if you die before me?'

'Then I'll see you when you get there.'

His mother was smiling but the boy felt a tremendous fear as he tried to take in all she'd said.

She hugged him again. 'Come on, we should go look after Aunty Wendy a bit.'

They went into the kitchen and sat at the table, and Wendy served his mother a cup of tea and put some biscuits before them on small flowered plates. They sat around the table eating and drinking in silence.

The boy eventually spoke up. 'You okay, Aunty Wendy?'

She smiled. 'I'm alright, Sam. Just a bit sad.'

'Hey,' his mother said, 'you know what we should do?' Grinning now, she slapped her hand down on the table and stood. 'I know what we need to do. Come with me.'

'What do we need to do?' the boy asked.

'Just something my dad showed me. Same thing he did when my old cow died.'

Wendy and the boy followed his mother out the back door. She went into the garden shed and found a chisel in a toolbox draped in cobwebs. She then led them to the front garden and hefted a large charcoal-coloured stone from the border of the flowerbed. She kneeled down and, with a hammer and chisel, inscribed Daisy's name on the stone. Then she lifted the stone onto a fence post and stood back to admire her handiwork. 'To remember her,' she said.

Wendy nodded and the boy looked at the stone and the name so roughly etched.

When his mother walked away Wendy went with her, but the boy remained and ran his hand over the rock. He tried his best to remember the eyes of the cow but found in his conjuring no life there at all.

SIXTEEN

1961

His mother's gravesite looked the same as it had weeks ago. The earth he had shovelled still looked fresh on top and the headstone, now erected, looked just as newly hewn. His father stood to one side and allowed the boy his time.

What worried the boy most was the thought of his mother's body not yet decomposed. He wondered what she might look like with some of her skin no longer there. He also understood that this body in the grave was not his mother and that her spirit was elsewhere – in heaven, like she'd said – but found it difficult to reconcile the two strange pictures: the body decomposing and the heavenly creature.

This idea too strange to fathom but also what must be. If his mother was not heaven-bound then there was only the rotting corpse beneath this mound of dirt. His luminous mother, with her gentle nature, could not be so decayed or destroyed. So surely her spirit was no longer confined to this earth. Surely this dead body with its almost-face was no longer her.

Staring at the stone he wondered what he might say but could not muster words. So he did his best to capture the feeling he had and he held out his hands and laid them on the stone and cried for a short while. Then he wiped his eyes and walked back to his father.

SEVENTEEN

The night before they took the boat across to Tangalooma, the boy slept in Phil's living room on a mattress on the floor.

He slept fitfully and was already awake, staring at the ceiling in the darkness, when his father stumbled out from the spare bedroom.

His father walked over to him, bent down and shook his shoulder. 'Come on, mate. Get up.'

The boy sat up, and immediately was struck by how cold it had become.

'Grab your things,' his father said. 'You going to shower?'

'Should I?'

'I'm going to.'

The boy decided he would too. He cleaned his teeth looking in the frosted mirror and scratched a shape in the mist with his fingertips.

When he was done he went to the kitchen where, around the mess of plants, his father had set two bowls of corn-flakes and two glasses of orange juice. The boy drank the orange juice, forgetting he had just brushed his teeth, and almost gagged at the bitter taste. He forced it down anyway. He felt so sick after he could barely manage the cornflakes.

His father put their car keys and the keys to the padlock of their shack in a bowl on the kitchen bench. As the two of them stepped outside, lugging suitcases, the boy stopped and vomited into one of the potted plants on the verandah.

Phil, who was locking the door behind them, laughed aloud, but his father put a hand on his back and said, 'You alright?'

The boy nodded. Spat.

'You don't need to worry, you know? It's not that hard. And today especially is easy.' His father's voice was warm and pleasant. 'I'll just introduce you to a few folks and we'll find you a place to sleep and we'll be all set. There's nothing required of you. Not for a while.'

The way his father's moods swung from sympathetic to resentful, and the speed at which they did so, utterly confused the boy. Made him untethered to the world.

Though his father's heart was clearly in this speech, it did little to alleviate the boy's deep fear. He was afraid that he would fail and that his poor performance would indicate that he was of little worth. He spat again into the dirt and the orange juice and cereal mixed with this brown made him want to keep throwing up, but he convinced himself not to.

They bundled into Phil's car, a black Holden, with their things piled in the back, and the boy whispered a prayer. Phil heard him, and laughed.

'What're you afraid of?' Phil said as he started the car.

The boy shrugged. 'I don't know.'

'All blokes have to do something for a living. You can't rely on this old man here to support you the rest of your life.' He turned to the boy's father. 'You got what? Ten good years left in you?' He grinned. 'Twelve?'

The boy, sitting behind his father, could not see the man's expression, but he heard, 'I reckon I got a few more than that.'

'There's nothing to be afraid of,' Phil said as he man-oeuvred the car up the driveway and onto the street. 'I remember when I first went out there I was nervous. But it went fine. It's not that hard, really. Your dad's right. It's not like plumbing or something. Any old bugger can do this.'

'Then why don't more people do it?' the boy asked.

Phil laughed, a sound the boy realised was native to the man. 'The smell, mainly. Don't know. It's physically hard sometimes, I guess. Plus the blood. But it's no worse than being a butcher.'

The boy said nothing, but as the car stopped at a set of traffic lights Phil turned around and looked him up and down. The boy squirmed beneath his gaze. 'You afraid you're small like your old man? Don't worry about that. This bloke here –' and he clapped the boy's father on the shoulder '– is one of the best I've ever seen. And he's only got one good hand.'

The boy could see his old man's fist clenched by his side, between the car door and the seat.

'You'll be fine, mate,' his father added.

They drove across a bridge, the water below dark in the pre-dawn. There were other cars already on the road. Their headlights hurt the boy's eyes, making him squint. The few skyscrapers in the city were almost completely devoid of light. A few neon hotel signs stood out as they drove and the boy watched the barrier of the bridge flick past his eyes and become blurred. He did his best to lose focus.

They drove alongside the river and eventually they came to a jetty, a boat bobbing beside it. They went a little further and parked the car. The boy mimicked the older men as they walked with their suitcases dangling over their shoulders, one hand securing it by the handle. The boy almost stumbled beneath the weight.

They walked the short distance back to the boat. It was mostly white except for green splotches of mould near its base and blue trim along the edges. There was ample space at the rear for people to stand and there was shelter from rain and sun. Several men were already on board, and as the trio approached the boy could hear the low murmur of these men merging with the sound of the running motor.

'Walter!' said a man as they reached the side of the boat. He grinned at the boy's father. 'Bloody cold this morning, no?'

His father nodded. 'Rob. This is my son, Sam.'

Rob laughed and extended a hand to haul the boy aboard. 'Coming with us, are you?'

The boy nodded. 'Nice to meet you.'

This made the man laugh mightily, and he was still laughing as he reached down to help the boy's father and Phil aboard.

Phil clapped the man in a bear hug and lifted him from the deck, jiggling him up and down as though emptying a sack. The man chortled and choked.

There were other men on board whom the boy was introduced to with his father's hand at the back of his neck. He stood then, uncertain, near the front and watched his father navigate conversations, then followed his father below deck to stow their suitcases.

Back on deck, he watched as more men turned up in their cars. Rob seemed to know everybody's name and story and greeted them all with the same warmth with which he'd greeted the boy. The boy felt at once welcomed and forgotten.

Soon there were twenty men on board. Rob turned to the boy and said, 'Hope you packed your balls, mate. It's set to be a tough one,' and grinned the worst grin the boy could imagine.

EIGHTEEN

Two men stepped onto the jetty and untied the mooring and cast the ropes back on board before riding the gap over the water as though straddling a horse. Finally, they were reunited with the boat and the men on board cheered and laughed. The conversation swirled about the boy without pause, muffled and thick. There were accents the boy had never heard before – Norwegian, he supposed – and he struggled to decipher some of the words and phrases. As the boat began to move he staggered forward into a man who turned to regard him and then offered him a smile and a calloused hand. He said, '*Jeg heter* Magnus,' and shook the boy's hand. His grip hurt the boy's fingers. Magnus's beard was brilliant red and thick and bushy, not like his father's wiry effort.

'Sam. Nice to meet you.' The boy found himself shouting to be heard over the people nearby.

'And you! You are young?'

'I guess,' the boy said.

The man shifted closer to the boy's ear. 'You will be okay! Strong handshake.' He clapped the boy on the back so hard the boy stumbled, then he moved off to talk to the other men.

The boy pushed his way through the crowd in search of his father. He found him standing alone at the front of the boat watching the waves. The boy rested his arms on the railing and made fists of his two hands in the same manner as his father. His father regarded him with a smile.

'You alright?' he said.

'I think so.'

'Been a while since you were on a boat.'

The boy pictured his own boat, the one he had made. He remembered he wanted to look for their beach when they were out to sea. He tried now, but they were not far enough from land. He said, 'No. I haven't.'

'You'll be alright.' His father sounded as though he were trying to convince himself as much as the boy. 'Just lean over if you need to be sick.'

His father lifted his gaze from the waves and looked sidelong at the boy. He gave him a wink.

The boat lurched up and down in the choppy waters. Some of the men were throwing up and the boy smelled it and immediately chucked up what little remained of his breakfast. Some of it splashed on deck and he quickly scuffed it with his shoe so that nobody would notice and looked around to see if he had been caught. He wiped his mouth with his jacket sleeve and his father winked again, and turned back to the ocean.

Curious, the boy watched the men converse. He hadn't had many opportunities to observe a group of men like this. At school he had been surrounded by boys his own age, and when his father was home from a season flensing whales he didn't socialise much with other men, but was quiet and solitary.

They were all wearing jackets with their hoods up and their hands in their pockets to protect them from the chill of the wind. Most had beards and the few that didn't had heavy stubble. They were chatting and laughing in groups of three or four. Periodically these groups would disband and new groups would form. Few men stood alone like his father. The boy was by a great margin the youngest of the bunch.

The boy raised his own hood and looked at his father then back out to sea. The island was still some distance away. The boy knew what he was about to undertake was both momentous and strange. Few men had done what he was about to do and maybe none so young. He had never been so thrilled nor so terrified.

After a while he felt like vomiting again. His father noticed his face this time and the way his bottom lip trembled. He said, 'Move to the back of the boat. It doesn't bounce so much back there,' but he made no motion to suggest that he would take the boy there.

The boy slipped between the men and hastened towards the back. He was pelted with salt spray. He stood behind the man piloting their vessel. The man did not appear to notice the boy. The boy watched the man spin the wheel, and spin it back. After a time, he began to feel better and looked past the man to regard the island.

As it came on it slowly grew in width. The water grew choppier still and the man at the wheel uttered what the boy thought must be a curse word in Norwegian. It was bitterly cold. His father was still solitary and unmoving at the front and the boy had to look by him to see the island in its entirety. From their beach the island had appeared mostly flat, but as they drew closer the boy could see just how many hills there were. Inland was thickly forested with some type of gum. The edge of the island was fringed with golden sand. Seagulls circled over what the boy assumed was the main factory and the boy was struck by the smell, which came on him fast. It was rich and full of blood and salt. The boy had smelled blood before but this air felt viscous and was difficult to suck into his lungs. The smell of fishing mixed into the odour. The boy wanted to retch again and coughed. None of the other men seemed bothered by it except Magnus, who maybe was also new because he coughed just like the boy.

They approached further to the south of the factory than the boy expected, but as they drew close to the island the man beside the boy twisted the wheel firmly to the left and they travelled north along the coast. The water closer to shore had settled somewhat and the boy began to feel more settled in the stomach. As he strained to see the factory, or maybe one of the whaling boats, Phil came alongside and clapped him on the back. Startled, he almost fell over, which made Phil laugh.

'I've been looking for you,' Phil shouted over the sound of the motor. 'Thought you might have got lost.'

'I'm alright,' the boy said.

Phil laughed again and pointed to the boy's hand, which was holding his nose shut. He took big gulping breaths through his mouth. He could taste the blood.

'Bit of a stink, hey, mate?' Phil yelled. 'This is nothing. They haven't brought in one whale this season yet. Wait till it starts up proper. You get used to it, but.'

The boy was glad to hear this, because the smell and taste was so cloying he had considered leaping overboard and swimming back home.

'You're a bit uptight, aren't you?' Phil said. 'Like your old man.' He nodded towards the father who stood, a sentinel, at the front of the boat, leaning on the rail. None of the other men had approached him, the boy noticed. He kept them at bay with his surly back.

The boy shrugged. 'What's uptight?'

'I don't know. You know,' Phil said, and scratched his head. 'He doesn't talk much, doesn't play cards or do anything, really, with the rest of us. Bit hard to talk to. Uptight. Can't have a laugh. You know?'

The boy had not been aware that other men shared this impression of his father. Because his father was all he had known, he had assumed this was what all men were like. To hear that his father was as strange and foreign to other men as he was to the boy was a kind of victory, but not one the boy cared to celebrate. Strangely, he found himself feeling defensive on his father's behalf.

'I guess he is like that.'

'So is that you?'

Another shrug. 'I don't know. I don't think so.'

Phil laughed. 'It sounds like it. Well, you just feel free, when we're settled, to come spend some time with me and the other blokes whenever you like, if our shifts work in.

We go biking some nights, hunting, watch movies. Your dad doesn't join us that often, but you can.'

The boy asked, 'Are you and my dad friends?'

'Yeah, mate. Of course we are. What do you mean?'

'Why?'

'Because we're mates. I don't know. I know him.'

'You don't seem to like him much.'

'Come on.'

'You tease him.'

'Sensitive like your old man too, eh?' Phil smiled then, as if realising the boy was hurt by it, sighed and lowered his voice a bit. 'Teasing is just what blokes do. You never got teased at school? He's just a bloke I know who I can chat with about things. You don't get that very often. Not round here. You know, serious things. I know he seems shut off but he's a good listener.' Phil stared out at the ocean for a few moments, then continued, 'I just wish he'd lighten up is all. And it's not just 'cause your mum passed. He's been the same as long as I've known him.'

Phil bit his bottom lip as if he regretted mentioning the boy's mother.

The boy stared with him out to sea. He didn't mind his mother being mentioned and he wanted to say this to Phil but sensed this would only increase the man's shame.

In front of them, the man behind the wheel said loudly, 'Nearly there.'

The boy went to the rail that looked right onto the factory. There was a large wooden ramp that sloped down to the sea, with a flat bit in the middle. The boy pictured a whale sliding up it, getting winched by the tail and the tongue, if it had a tongue, splashing bright red blood as it flapped out onto the wood. There was a walkway to the right that travelled up the length of the ramp and there were two men doing something to the wood with tools the boy could not see.

The boat pulled to the left and the deck lurched beneath the boy's feet. They sidled up against a long jetty. Two men, the same who had cast them off back on shore, leaped off the boat now and tied it off. The other men on board were already heading below to fetch their bags and the boy looked over at his father, who still hadn't moved.

After a few of the men had leaped onto the pier the father turned and found the boy in the crowd. He smiled and made his way over. 'Come on, mate. Let's get our things.'

Phil helped them with their luggage and then they joined the stream of men going ashore. The boy looked for Magnus but couldn't find him in the crowd of beanies and thick sheepskin jackets. A cloud of cigarette smoke travelled with them. The boy noticed his father did not smoke like the others, despite having smoked occasionally these last few months. Maybe he was hiding what weaknesses he could.

Phil said to his father, 'What were you thinking about, up there?'

'I don't know.'

'You looked like you were thinking about something.'

'I was trying not to think.'

There were seagulls in greater number above them now, circling and squawking. The boy looked to the whaling ramp, the waves sloshing onto the damp wood at the bottom.

Phil put a hand on the boy's shoulder. 'You see that bit down there?' He pointed. 'Down at the bottom of the ramp? Bloody nesting ground for sharks. You can't swim there. Or anywhere here. This whole damn island.' He swung his arms to indicate its mass. 'The whale blood attracts them. Your dad told you that, yeah?'

His father, who had stopped beside them, shook his head.

'You didn't tell him?'

His father shrugged. 'Figured I'd tell him when he wanted to go swimming.'

Phil looked the boy in the eyes. 'Don't you bloody swim here, mate. Don't let me catch you even trying.'

The boy looked at the waters lapping against the bottom of the ramp and he imagined beneath them fins and teeth and black eyes. Nightmare creatures. Why would he want to swim? There were stains on the ramp that were darker than mere dampness and the boy was at first puzzled and then realised that the stains were from a decade of whale blood.

They soon reached the end of the jetty and stepped onto sand and grass, and the boy strained to see the flensing deck where his father worked. It towered above him, a wooden platform atop a concrete base. He could see chimneys and boiler stacks, heard mechanical sounds within. There were floodlights on towering stilts so the men could work well into the night. His father hadn't noticed the boy had stopped and he and Phil had kept walking, so that the boy had to hurry to catch up.

NINETEEN

The path they followed was engulfed in thick jungle. Despite the many years of slaughter the island felt fresh and alive. The green leaves were rich and the tree trunks dripped moisture. The boy touched one and imagined he could feel its beating heart.

They headed towards the station's living quarters, his dad indicating them with a tilt of the head. The accommodation blocks were sheltered from the bitter wind by a thick tangle of tropical trees. Palms, some gums. The branches like hands locking fingers. On their left was a building with the company logo on top painted in deep blue. The building itself looked like the sky in colour, faded from unyielding sun.

His father put a hand on the boy's back and steered him up a slight incline towards a building standing on stilts, the ground beneath moist with water. The smell of salt in the air, the blood faint now. The boy looked closely at the construction of the building and wondered at his father's delusions of carpentry. That they might one day make something so grand.

They stepped onto the verandah and his father produced a key from his pocket and opened the door. Inside were two beds and a television. The boy threw his bag onto one of the beds and was glad to see through an open door a bathroom with a shower. Until now he hadn't realised how much he'd missed these modern conveniences. His father had never specifically said, but had always given the impression that his time at Tangalooma was torturous, uncomfortable. The boy had pictured little shacks not unlike his new home, with no showers in which to rinse off the blood, oil, dirt. He hadn't imagined anything as nice as this.

His father was unpacking his clothes into the closet, so the boy opened his suitcase to follow suit. His father said, 'Leave some room for whoever else they stick in here, mate.'

'There's going to be somebody else?'

'Yeah. You aren't getting paid this first time out so you won't be sleeping on a bed either, unless they didn't crew enough to fill the rooms – but I bet they did.' His father must have seen disappointment in the boy's expression, as his voice softened. 'Come on, mate. Don't whinge. It's better than home.'

The boy looked at the couch. It was long enough, he reckoned. He lay down, found it comfortable. There were telephones on the stands beside both beds and the covers of the beds were thick, quilted and blue. The boy turned the television on and found the reception too sketchy for pictures. He played with the rabbit ears until he could see people and he forgot completely where he was while he focused on this task. When he looked up he saw his father had fallen asleep on his bed, his shoes kicked out in front of him and his arms spread wide.

The boy went outside to stand on the verandah. From here he had a clear view of the flensing deck. There were boilers already cooking, big brown tubes from which steam billowed. There were men cleaning the deck with large, thick-bristled brooms, the sound of their steady scraping reaching the boy.

He went back inside and watched television with the sound turned way down. Some game show he couldn't follow.

His father eventually woke and, without a word, took some clothes from the closet and went to the bathroom. While he showered the game show ended and was succeeded by a cartoon the boy knew. He watched happily.

His father came out of the bathroom and sat on his bed to put his shoes back on. He looked at his son.

'You getting ready?'

'For what?'

'We have to have dinner.'

They'd eaten sandwiches his father had made for lunch and so the boy had expected something similar for dinner. He had grown comfortable in this new environment; so comfortable he'd forgotten, if only for a short while, their intent in this place. He rummaged in the closet for some clothes to change into. His father added, 'We might be on late shift tonight, too, so dress warm. Wear boots, your jacket and your shorts. Your legs'll stay warm as you work. Go on.'

'I don't have boots.'

'What do you mean you don't have boots?'

The boy looked through his suitcase. 'I don't have any boots.'

'I told you to pack boots.'

'No, you didn't.'

'I bloody did, mate.' His father put his hands to his face and sat on the bed, then looked sideways at his son. 'You don't listen.'

'I don't know what you want me to do,' the boy said. 'I don't own boots.'

'You should've said when we were out shopping. You should've said this morning. You need boots, mate.'

The boy wanted to protest his innocence, but by his father's countenance he knew arguing would only anger the man. So he put on his shoes instead, the good leather ones he had worn to his mother's funeral. Once he was fully dressed he stood before his father with his arms outstretched. His father nodded and said, 'Yeah, alright. That's fine.' He frowned at the shoes, though.

They stepped outside into the dark, which was illuminated by the harsh lights of the verandah. The father looked over at the flensing deck. There was a lot of activity the boy couldn't make out. At least twenty men at various tasks. There were some other men leaving their rooms along the verandah, and they walked through the darkness as a group. The dirt slope leading away from their quarters was lit only by moonlight and their shadows beneath them were almost circular. The moon somehow seemed brighter on the island, though the boy knew this could not be so. There were bats too, lots of them, flying overhead and alighting in trees. They seemed closer to the boy, nearer to head height. If he were to raise his hand he might touch one's furry belly and feel its fangs in his fingertips.

The group entered the mess hall. It was loud with conversation. There were men standing over large cooking pots, stirring their contents with giant spoons, and stacks of white porcelain bowls and plates and silver cutlery in trays. There was a crowd of men lined up to receive their portions of spaghetti and sauce, which they then carried over to one of the large tables, chatting nonstop all the while. Spirits generally seemed high, though there was a table of men near the corner who ate quietly and didn't speak to one another. The boy knew where he and his father would sit.

They lined up with the others. The boy saw Phil at a table talking animatedly, his hands gesturing wildly, the men before him snorting with laughter. Phil saw the boy watching and winked at him. The boy nodded in acknowl-edgement and then looked at his father, this stoic statue. They shuffled along in the line to get spaghetti. He picked up a bowl like his father and held it out towards the man serving. The man smirked at him and gave the boy more than he could handle, a big sloppy helping. He followed his father to the predicted table. As they moved through the mess hall, his father was stopped by men greeting him. Some even shook his clawed hand – the good one carrying his bowl – and beamed as they said his name. Respect in their eyes and words. One even called him 'sir'. The boy was surprised.

They sat opposite one of the quiet men, who looked up and smiled. 'Who'd you get stuck with?' he asked.

'Just me and him at the moment,' his father said, nodding in the boy's direction.

'This your boy?' the man asked. He was thin. The bags under his eyes suggested he'd had little sleep.

'This is Sam.'

The man laughed and extended a sauce-splattered hand over the table. 'Aleks. It's good to meet you.'

The boy noticed a faint Norwegian accent in his speech.

He said, 'Nice to meet you,' but the man had already turned back to the boy's father.

'You'll get somebody in there with you tomorrow, though, yeah?'

'I know.'

'Can you believe it's been a year already? I couldn't believe it. My wife couldn't, either. I looked at that calendar for a long while to be sure.' Aleks turned back to Sam. 'Why's he here, then? Why are you here, my boy?' He grinned, small flecks of tomato on his teeth.

'He's learning the trade,' his father answered.

'Ah. And you've checked with Melsom?'

'No,' his father said. 'Not yet.' He took some grated cheese from a bowl in the centre of the table and sprinkled it over his spaghetti. 'You think he'll mind?'

'No. But you should ask. He won't be paid, yes?'

'I know.'

Aleks turned to look at a man who had sat recently down beside him and then turned back to whisper to the two of them, 'Didn't think old Mick here would make it back, eh?' He checked to ensure the man hadn't heard him then added, 'Bloody moaned near the whole season last year.'

Aleks went back to his spaghetti. His bread roll was balanced carefully on the side of his plate and when he put spaghetti on his spoon he twirled it around with his fork instead of just scooping it up like the rest. The boy tried this method out himself and found it successful. The spaghetti was quite nice and so was the cheese, which was a type he had never tasted before. More nutty. It was the best meal he had eaten in months.

His father said to Aleks, 'Thought you'd be out this afternoon?'

'No, my friend. Soon,' he said and laughed. 'You won't see much of me again.' He looked at the boy. 'I don't see what your dad does and he don't see what I do. But we're still friends. I know the boats, your dad knows the factory. He's one of the few, though. Yes? We'd love it if it was only us –' he waved his spaghettied fork '– doing all of it and making all the money.'

'I know that,' his father said.

'We'd all be Norwegian here if there were enough of us. Oh, my boy . . .' He clapped the boy on the back. 'What a heaven. Not that we begrudge you lot your earnings. But what a heaven! Our food, our ways, our language. My boy! You should see it.'

'But I'm Australian,' the boy said.

This made both older men laugh.

Eventually the boy's father said, 'I'm lucky I get to flense.'

Aleks swallowed his mouthful quickly so he might say, 'You are good at your job. You have earned that position, my friend.'

His father nodded and the mood lightened. The boy felt happier. The air of excitement in the room helped him to stop thinking of what must come.

Soon a man stood up, waving his hands and yelling for attention. When this didn't work he put his fingers in his mouth and whistled shrilly. The men quietened. While many of the men were heavily bearded this man outdid them all. His beard was black, flecked with grey near his skin. His face looked taut and his eyes shone, and he had close-cropped hair. He looked stocky and fit, thick around the neck.

'Welcome back, fellas!' he said. He looked at them all in turn while they were silent and he let the silence grow until the boy was uncomfortable, and then the man's eyes settled on him and he raised his brows in a question. The boy held his breath.

But instead of asking it, the man just said, 'Your shifts are posted, as per normal, on the noticeboard.' He pointed. 'So make sure you check it out and know where you're supposed to be. Most of you know what we expect here by now, and if you're new you'll soon learn. How many of you are new here?'

A few raised their hands, but not the boy.

The man said, 'Be on time, work hard. The harder we work the more money we make. Simple as that. We want that barrel bonus, so go at it.'

As he spoke his eyes travelled over the group and the boy watched Phil, who leaned back in his chair with his arms folded.

'Look after each other too,' the man said. 'What else did I have to say?'

He scratched his beard and jutted his chin forward and another smaller man seated nearby stood and whispered something into his ear.

The man's face lit up and he said, 'That's right. Yeah. We had a small slump in how many we took towards the end of last season. I'm sure you all remember.' Grumbles filled the hall. 'So this season we're trying out something new. You might have noticed these hard-looking blokes.' His eyes scanned the crowd until he found who he was seeking. 'Boys, stand up, please.'

Four men at one table scraped their chairs back and stood. One bowed. All looked awkward.

'These men are our new pilots,' the man said. 'We've got a small landing strip we've built north of here and these boys are going to fly out ahead of our boats and spot the whales and call 'em in. This'll make it that bit easier to meet the quota. We'll have met it before you know it.' Murmurs among the men. 'Anyway, boys, that's it. Come see me if you want anything. Door's always open.'

The man sat without further ceremony and his audience did not speak for a moment, then the sound of voices rose again and the hall was soon returned to its previous mood.

His father went to get dessert for himself and the boy. He came back with two bowls of a strange, wobbly trifle. The boy tried it and found the taste bitter. He pushed his bowl away and watched his father eat.

The boy said, 'Are we going to talk to Melsom?'

His father swallowed. 'Yes.'

'Now?'

'Let me finish my meal.'

When he was finished they emptied their scraps into a large plastic tub and put their cutlery in labelled grey buckets full of soapy water. They stacked their plates as the boy eyed the heavily bearded man, whom he assumed must be Melsom.

The man was involved in an animated discussion as they approached, but as soon as he noticed the boy's father his face lit up. He said, 'Walter Keogh!' and stood and enveloped his father in a hug.

His father smiled, clearly both proud and embarrassed, and returned the man's embrace awkwardly. 'Sir. It's good to see you.'

'And I hear you've brought your son with you,' Melsom said, smiling at the boy.

The boy returned the smile and shyly extended his hand.

The bigger man was slow to extend his own and he shook the boy's as though he were weighing him up, taking the measure of his character. He didn't squeeze the boy's fingers but his grip was firm.

'It's good to meet you, sir,' the boy said.

'And how old are you, my boy?'

His father answered, 'Sam's fifteen.'

The boy felt rotten that his father had lied on his behalf, but he did not want to correct his father in front of this man he so clearly respected, so instead he smiled and nodded and did his best to hide his discomfort.

Melsom released his hand finally and then looked at his own palms. This frightened the boy. If he judged the boy's handshake inadequate, then what would become of them?

Melsom said, 'So you'll be following your dad around then?'

'Yes. Sir.'

'You just do what you're told and work hard and we'll have a spot here for you, mate. We can always use good new blood. Just work hard, yeah? You had a job before?'

'No, sir,' the boy answered, before his father could lie. 'Not really.'

Melsom laughed. 'Well. Welcome, eh?'

The boy was usually frightened of such expectations, sure he would fail to live up to it. But in this man's grip and unwavering gaze, he found inspiration. His father might expect little of him, but this man expected that he would work. So that was what the boy would do.

TWENTY

After dinner they walked back in the new night and found their room unaltered. His father grunted at this and said, 'Normally have another bloke in here by now.'

His father showered again, despite having already done so, and the boy sat on the edge of his father's bed. He eyed the other bed covetously and hoped that nobody else would show up so that he might sleep there. Outside, he could hear other men walking along the verandah to their own rooms.

His father came out of the bathroom wearing tan shorts and a white t-shirt. There was coarse black hair coating his arms and through the thin white cotton stretched across his chest the boy could see the matted black beneath. On the back of his neck, too. He sat next to his son on the bed and yanked on his thick woollen socks with difficulty and pulled them up his shins. Then he put on his heavy gumboots. He stopped once they were on and looked at his son's footwear, still near the door.

'Should've thought about it, hey, mate?'

The boy looked down at his feet. 'Will I be alright?'

'You'll be fine.'

'I don't need gumboots?'

'You won't be handling the flensers, so no. But for next time we'll make sure we buy you some,' he said. 'What did you think of what Melsom said?'

'About me working here?'

'Yeah.'

'I don't know.'

His father stood and said, 'It might be a good opportunity. Did you read the posted shift we got?'

The boy shook his head.

'The men work two twelve-hour shifts here. We've scored the worst of it to start with. Midnight to midday. The other blokes will come on when we finish. It's a hell of a slog.' He crouched over his suitcase and rummaged through it till he found a leather belt. He looped it through his shorts then positioned a black holster on his left side. In it was a knife with a wooden handle. The father removed the knife from the holster and laid it on the bed with something like reverence, and then went back to the suitcase and removed a black velvet stone from one of the front pockets. He threw it to the boy.

'That's a whetstone.'

'I know what it is,' the boy said.

'You know how to use it?'

The boy nodded. 'Yes.'

'Well, sharpen my knife for me.'

The boy rose and went into the bathroom. The mirror was still steamed up from his father's shower. The boy stood before the mirror and wiped it with his hand. He looked at himself. He didn't measure up to the other men in any way. He was scrawny up top and there was no hair on his face. There were a few pimples on his chin. He turned the faucet on and wet the stone, then went back into the room and took his father's knife from the bed. Under his father's gaze, he scraped the blade across the stone.

When he was finished he showed the knife to his father, who nodded once – his only expression of satisfaction – then took the knife and returned it to the holster.

The boy tried to hand the whetstone back, but his father shook his head. 'You look after that, mate. That's your first job.' Then he added, 'Go on. Get ready.'

'I thought we weren't starting till midnight?' The boy looked at the clock near the bathroom. 'It's only ten.'

'I like to get there early the first night. Make sure my flenser is sharp.' He laughed. 'You've never flensed a whale till you do one with a blunt bloody knife. I should choose a blunt one for you to start with. Get you used to things.' His father grinned. Then he saw his son's expression. 'Don't look so worried, mate. You aren't starting tonight. But you will soon, yeah? Stay close to me, do as I say. It's just like any other job, really.' His father was lecturing now. 'I always get there early. I'm the leader of this team. If you want to lead men, you gotta get there first and do things by example. You want 'em keen, you show 'em *you're* keen first.'

His father put on a sheepskin jacket and shrugged it up so it covered his neck and put his hands in the pockets.

'What do I need?' the boy asked.

'Wear what I'm wearing. You got a belt on?'

'A belt?'

'What did I say?'

The boy found his leather belt in his suitcase and quickly slipped it through the belt loops of his shorts. He still felt ill-prepared. His shorts now felt much too tight, the waistband squeezing his stomach. His leather shoes felt stupid. He sat on the bed and looked up at his father. 'Dad?'

'Yeah?'

'Why am I here?'

'Experience. What do you mean?'

'I mean, what if I can't do it?'

'You'll be fine, mate.' His father sighed and frowned. 'I don't know why you worry so much.'

'But what if I'm not fine?'

'It takes weeks to learn how to do it well. You just gotta keep at it.'

'But what if even then I'm no good?'

His father took a breath and raised a hand as if he might place it on his son's knee. Instead he dropped it to his side and said, 'What are you worried about?'

'I don't know.'

'If you don't know, why are you worried?'

The boy shrugged.

'When I was in New Guinea,' his father said, 'we had a bloke with us and he was always doing what you're doing now. Expecting the worst and always worrying. A glass half empty kind of guy. You heard that expression?' The boy nodded. 'And he was always making mistakes because of it. He was so focused on what might go wrong he forgot to concentrate on what he was actually doing. So I don't want you worrying when we get on deck. Okay? I want you just to watch me and do what I ask. You'll do fine. Alright?'

The boy nodded and his father stood in front of him and lifted him off the bed by his underarms as though he were an infant. Then his father straightened his shirt and adjusted his belt. Small gestures that made the boy feel loved.

When the father was satisfied with the boy's appearance they left the room together and walked along the wooden verandah, down the steps and onto the muddy path that led to the factory floor.

TWENTY-ONE

As they made their way up the stairs towards the flensing deck, the boy tried to look into the room beneath, but there were no windows, just the sounds of machinery and men's muffled shouting through the walls. At the top of the stairs was a small iron gate and his father opened it and ushered the boy through. There were men swarming over the wooden deck already, wearing clothing similar to his father's. A few of them looked up and smiled at the new arrivals before turning back to whatever it was that kept them busy.

There were more buildings adjacent to the deck and their rusted iron roofs extended from beneath the boy's feet, bristling with antennas. The deck itself was around one-third the length of a footy oval and about half that width-wise. Barrels and ropes and other items lined the edge. As the boy watched, a heavyset man bent down and picked up a coiled rope and slung it over his shoulder. As he moved towards the stairs they'd just walked up, he gave the boy's father a small nod of recognition.

The floor beneath the boy's leather shoes was panelled wood. The boy bounced a little to test that it could hold his weight and then he stopped and looked about. The panels held whales, of course they'd hold him, and he had just looked stupid in front of these men. Two of them smiled at him but kept about their work. The others did not turn.

Two men came over to shake his father's hand and the three of them began to talk, the boy silent beside them. His father made no move to introduce him, so he walked away to look at the ramp. The ramp's wood gleamed wet beneath the huge lights shining down from above. The timber was much rougher than the panelled flooring, as though trees had been arbitrarily chosen and laid side by side in whichever order they'd arrived. It looked like his boat. The boy smiled and breathed in the ocean. There were several large winches at the rear of the deck. A strange tower too, to his left, made of dull red iron. He heard the two men laugh and his father join in.

The boy walked to the left side of the deck. Another winch near his feet. A hole in the floor. He stuck his head through. There were boilers and black barrels and men hard at work. A dulled saw towards the rear. He could see the men's shapes as they moved, reflected in the polished metal. The teeth were large. Ready to sever a car. The smell of burnt sausages. The boy stood and breathed salty air and looked around for his father.

His father was bent down and had in his hands a long pole with a curved blade at the end, like a sickle. The wooden pole was as tall as the boy. His father held it upright and motioned for the whetstone, which the boy placed in his hand. His father sharpened the blade with methodical care. This blade had probably cut the flesh of a thousand whales. His father looked with pride at the blade and smiled as he sharpened it.

'You gotta sharpen these,' he said, almost to himself. 'You gotta be able to cut clean in with it. Very important tool, this whetstone. Don't lose it.'

He handed the stone back to the boy, who pocketed it. The boy kicked at the deck and looked at the busy men. 'What's going to happen now?'

'We'll just get used to where we are a bit.'

'I mean, when will the whales get here?'

'They'll get here when they get here.'

'And what should I do?'

'Just watch, mate. Take it easy. We're going to be here twelve hours. All night. You're going to be exhausted. You need a break, you take one. You remember where the coffee was in the mess hall?'

The boy nodded. 'But I don't like coffee.'

His father laughed at this. 'You will by the end of the night.'

The boy watched as a man who'd been standing with a group nearby stopped chatting and looked around at his father. He walked over in a hurry and shook his father's crippled hand. His grip was too tight, judging by the expression on his father's face. The beanie on his head looked new. He said, 'I'm Dan.'

His father said, 'Walter.' They stopped shaking. 'Who are you?'

Dan laughed. 'Sorry, mate. Forgot my manners. I'm the Fisheries inspector.'

His father's brow creased. 'Where's the other one?'

'The other one?'

'The old one. What's his name?'

'James?'

'Yeah. James.'

'He's not here this time. I'm here this time.'

'Oh,' his father said. He looked the man up and down. 'You done this before?'

'I was at Byron a few seasons.'

'So you know what you're doing?'

The man might have been insulted by this, but it was difficult for the boy to tell considering the man's smile. 'I do,' he said. 'Don't worry.' He looked behind his father and then at the boy and grew confused. 'Where's the rest of your team?'

'Over there,' his father said, pointing at the two men the boy had heard him laughing with. They were both bent to some task.

'Can you introduce me?' Dan asked.

His father nodded and was about to walk off when Dan said, looking at the boy, 'Who're you?'

'Sam.'

Dan looked at his father. 'How old is he?'

'He's fifteen.'

'He's your son?'

'He is.'

'He's a bit young, isn't he?'

'He's not working. He's just watching me work. He'll work here when he's old enough.'

'He's just watching?'

'He'll help out a bit later on, but yeah, mostly.'

'Help with what?'

'I don't know. What he needs training in.'

'Will he touch the whales?'

'Is it your business?'

'It is actually, mate,' Dan said. He removed his beanie and wiped at the sweat coating his hair. 'Will he handle the whales? Or the knives?'

'Not at first,' his father said. The boy noted the slow breath out and knew his father was attempting to control his anger. Two clenched fists, one imperfect. 'Tell you what. You tell me when you think he's ready. I won't let him do a thing without your bloody say so.'

The man, possibly noticing his father's clenched fists, said, 'Sounds fair.'

'You want to be introduced –' his father tilted his head towards the other men '– or what?'

The two walked off and left the boy. The boy noticed that his father had not introduced him to anyone except when asked about him. In an act of defiance, he approached a man near the ramp with a hose and said, 'How's it going?' He tried to sound casual, like he was one of the guys.

The man turned and extended his hand. 'Brian. Good to meet you.'

Shaking the man's hand, the boy said, 'I'm Sam.'

'Your Walt's kid, yeah?'

The boy nodded. 'How'd you know that?'

'No other kids here, are there?' Brian said. 'Bloody stupid what they let him get away with. No offence to you, mate.'

The boy ignored this comment and bent to touch the ramp. He said, 'What are you doing?'

'I'm hosing down the slipway here so the whales can slide up without getting splinters or catching on the wood.'

Brian let the hose fall and spray wildly on the deck and walked to the side and cranked the faucet on further and the water gushed out. The boy was quick to grab it as it snaked from side to side. He aimed it down the ramp and his hands quickly grew cold. When Brian returned the boy handed the hose to him. He shook the water from his hands and tried to think of something to say, but when he looked Brian's back was to him, so he walked away.

Phil soon showed up. The boy noticed that he was later than most of the other men and as he entered he threw his hands in the air as though crossing a finish line and some of the men hooted and clapped. He turned and stood, a celebrity. He set to sharpening his flensing knife, the boy watching from a distance so he wouldn't disturb him. Phil was less precise than his father. While he sharpened his knife the other men crowded around and chatted and he became distracted from what he was doing.

The boy surveyed all the activity going on, the air of busyness and purpose, and found himself uplifted by the sense of a shared mission. The men seemed happy to be there, despite the late hour and despite the hours of work ahead of them. They were engaged in some task or other. The boy had never seen men so fulfilled. His father was one of them. He wondered if he would become fulfilled also and if he had what it took to make it in this world.

TWENTY-TWO

The boy stood with his father at the lip of the slipway watching as a boat came in. It was large and, as the vessel slowly exited the shadow and emerged into the light, the boy saw one of the harpoon guns glinting. The waves hitting the bottom of the ramp increased in measure with the boat's approach. The boy kept his eyes peeled for sharks.

'The chaser'll pull up,' his father said. 'It'll stop there –' he pointed out to sea '– and wait for the *Looma*. *Looma*'s a bigger boat; she stays with us. She just goes out to collect the whales from the chasers. Chasers can't afford to be waiting around for us with the dinghy and the ropes each time, so they head back out while the *Looma* comes up here.' He pointed near the end of the ramp. 'Then we send a dinghy out to drag the whale to the slipway.'

'Why?'

'Just how it's done. Don't ask me, mate. The Norwegians invented whaling and they organise all this. We don't have to worry about that side of it, anyway. We just have the whales to sort.'

The boy looked at his father, who was watching his face keenly. There was a part of the boy that wanted to walk away from this, all he saw. Another part that was buoyed by the sense of purpose amongst the men. He shuffled closer to his father's bung left hand.

'How often do the chasers come in?' he asked.

'When they've caught enough.'

The boy was struck with what he would now witness. A whale up close and dead. A once-living creature created by God slaughtered for what was inherent in its design. Bone, fat, meat. Churned into margarine and food for pigs. A reapplied purpose worth more to man than the creature alive. He looked at the men about him and wondered what they might have done to earn the right to take what they wanted from the whale.

Difficult to see in the dark, but out to sea a ship approached and another vessel of longer design met it. An elderly couple embracing each other with tender arms.

The men on the deck had grown silent and now over the water came the sound of booming engines and men shouting. The boy watched. Soon the vessels parted and the larger one turned back to them with its cargo.

Smoke billowed from the *Tangalooma*'s funnel and failed to disperse despite the breeze and the movement of the vessel. As the ship came near the factory, the funnel reflected the bright lights and the surface of the ocean rippled. There were men aboard the boat wearing dark woollen beanies and long trousers and gumboots. The vessel seemed to sit low in the water. There was a large white shape lashed to the side closest to them. Its skin swallowed water and light both and reflected colour back to the boy. One flipper was extended upwards, eternally asking a question.

The boy turned aside from the whale carcass and looked instead to the dinghy headed out from beneath him with three men aboard. They approached the white mass and the motor coughed and struggled. They found the embedded harpoon and attached a thin steel cable they had dragged with them, its other end anchored to the slipway that glinted beneath the lights. The questioning flipper smacked against the surface of the water as the whale was released from the *Tangalooma* and the boy heard a man on the dinghy laugh aloud. The dinghy dragged the carcass to the bottom of the slipway. The whale listed uselessly and bobbed like a bath toy.

'How's it floating?' the boy found himself asking.

His father said, 'They pump it full of air to keep it afloat on the way home.'

The whale thudded against the wood of the slipway and the boy could feel a faint vibration in his legs. Men near him were yelling directions and orders. He could sense the anticipation in his father and the men in his father's team as they strained forward, eager to begin. Beside them, Phil and his team handled their flensers and stared intently.

Two more men leaned out from the slipway and attached a heavier steel cable to the beast's tail that threaded its way up the slipway to one of the winches at the rear of the deck. Brian kept hosing beside him. Once the cable was attached and secured, the men called out with Norwegian accents and the other cable – the hawser, the boy heard it called – was released back to the dinghy, which made its way back out to the *Tangalooma* to collect another beast.

His father beside him yelled a warning to the men below, which startled the boy so he almost slipped and he grabbed his father's sleeve. His father laughed as the boy cursed his ill-suited shoes.

The winch began to turn, and the whale was dragged onto the slipway.

So large a beast seemed to the boy to demand dignity in treatment and in word both, but instead the men surrounding it only laughed and joked, acting as though what happened before them was entirely without consequence. Both of the flippers were squished awkwardly beneath it as the carcass gained traction on the wood and the boy was positive that if there were bones in these appendages then they were by now surely broken. The whale's tongue lolled out behind it and wobbled and shuddered as the winch cranked. Its skin stuck despite the steady hosing of the wood. The tail was small compared to the size of the creature's head.

Perhaps no dignity was possible in death. The boy remembered his mother's made-up cheeks and the look on his father's face as he shut the coffin lid. He remembered too the colour of her sickness. All death was ugly; why not present it so?

Once the whale had reached the flattened part in the middle of the ramp its progress stopped. A bloke ran out and attached another heavy chain to its tail and the process was started anew. The whale seemingly grew in size as it approached. Looking beyond this nightmare, the boy saw the dinghy had retrieved a second whale, smaller than the first. It bobbed on the surface of the water in the same way and the dinghy started the journey back to the ramp. Brian still hosed, looking bored with his task. The first whale scraped up the wood, almost upon them. It caught on the lip with a low squeak and his father yelled at the winch man and then, without hesitation, he and his team heaved the carcass over the lip onto the deck. The boy caught a glimpse of its eyes as it slid past and he remembered his mother's colourless pupils. Unlike her, this beast seemed still to be present within its flesh, staring back at him from its premature afterlife.

The smell of it up close was not that bad, but the boy knew it had not been opened yet and that the insides of an animal stank far worse than its outside. As it slid past, still jerked by the chain, its eye and belly wobbling, the boy noticed the ridges on its monstrous head.

The men all followed their quarry. The winch cranked and there were seagulls circling above. One of them landed near the whale's flipper and arched its wings before flapping away at the next jerk of the winch.

Finally, his father gave a shout and waved a hand in the air, and the whale came to a stop.

'Stand over there,' his father said, and pointed to a place near the rail of the deck.

The boy obeyed and watched as the men circled the upside-down whale.

Dan the Fisheries inspector walked up and looked it in the eye then, without hesitation, sank his knife in up to the hilt.

The boy thought at first he was stabbing the eye itself, and was about to look away, but then he saw the inspector had cut a little below. Blood oozed from the wound to coat his bare hands, and as he sawed he shook his hands intermittently to flick the blood onto the timber deck. It landed in droplets the size of pennies. The eyeball wobbled in protest and suddenly out it popped, hanging by a thick membrane, swaying. Dan, without looking, flicked his knife and severed the thread and the eyeball landed with a thud on the deck. The boy wanted to vomit but managed to fight the urge.

Dan reached a hand into the cut he'd made and fished out what looked like a large oyster shell and studied its thickness. He held it up to the light, this gore-encrusted talisman.

'About twenty-five years,' he yelled.

The boy saw a man near the back of the deck write something on a chalkboard.

Dan then set to measuring the whale. A little blood seeped from the cut near its eye, the empty cavity that had once held a window into the creature's depths. Dan yelled out figures the boy didn't understand to the man at the chalkboard, and when he was finished Dan stood in front of the upside-down beast and patted its colossal jaw. He said, 'Sorry, mate,' and then nodded to the boy's father, who stepped forward.

As his father began pulling the flipper out, Dan presented the shell-like bone he had extracted to the boy. 'Souvenir,' he said. 'If you want it.'

The boy took the object and found it was harder than stone. He looked up at Dan. 'What is it?' he asked.

'That's the whale's eardrum. It's how we measure their age. See?' He pointed at some barely legible, mostly translucent lines that ran the length of the object. 'People keep 'em as souvenirs. You can paint a face on it. Your dad never brought you one?'

The boy shook his head and stared at the greyish white eardrum coated in gore. When he next looked up Dan had moved away to join Phil's team as they walked the new whale onto the deck. The boy put the eardrum down beside him and vowed to forget where it was.

His father's team did not mess around. They extended the flippers and hacked at the joints with their long flensers until the flippers had fallen to the wood. Next they sliced the sides of the whale in thick strips almost to the tail. The whale's shiny black skin and the white skin of its underbelly were soon covered with a pink-red syrup that gleamed beneath the lights. His father was covered in the slime. There was something pink and gristly in his beard.

While his father and one of his team sliced, another man attached winch lines to each strip they cut. The winch was cranked and the blubber and skin were peeled off in a thick sticky mess. And the process was repeated. It wobbled like jelly in a bowl as it thumped onto the deck. The man not cutting into the actual carcass used a knife and hacked into the blubber until he had formed multiple squares. These were shoved with his foot into a nearby hole. Then the process was repeated.

The boy watched the blood as it pooled out of the whale onto the deck. It threaded its way to the side and into a deep gutter. One of the team slipped in a puddle of blood on the deck and laughed and caught hold of the whale to save himself from falling.

Soon they had finished stripping the underbelly. What was left was bone and pink. His father gave the boy a blood-soaked grin as he passed and they hooked on another winch and, with all the men shoving, flipped the carcass over. The process began again on top of the head.

The father turned to the boy and said, 'You want a go?'

The boy shook his head. 'No.'

'Come here. Have a look.'

The boy carefully inched closer. His leather shoes fared poorly in the blood and he was deathly afraid of slipping and falling – not because he would face embarrassment, but because he would end up covered in viscera. He managed to make it to his father, who pointed out the cuts.

'We cut here. Then we strip off the blubber and throw it in that hole.'

'Why's there so much blood?'

His father laughed. 'Big animal.'

They finished the head and the stink slowly soaked into the boy's clothes. Once all the square pieces of blubber had been shoved into the hole in the floor, they hacked up the red meat, the intestines, the liver, all the innards. The boy stared in wonder as the whale's heart was unearthed and flopped onto the ground without ceremony, to be set upon by some bloke and his knife with the viciousness of a dog. This muscle that once gave such monstrous life treated so poorly.

The whale's massive tongue was cut into strips and these were pushed into a different unmarked hole in the floor. This dreadful job did not tire the men. Rather, it gave them energy so that they almost leaped about as they worked. All meat and innards were passed through the same hole and they were left with a giant bone carcass and some bristly bits that were in the whale's mouth.

'That's baleen,' his father said while he sharpened his flensing knife. 'You bored, are you?'

The boy shook his head. 'No.'

'You look bored.'

'I'm not bored,' the boy said. 'I feel sick.'

'Sick?'

'This is making me sick. I want to throw up.'

'Come on, mate. You've seen your granddad cut up a pig.'

'I feel sick,' the boy repeated stubbornly.

His father sighed. 'Why don't you go help Brian?' His father nodded to the man still on the hose.

'What if I mess it up?'

'You can't mess that job up. Why they put Brian on it.'

His father smiled in that sinister way he had and the boy, grasping his chance to escape, dashed over to Brian. He avoided the innards and meat and life as best he could. The strong smell, gulls pecking at whale bone. He felt he was in hell.

The boy tapped Brian on the shoulder when he reached him.

The man turned. 'Yeah?'

'I could help?' the boy said.

'Right. Here,' Brian said and handed him the hose. Without further ado the man walked away and left the boy to the task.

Another vessel had anchored and another whale was sliding up the slipway, much smaller than the other two. The boy did his best to copy what Brian had been doing, splashing water beneath the beast. A sound somewhere below them of a saw churning and then the sound of the blade squeaking into stubborn timber. The boy kept on hosing and as the smell began to make him gag he put his face closer and closer to the hose and did his best to focus on the smell of fresh seawater instead of the smell of fresh innards of whales.

TWENTY-THREE

In all, seven whales were hauled up the slipway while the boy watched with subdued horror. He kept an eye out for Brian, so that he might be relieved of his task for a while and sit and rest his legs. But the man didn't return, so the boy was stuck hosing. It took each team an hour to process a whale completely, sometimes longer, though as the night progressed and the boats stopped arriving the men grew quicker. The boy had never felt so tired in his life. His legs and arms were aching and the hose that had once felt so light grew heavy. His mind became muddled and he flicked his head sideways to clear it. He pictured his mother in her summer dress with a hook through her feet being winched up the slippery surface that he was helping to keep wet. She stared at him in mute appeal. He kept hosing, shaking his head, trying to dispel the image.

His father had lost all awareness of his son's existence and was working like a man possessed. Despite his crippled hand and slight build, his father appeared to be a giant among these men, a clear and respected leader who worked quickly and efficiently. The boy envied his father his skill and the delight he seemed to take in his work.

The sun winked up from beneath the horizon and the boy was relieved to see her. He looked down. Sharks were gathered near the base of the slipway, gliding silently through the water, waiting for the next catch. Their fins sliced the surface without sound. The boy was aghast he had not noticed them before.

He was on the verge of being unable to continue, struggling to hold up the hose and aim it true, when Brian appeared beside him, smiling. 'I appreciate that, mate,' he said. He had a mouthful of something and he shoved more in and chewed. 'Always want more experiencing flensing. And always like getting some grub. You alright?'

'Pretty tired,' the boy said.

Brian laughed. 'First night can be hard on a bloke. But you did alright. Here. I'll take over.' He took the hose and nodded towards the mess hall. In the distance came the

Tangalooma with two more whales bobbing. Brian said, 'Go and get some coffee.'

The boy nodded and stepped back and clenched his fingers into fists. He released them then clenched them again. He felt weary in the limbs. His legs were wobbly as he walked back across the deck, taking care to avoid the remnants of whales. Most of the men had disappeared from the deck during the lull and his father was nowhere to be seen. He felt a dull anger in his gut.

As the boy reached the stairs Brian called out, 'Tell your old man there's more coming now.'

The boy nodded without turning then walked down the stairs. He made his way back along the muddy track to the mess hall and swung open the doors.

To his surprise, his father and Phil both were seated at a table with their feet up on other chairs and coffees steaming on the table before them. His father was more relaxed now that he was at work and Phil also seemed contented. The differences between the two the boy had found so puzzling were now diminished by their shared labour. His father said something and Phil tilted his head back and laughed.

In the corner the boy found sachets of instant coffee and emptied one into a blue tin mug then carried it to the large urn where a few other men had congregated to fill their mugs with boiling water. He followed the other men to the milk and then he walked over to his father and sat down next to him.

His father greeted him with a proud smile and said, 'How's your first shift going, mate? You feel like falling asleep?'

The boy nodded and banged his head down on the table in mock exhaustion and started to snore. Both men laughed and the boy raised his head.

Phil said, 'You did alright on that hose, mate. Your dad said you felt a bit sick?'

The boy felt ashamed and for a moment did not respond. Then he said, 'It's a bit big.'

'It is big. It's a big deal.' Phil winked at his father. 'You'll get there.' He looked down and raised his eyebrows. 'What's this on your feet?'

'I forgot to get him boots.'

Phil laughed. 'Bloody hell, mate. That's a bit rough. What else did you forget?'

'Don't know. Haven't unpacked everything yet.'

Phil laughed and punched his father on the arm and his father smiled. 'I've got some spare boots, mate,' Phil said. 'I'll bring 'em by when we're done.'

'We're not done?' the boy asked and was answered by a gale of laughter. He looked outside, remembered Brian's instruction, and said, 'Brian said there were more whales coming.'

His father quickly stood. 'Now?'

Phil was already heading for the door and his father followed. 'You should've bloody led with that, Sam,' he called out.

The other men put down their mugs and followed Phil and the boy's father, and the boy found himself almost alone. Just one other man sat nearby and when the boy looked more closely he saw it was Magnus, who looked as tired as the boy felt. The big man's eyes were shutting slowly and opening and his head dipped towards the coffee he held in both hands so that his red beard almost dipped in. His breathing was slow.

The boy put a cheek on the table. The happiness he had felt at Phil's laughter and his father's good humour had been banished with his mistake. He studied Magnus and wondered if this man also struggled to fit in or if he even considered such things. The coffee was bitter and smelled foul. After one sip the boy wanted to stop but he forced himself to down the rest. Instead of making him feel better he felt the nausea rising again. He gagged, realising he was about to throw up. He ran out of the mess hall without a word to Magnus, who looked properly asleep, and threw up in the bushes beside the front door. He held his stomach and groaned and more vomit came out, sticky brown and hanging in strands from the leaves of the bush. He looked up at the deck and heard the men shouting, and somehow summoned the strength to go on.

He squinted into the early-morning light and shielded his eyes as he stumbled onto the deck, still holding his gut. He searched for his father and tried to take shallow breaths through his mouth lest the foul air make him sick again. Dizzy with fatigue, he rubbed his eyes. He had to stay alert or he might fall asleep mid-stride and land inside a whale and be swallowed up like Jonah. His father would only laugh at him and bury him in entrails.

A hand landed on his shoulder and steadied him. His father's voice whispered, 'Just take a break, mate.'

'I feel sick,' the boy said. He couldn't place where he was on the deck. How close might he be to the slipway? 'I just threw up.'

'Well. That's alright,' his father said. 'Big day. Big couple of days.'

The boy looked up at his father and saw him shake his head.

'I didn't think. You go back to our room, yeah?'

'I don't remember which one is ours.'

'Just look for my shoes. They're out the front.'

The boy did not want to admit he did not know his own father's shoes and so he walked away without saying anything.

He went down the stairs and immediately the sound of the deck became distant and the air seemed fresh.

He found a pair of shoes on the verandah and, not caring if he was wrong and they weren't his father's shoes, he turned the handle and went inside, heading straight for the bed. Then he remembered he was covered with whale insides and so he showered and found his pyjamas in the closet – it was the right room after all – and collapsed onto the mattress. He shut his eyes and fell asleep.

TWENTY-FOUR

When he woke and tried to stretch he realised all his muscles ached. His arms, his chest, his back. Beside him his father was asleep, snoring in that heavy way of his. The curtains were drawn but flapped in a breeze coming through the open window and the sun leaked in around the edges, warming his legs, his chest. Outside the sounds of whaling continued and the smell of cooking carcasses, the boiling of blubber, barbecued sausages, filled their room. The boy could still taste whale blood on his tongue, which made him regret not brushing his teeth. He smacked his tongue against the roof of his mouth.

Lying on his back he stared at the ceiling for a moment before he kicked at the covers and sat up. He looked at the clock on the bedside table. It was 2 pm. So his father had only just knocked off two hours ago. The boy groaned. Another ten hours before they started once more. He needed to go back to sleep.

He realised that his father's snoring was interspersed with someone else's snores. The boy looked over and saw another man asleep on the couch. This bloke had kicked off most of his blankets and his big white belly moved as he breathed. It was matted with sticky hair. A moustache curled at the sides of his mouth and the boy imagined his eyes were blue because his hair was sandy. He was too big for the couch and looked uncomfortable on it. Ashamed at having taken his bed, the boy debated waking the man to swap places with him, but decided against it and lay back down.

Eventually, unable to fall back to sleep, he stumbled from their room in search of fresh air. Standing on the verandah, he looked at the flensing deck. Men who had just started their shift were clambering over yet more whales. The *Tangalooma* bobbed near the end of the slipway. In the distance, near the horizon, a ship moved into view, a whale lashed to her side.

As he turned to enter the room again, he noticed next to the door some gumboots about his size. Phil must have put them there before he fell asleep. The boy felt a rush of gratitude. He picked them up and took them back inside with him and put them beside his bed. This time he easily fell asleep.

That evening, the boy felt ready. Wearing Phil's gumboots, a cup of coffee warming his hands, he sat at a table with his father in the mess hall, two hours before their second shift. He felt included now in the rhythm of the work and knew what to expect and so was less afraid.

His father leaned back and put his hands behind his head, his eyes roaming the room, nodding whenever he caught another man's gaze.

He turned to the boy and smiled and clapped him on the shoulder. 'So,' he said, 'what did you think of your first day?'

The boy said, 'It was alright.'

'How're you doing with the smell?'

The boy had stopped thinking about it and said so.

'Yeah,' his father said. He looked at the ceiling. 'It takes a day or two but you get used to it.' His gaze returned to the boy and the boy did his best to not flinch or turn away. 'You think you'll make it the full twelve hours this time?'

The boy shrugged. 'Don't know.'

'How're you feeling?'

'Okay. Sore. Sore in the back,' the boy said and rolled his shoulders.

'Anywhere else?'

'Everywhere.'

His father smiled. 'You want to be on the hose again tonight?'

The boy nodded. 'Brian seemed to like getting a chance to do something different.'

'Mmm. He would,' his father said. He sipped at his coffee. 'It's not bad though, is it?'

'What?'

'Working.'

'I guess.'

The father did not seem fazed by the boy's response and continued, 'There's something about it.'

'What?'

His father sighed, leaned forward. 'I don't know, mate. It just feels good to be out there. It feels good getting your hands dirty.' He looked down and noticed the boy's new footwear. He looked at the boy's cup. 'You liking the coffee?'

'Not really.'

'It'll help.'

'It makes me feel sick.'

'You'll get used to it.'

The boy swallowed another bitter mouthful. 'I don't think I like killing the whales.'

'They're already dead when we get 'em. You're not killing anything.'

'I just don't like the industry, I think.'

'What industry? The meat industry?'

'I guess.'

'How's it different from killing a cow?'

The boy briefly remembered his mother doing just that as an act of mercy. That had been very different, and long ago. 'I don't think I'd want to kill a cow either.'

'Where do you think meat comes from? What did we just eat?'

The boy looked down at the remnants of his meal: roast lamb, mint sauce, peas, mashed potato. He said, 'I know.'

'How's it different?'

The boy looked aside and took another sip of coffee and hoped his father wouldn't get angry at him. 'It might not be for me, is all.'

'You get used to it. It's not easy to start. Plus you're more sensitive.'

'Sensitive?'

'You care more about animals. I don't know.' His father leaned back in his chair again. 'Whenever we went fishing when you were little, you'd always scream when I reeled one in. It got so your mum made me throw 'em all back. Then we stopped going altogether.' At the mention of the boy's mother his father lowered his head. Then he looked up. 'You'll grow out of all that, though. Would've happened years ago if it was up to me. Can't keep you sheltered from everything. It's not healthy. My old man did it for me. You remember your other grandfather, my papa?'

The boy shook his head.

'Didn't think you would. We'd stopped talking really by the time you came along.'

This made the boy curious; he wondered what had happened. He shifted a little closer in his chair.

'Anyway, I used to be like you, but Papa knocked that out of me early on. Bit hard on a farm if you've got a kid worrying about the cows you have to send off to the abattoir. So he taught me to grow up about it, be a man.'

The boy said nothing. Then, 'What does that mean?'

'What?' his father said. 'Oh, you mean how'd he teach me? He took me, once. Had me stand and watch as they did the cow.' His father's gaze seemed to turn inwards. 'They used to take this pistol and put it right up behind the cow's skull and pull the trigger –' he mimed the actions with his hands '– and fire a big old metal bolt into the base of the skull.' He added his version of the sound, a slap of the tongue to the top of the mouth. 'This was just to stun the poor thing so it wouldn't feel pain. The cow would just buckle at the knees. Then Papa made me slit its throat to bleed her.'

The boy nodded slowly, thought of the whales, and said, 'You weren't nervous?'

His dad smiled. 'I was shaking, mate. I remember the blood coming out of her ...' He shook his head. 'Like I said, I was a bit more sensitive then. But you know, doing it that time, and then working on the farm over the years, just forced it out of me. Good thing, too; I would've been useless otherwise. Would've been useless out here.' He waved his coffee mug to take in the dining hall, all his colleagues. 'Useless in the war, useless at home. Bloke needs to toughen up.'

The boy said, 'Mum told me she had a pet cow once.'

His father laughed. 'Oh yeah. Becca. She told you that?'

The boy nodded, tried to smile with his father.

'We were gonna name you after that cow, you'd been a girl.'

'Becca?'

'Rebecca, yeah. That bloody cow,' his father said. He shook his head ruefully. 'Shame we didn't get a property, have a hobby farm or something at least. Your granddad moved his family back nearer to the city when your mum was just little. She always wanted to get another cow, or a few more. Another reason I got you that dog.'

'Why?'

'She just loved animals, mate. Always had an affinity with them. Saw that in you.'

'Affinity?'

'Like she was connected to them a bit more than the rest of us. Nothing wrong with caring, mate, but you can't let that kind of thing cripple you the rest of your life. You understand?'

The boy nodded and then without pause drained the entire cup of coffee. They sat there, the two of them lost in their thoughts. The boy looked at his father and wondered what his life might be like if his father were a different man. Would his father be different if his own father had been? Would he have brought the boy to this place? He knew in his heart that his mother would have hated what he was doing now, and maybe she'd have hated *him* for doing it. He knew shame so deep then it made his fingers clench.

TWENTY-FIVE

1955

The boy in his haste kept pedalling, but knew he would soon topple. As he went down his arm hit the ground hard, but it was not this that made him afraid; it was the bush he had fallen into, with its spiky leaves. He knew as he put his hand down to right himself that he was stung. He rubbed his arms, which only made the sting worse. The tears started. He struggled to his feet and picked up his bike, then saw the chain had come off. He kicked it, in anger, but knew he'd be in trouble if he just left it, so he picked up the bike and wheeled it back up the dirt path down which he'd ridden.

He was some distance from his home. He ran and cried and wheeled the bike. The rash on his arms spread. His face, too, felt aflame. Maybe his skin would peel off and maybe he would die. Maybe he was poisoned, like from a spider or snake. He ran past an old farm and into town, where he saw Mr Lusby drive by him in his old ute with his eyebrows raised. He ran past the shops without slowing. The stinging grew worse.

At last he reached his house, with its manicured garden out front. He swung open the gate and threw the bike down on the lawn. He ran inside and went to his mother's bedroom and instead found his father asleep there, snoring.

'Dad?' the boy said. He shook his father's body.

His father groaned and looked as if he wanted to swat the boy away. 'What, mate? Bloody hell.'

'Dad?' The boy was still crying. 'Dad, look.'

'What is it?' His father sat up, grunted. 'What's happened?'

'Dad, I ran into some bushes on my bike.'

'Ah, mate,' his dad said, and swivelled to a sitting position. 'Let me look.' He reached over to turn on the lamp so he could see better. He held the boy's arm tenderly. 'Mate,' he said, 'I know it hurts, but it's okay, alright? It's just going to sting a bit and then it'll cool down.'

'Dad, it hurts.'

'I know, mate. I know.' His father rubbed the boy's head. 'Alright, come with me.'

Still in his pyjamas, his father ushered the boy down the hallway and into the bathroom. His father helped him to take his clothes off a bit and then went down the hall to the kitchen as the boy stood there in terror, checking his body. The fiery rash had spread up his legs and came near his private parts. It was under his arms, too. When he looked in the mirror he saw his eyes were surrounded by it.

His father returned, carrying a jug of milk, the liquid sloshing over the sides.

'Dad, that's milk,' the boy said.

'I know, mate. Get in the tub.'

The boy obediently climbed in and sat down and his dad poured the freezing milk over him. He shut his eyes and felt it slither down his back and pool beneath him.

'Rub it all over, bud. Where's it really stinging?'

'On my hands and arms and eyes.'

'Alright. Well don't rub your eyes. But put your arms and hands in it a bit. Here.' His father scooped up some of the milk in his own hands and then cupped them against the boy's eyes. 'Blink your eyes in it, if you can.'

The boy did what he was told and felt the stinging subside.

'You feel any better?'

The boy nodded. 'Mmm. Yes.'

'All better?'

'I think so.'

'Alright, bud. You just sit there for a bit. I'll leave the milk.'

'Wait,' the boy said, and scrambled onto his knees. 'Where are you going?'

'Just going to call your mum and let her know what happened.'

The boy nodded.

'I'll be in the kitchen if you need me, okay?'

He nodded again and then his father was gone.

The boy splashed the milk all over himself and heard the sound of muffled speech coming from the hallway. His father's voice grew heavy, quiet, then loud. The boy couldn't understand what he was saying. Then he saw his father storm past the bathroom door – heading back to the bedroom, the boy assumed.

His mother soon returned. By this time the sting had gone and the boy had calmed down entirely. She flung open the front door and the boy could hear her running to the bathroom. She wrapped her arms around him, not even caring about the milk.

'Sweetheart. Oh, sweetheart. I'm so sorry. Let me look.'

'I think I'm okay, Mum.'

She examined his rash on his arms, near his privates, around his eyes.

'Does it hurt? Does it still hurt?'

'It's okay, Mum. The milk made it better.'

She turned to yell down the hallway, 'And what were you bloody doing letting him go out riding his bike on his own?'

'I was asleep,' his father shouted from somewhere. 'Alright? He's fine.'

'He's not fine!'

'It's probably just a stinging nettle. It'll fade,' his father said, appearing in the doorway. 'He's alright. You're alright, aren't you, mate?'

The boy nodded. 'I think so.'

'We need to take him to the doctor's.'

'Come on, Liz.'

'I can't leave him alone with you for one bloody morning,' she said, almost to herself. She smiled at her son. 'Let's get you cleaned up and we'll go see Dr Richards.'

'Dad didn't let me go riding, Mum. I just went for a ride down to see the bridge.'

'I know, sweetheart.'

'He shouldn't get in trouble, though, Mum.'

The boy looked at his father, who was leaning against the doorframe with his hairy arms crossed. His father smiled a little and said, 'Your mum's just worried about you, mate, that's all.'

'But you didn't let me go riding. I just went and I didn't even ask. I'm sorry.' He looked at his mum. 'I'm sorry.' And the tears started again.

'Ssh,' his mother said. 'Honey, you're okay. You did nothing wrong.'

'Well, he shouldn't've gone off riding without asking, right?' his father said. The boy looked and saw his father's face wide with a grin. 'But I guess we know for next time now, hey, mate?'

The boy was swept from the tub in his mother's arms and so did not see the look she gave his father, though he imagined there was one.

They went into his bedroom, where he was towelled dry and then dressed, then they hurried out to the car. As his mother pulled out of the driveway, the boy looked back to see his father watching from the front door, his arms still crossed.

TWENTY-SIX

1961

In the early dawn the sun suffused the dark about it with its seeping gold. The boy, on the hose, squinted down. There had been more whales this night than the one prior. More teams and new faces the boy did not know. Another man, not Brian, beside the boy, also hosing, unhappy with his lot. The man from their room was in a team of his own working across the deck. The boy was yet to meet him or learn his name. Strange to think this man had slept right near him.

The dinghy with two men aboard and whale lashed to it approached and another man ran out and hooked the chain around the whale's tail. The whale bobbed free from the dinghy and then, without shark intervention, was yanked onto the slipway. When it reached the flat section another heavier cable was attached and the winch started anew. After one night it felt to the boy that this rhythm had always existed.

The men, all assigned specific tasks, operated at high capacity. The boy happy to be included at all. He found himself striving to please these men and perform his task well. He hurled the water further than he had the first night and watched as it soaked in and wet the sections starting to dry beneath the new sun. He shifted his feet as this fresh whale drew closer and soaked its approaching skin. The bulk of it filled his vision and when it did so he looked down. He found himself looking less often in the direction of the flensers. The blood, innards and bone. The blubber as it sprang forth and slapped onto the wood and wobbled. The seagulls perched atop the pink and runny mess. He would not look that way unless he had to.

As the boy was forced to step aside to allow the whale entry onto the flensing deck he extended a hand and patted the dead creature. 'Sorry, mate,' he said, mimicking Dan from the previous night. He felt stupid saying this but glad he had made an effort.

The sun in the sky soon filled the new day so completely that the boy was forced to squint as his eyes adjusted.

His legs were gravy beneath him and his arms had grown thick with exhaustion. He looked to the mess hall and considered finding breakfast. The will to continue with his task slowly ebbed from him and, cursing his lack of discipline, the boy shook his head free of fatigue and turned back to the slipway. There were no new whales approaching and with deliberately unfocused eyes he looked at his father, who had set upon the new carcass, the flipper already lumped near his feet. The boy turned to the man beside him on the hose and said, 'You mind if I duck inside and grab something to eat?'

The man scratched at his eyes. 'I'll go when you get back.'

The boy squinted out to sea. 'There's no chaser heading in.'

'I see that.'

'We could both go.'

The man shook his head. 'Don't want to risk it.'

The boy walked away, his eyes fixed on the ocean instead of the bloodied whale as he passed.

His father saw him and said, 'You going inside?'

The boy nodded and kept walking.

'You sharpen this for me?'

His father unsheathed his knife and handed it, with the blade facing towards himself, to the boy.

'It looks sharp already,' the boy said.

'Mate. Come on.'

The boy took the knife. He went down the steps, along the path and entered the busy mess hall, where he fixed himself a cup of coffee and sat at a table. He looked at the knife with its dried blood on the blade. It was sticky to handle. He patted his pockets for the whetstone bestowed on him by his father and, with rising panic, realised he no longer had it. He double-checked each pocket and found nothing. Looking at the knife on the table, he contemplated his mistake, trying to work out where he could've lost the whetstone.

When he finished his cup of coffee he had another and helped himself to some of the cold pancakes. He rubbed and rubbed at his tired eyes. Growing still weaker in spirit. Unable to make it halfway through a shift without needing a break. Losing things. He needed sleep.

A man sat down opposite him and the boy blinked his tired eyes and realised it was Phil, smiling. 'You leave the hose out there, mate?'

The boy nodded. 'I needed a coffee. And breakfast.'

'You should've said something,' Phil said. 'Or put some-body else on it. Another chaser's come in. How long you been sitting there?'

The boy swore loudly for the first time in his life, which made Phil laugh. He stumbled from his seat, leaving his dirty plate. Phil called out as he left, 'Hey? This your knife?'

The boy wheeled around and grabbed it and as he exited the mess hall he heard Phil ask, 'You liking the boots, mate?'

On deck, the hose was now manned by some other bloke; the man the boy had left in charge was nowhere in sight. His furious father was flensing, aiming his anger at the whale carcass before him. The boy imagined having strips torn from his own body as he stood uselessly by the whale, watching the new man hose. A bloke was on the carcass and slipped in the gore of it. The blubber made a ripping sound like sticky paper when it was winched off. There was so much blood and smell up close. The coffee at risk of coming back up.

The boy watched his father for a time and considered asking if he could head inside but felt weak for even having the thought.

While his father's attention was fixed on the whale, he wandered around the deck, looking for the whetstone, but found no trace of it. Near another team he spied a whetstone sitting beside a coil of rope. Inspecting it, he decided it was probably not his own, though it was of a similar make. Still, desperate not to anger his father, he slipped it into his pocket. Then he walked over to a hose, wet the stone and sharpened his father's blade. When he handed the knife back he received no thanks or acknowledgement from his father, who merely sheathed it and carried on with his work. The other team did not seem to notice the missing stone. The boy watched them work, feeling guilty and ashamed, but all the same he did not return the whetstone for fear that his father would have need of it again. No telling what he might do if he discovered the boy had lost it.

As the day dragged on he found himself standing motionless, watching his father work. His eyelids were heavy and his gut was heaving so eventually he said, 'Can I go in?'

'We need to know when somebody leaves. You should have said something.'

The boy said, 'I left some other guy doing it. And I did say something. I told you.'

'Don't blame others for your mistakes,' his father said, attaching the winch that would flip the whale onto its underbelly. The boy thought of his mistake with the whetstone. 'I didn't see nobody else hosing but you.'

The boy muttered, 'I wasn't even supposed to be working.'

'What was that?' his father said. He let go of the winch and leaned on the carcass. He wiped his forehead with his bloody forearm, leaving a red smear, and stared at the boy. 'What did you say?'

'You said I wouldn't have to work for a bit,' the boy said, hating the whine he heard in his own voice. 'And I told you. You gave me the knife to sharpen, remember?'

'Don't give me excuses, Sam,' his father said, then returned his attention to the winch.

When the whale was flipped and had rested and his father had started in with the flenser again he said, 'Thought it was good that you found something you could do, keep you occupied. Now you're bloody whingeing about it. Anyway –' he made another three clean cuts '– head inside then, if you have to.'

His father refused to look at the boy, instead giving instructions to a man closer to the whale. The boy looked at this man, who also refused to meet his gaze. He looked at the other men on the deck working, the men from whom he had taken the whetstone, and felt invisible to all. He walked from the deck with his hands in his pockets and his head down, the sun biting hard into his neck.

As he showered in his room he regretted all his actions. He sighed and leaned his head against the shower door and let the water slosh over him until he couldn't feel the texture of it anymore.

He stepped out of the shower, dried himself and dressed in his pyjamas. With head in hands he sat on the couch that was his bed and sobbed. Then he covered himself in blankets and was soothed to sleep by the sound of his colleagues working.

He woke. It was early afternoon and his father and the other fellow were still asleep. The boy sat up and then lay back down on the couch and shut his eyes. Sleep eluded him.

He walked to his father's bedside and looked at this older version of his self, his mouth agape, his heavy beard. The boy quietly opened the bedside table and found a Bible, then returned to the couch and read it until he felt sleepy. He put the book down, fell asleep for a short time, then woke again. Frustrated, he walked outside, leaned on the rail, and watched the activity on the deck.

The new bloke woke up before his father did. When the boy returned to the room the larger man was patting his belly and looked contented, still sleepy. He smiled at the boy and said, 'You the bloke who stole my bed?'

The boy replied, 'Sorry,' and looked at his still-sleeping father.

The larger man's smile widened. 'Don't worry about it. I'm Steve.'

The two shook hands; the boy measured his grip and gave three firm pumps before release.

'You're a bit young, aren't you?'

'I know.'

'How old are you?'

With his father asleep the boy decided he would tell the truth. 'Thirteen.'

'Bloody hell. Why're you out here?' Steve walked to the mini-fridge in the corner of the room, opened it and withdrew a bottle of milk. He sculled a great quantity then turned his attention back to the boy. 'I mean, why're you out here when you're so little?'

The boy glanced at his father then said, 'My mum died. And Dad wanted me to come with him and learn, I guess.'

'Your mum died?'

The boy nodded.

'Bugger, mate. Sorry to hear that.' Steve scratched the top of his head. His hair was longer hair than the boy's father's. He sat on his bed and the springs squeaked. He put on a shirt he found nestled among his bedsheets and started on his shoes. 'Bugger me.'

'Yeah.'

'How?'

The boy was confused. 'You mean how did she die?'

'Yeah. I mean –' Steve looked guilty '– if it's not too personal.'

The boy sat on the couch. 'She was sick.'

'Ah, mate . . .' Steve sat forward, elbows on his knees. 'Kid your age shouldn't have no mum.' He smiled. 'Guess the work helps distract you from it a bit, yeah?'

'A bit.'

'You think about her much?'

The boy nodded. 'A bit.'

'Yeah. Good to think about her.'

They fell silent, and the boy knew he should ask a question of his own, so he tried, 'How long you been doing this?'

Steve looked relieved at the change of subject. 'It's my third year.'

'You like it?'

'I like the bloody money. Could do without the smell.'

Another silence. The boy stood and looked for something to do with his hands.

Steve watched for a few seconds then said, 'I might head down and grab some breakfast. You want to come?'

'No, thanks.' The boy shook his head. 'I'll wait for my dad.'

'No worries, mate.' A pause, then a chuckle. 'Did I hear that you've been thieving other blokes' whetstones?'

The boy turned and stared. 'No,' he said. 'Who told you that?'

'Don't worry about it. I shouldn't have said anything.'

'Who, though?'

'Mate, don't worry about it. Really. Guy's just a bugger stirring up trouble, yeah? Who cares if you did? It's just a whetstone. Anyway –' he clapped his hands on his knees '– I'm going.' He stood and walked to the door, stopped, and looked like he wanted to say something else. He soon managed, 'I am sorry about your mum.' Then he left.

The boy sat alone in the room with his sleeping father and watched the man breathe.

Then he said quietly, 'Me too.'

TWENTY-SEVEN

They ate a late dinner, the boy seated across from his father. The noise of the room was less jubilant than on the previous nights, the men now used to their new routine and weary from toiling beneath the glare of the gigantic lights.

Phil sat nearby and when the boy looked over he winked and smiled, maybe aware of the boy's sins. The boy felt shame for his mistakes from the previous night deep in his gut. Steve walked by and patted him on the head.

When he and his father walked onto the deck to begin their shift they were approached by a bloke who looked like a possum in a spotlight, all wiry and fearful, but with his chest raised in a show of aggression. The boy realised with a sick feeling that this was the bloke to whom the stolen whetstone belonged. This must be the man who had accused him.

'Walt? This your kid?'

His father looked around in bewilderment before settling his gaze on the man and the boy saw immediately the fire kindle within him, his bad fist clenched, the tendons on his wrist. 'You alright, Harry?'

'Your kid here stole my bloody whetstone yesterday.'

The gaze his father levelled at the boy could have meant anything. Then he said to Harry, 'Step back, mate.'

'There's no bloody place on deck for kids, mate, and he doesn't know what he's doing. Wanders around like he needs a whack in the head to put him straight.'

'My kid doesn't steal. He's a good boy. And he's learning, mate.' His father bit off the last word like he'd meant violence with it. 'You got no call to be speaking down about other's abilities on this deck, yeah?'

Harry wasn't put off by the implied insult. 'You gonna return my whetstone?'

'I'm telling you he didn't steal it. You didn't take it, did you, mate?'

Squirming beneath his father's gaze, the boy wished he had the courage to tell the truth, but instead he said, 'No. I used the one you gave me.'

'There. That's it.'

'I had it there.' Harry pointed an angry finger. 'Will saw your kid wandering around near it, and then it wasn't there. You reckon it disappeared by magic?'

'Mate, step back.'

'Your kid –'

The boy did not see his father's fist swinging until it connected with Harry's jaw. Harry himself seemed to be taken by surprise, and he stumbled back. Then he reared forward and the two men were locked together in a violent hug, their feet stomping into the deck like two bulls, horns entwined.

The boy was pushed aside as two men ran over and grabbed his father. Others latched onto Harry and the two men were held apart.

The boy's father seemed calm, laughing, but Harry struggled violently against the arms restraining him, spitting foul obscenities at the boy's father.

Eventually he quietened, and his mates coaxed him back to his team. As Harry passed he looked at the boy with such hatred the boy felt his stomach lurch. He knew that what had happened was his fault entirely and he had no way of making amends without causing further harm.

The men who had surrounded his father soon let him be, patting him on the back as they drifted back to work.

The boy, after waiting another moment, approached his father.

His father, looking at his flenser, said, 'You alright?'

'Are you?'

His father laughed. 'Harry's an arsehole, mate. Don't pay attention to him. You'll meet them in life, you know? All kinds. Can't let 'em get one over on you.' He paused. 'You got that whetstone handy? Might sharpen the flenser.'

The immediate fear his crime would be discovered. 'I left it in the room, sorry.'

His father shrugged. 'Just bring it next time.'

'Is it true? What he said?'

'What? About you needing a whack in the head?'

'Yeah.'

'Do you think it's true?'

The boy shrugged. 'I don't know.'

'Well. Don't believe everything everybody says about you. Yeah?'

The boy nodded. 'What should I do?'

'Go to the hose again, if you want.'

Instead of moving away, the boy stayed watching his father, the assured way he handled the flenser. He said, 'Thanks.'

'For what?'

'For sticking up for me.'

His father laughed. 'He's an arsehole,' he repeated. 'Had it coming. Don't worry about it.'

The boy walked away thinking about how he had failed his father and hoping there would be no further repercussions. He also hoped he would never be forced to admit what he'd done and so damage his reputation in his father's eyes. His father had called him a good boy and this was what he wanted to be from now on.

He found Brian on the hose and when he approached to take over he got a shake of the head, as if he were no longer trusted with the task. The boy didn't step closer but neither did he immediately move away. He stood with his hands in his pockets and rocked back and forth on his heels like he didn't care.

After the first few whales, which came in quick succession, he made his way to his father's side and stood and watched as he flensed with expert precision. Each of his cuts sank in just so to the edge of the blade, and each slice was straight and spaced evenly. The whale's skin opened up a cavity from which blood oozed slowly. A canyon with wet, pulsing walls. This thought disgusted him. His father didn't seem to notice he was there. There were a number of discarded eardrums lining the side of the flensing deck now, and in their pink and red discardment the boy saw himself. The smell of cooking blubber reminded the boy of their small campfire.

His father finished stripping the blubber, and the meat and innards cascaded onto the deck in a sloppy shower. The boy was loath to step near them even with his boots on.

Without fuss, his father's team cut the innards and other parts into small chunks, and as they shovelled them out of the empty whale slowly the white bone emerged. Some meat and other red bits still clung to the bones, the ribs forming a cage. The boy stepped between the ribs and held two of them in his hands, staring out at his father as if from behind bars.

His father turned and said, 'What're you doing?'

'Looking.'

'Get out of there. Help us push 'em to the saw.'

The boy helped the men to shove the bones to the hole at the rear of the deck. When they were dropped in there came a crash from below. The boy could hear the sound of the bones being ground by the saw and turned into meal.

'Listen,' his father said when he returned. He bent down to look him in the eyes. His red and glistening hand rested on the boy's shoulder. 'It's not okay you keep slipping off before our shift is up. Okay? I know it's hard, I know you're young, but you need to push through it. You need to stay here for the whole shift. That's your job tonight. You just focus on making it to the end. Once you're over the hump, it gets easier. It's because you keep on giving up that you're struggling so much. So just stay awake tonight, alright? You show Harry what you can do.'

The boy had almost forgotten about the earlier violence. He nodded and said, 'When do we get a day off?'

His father smiled. 'We don't.' He kept smiling despite his son's expression. 'We work seven days a week. I only do this a few months a year, we all do, and during those months we work as hard as we can to get it bloody done. We do get off night shifts eventually, though, and you get a good half-day then to get used to it.'

His father walked away to await the next whale and the boy watched as he approached a team member and started to chat. The boy became genuinely concerned that he might die from exhaustion. The task before him felt too monumental for his young body and young mind. He wondered what on earth his father had been thinking, consigning him to this earthbound hell. Limping on aching feet, he walked down the stairs that led to his room.

TWENTY-EIGHT

Over the coming days, the boy's ability to function despite a lack of sleep increased. He worked on the hose occasionally, but apart from that he only watched. A few times he fell on his back in the cool grass outside the mess hall and looked at the sky but didn't shut his eyes. Most of the men smiled and teased him as they shuffled into the mess hall, and the boy accepted this with good humour. He didn't manage to finish an entire shift but found he forgave himself readily and started again the next day with renewed enthusiasm for the task he had once seen as insurmountable.

Amid all of this the boy dreaded coming upon Harry. When the two of them were in the same room the boy felt sick with guilt and would often look over at the man to keep an eye on him, to assure himself the hatred he sensed emanating from Harry was all in his mind, though he knew it wasn't. A dark bruise soon clouded the right side of the man's face.

Having just started a new shift, awaiting their first whales, he and his father stood on deck. With winter now started in earnest the winds of a night-time were thinner and penetrated skin more quickly. He looked forward to warmer months, and dreaded spending such a long time in this place. Soaked to the skin with blood. Who would he be by then? It took a few whales each night, slipping by him as he worked on the hose, before his legs would warm up. Now he stood with his arms wrapped around his middle. His father's team were seated on barrels and coils of ropes to the side of the deck. Harry and his team were still in the mess hall. Phil was nowhere nearby. The boy watched his father sharpen his flensing knife with the stolen whetting stone, gripping it with his three-fingered hand. His father, as if sensing his gaze, said, 'What is it?'

'How long before you were able to work a whole shift?'

His father grinned. 'I've done a lot harder work than this.'

'In the war?'

'Yeah, in the war.'

'What did you do?'

His father pocketed the stone and swung the knife back and forth. 'You just never slept at all. Even when you could sleep you were in the mud or the jungle, and the Japs were always somewhere. Even when they weren't there, they were there. You understand?'

The boy nodded, licked his lips. 'So you started out working the whole night?'

'Yep.'

The boy looked down at his gumboots, which were splashed with dried blood. 'Why can't I, then?'

'What? Work through?'

The boy nodded.

His father sighed. 'I don't know. You're young, I guess. You're doing alright, mate. Don't worry about it.'

'What about on the farm?'

His father smiled. 'That's right, mate. Took me a long while to get it on the farm. And I was working less than you. You'll get there.'

The boy nodded, but deep down he felt that he had failed his father and that if he only tried harder he might manage to push through this weakness and just work and work. Maybe the problem was that he had been giving into this urge where his father had determined to subdue it. Maybe it was that simple.

He worked hard that shift, taking turns on the hose and helping to push the bones into the holes at the rear of the deck, but despite this by dawn he was struck with the familiar lethargy in his limbs. Instead of running to the mess hall to drink coffee, he threw himself into his tasks with even more vigour.

During a lull between whales in the early hours, the boy stood near his father and his father's team as they sharpened their knives. He shut his eyes for a moment and lost his bearings and swayed on his feet. He pressed hard at his eyes until they were sore. A real struggle to open them again. He was so weary and distracted he managed to miss an incoming whale – despite its size – and another man shoved him aside as the whale was winched into position, right where he'd stood.

As he waited for Dan to inspect the whale's dimensions, his father said with a sigh, 'Just go, mate.'

'I want to make it to the end.'

'Just go. Make it tomorrow.'

'What's the time?'

'It's seven-thirty.'

The boy was downcast.

One of his father's team added, 'We only want you here if you're not getting in the way and you're getting in the bloody way.' The bloke glanced at his father as if fearing a reaction.

His father refused to look at the boy, who was hurt by the implied rejection and angry at himself for having caused it. All he craved was his father's approval. He felt like he might cry and hated that about himself too. So he left.

As he walked along the verandah to their room he passed Phil, who had a steaming cup of coffee in his hand and a smoke dangling from his mouth. Whale blood glistened on his boots. He was leaning on the rail watching the flensing deck with acute interest, but when the boy approached he turned and put a hand on his shoulder.

'You alright?'

'I can't make it to the end of a shift,' the boy said. His voice cracked when he spoke.

'That's alright, mate. Who told you you had to?'

The boy shook his head. 'Dad. I know he wants me to.'

Phil looked back at the deck and sighed and rolled his shoulders. He said, 'Don't worry so much, alright? It took me a while to adjust. Everybody's different. You're young. Might just take a while. Your old man's got other concerns anyway.'

'What other concerns?'

'Heard he's been called into Melsom to sort out what happened between him and Harry last week.'

The boy's shame increased. 'You mean he could get fired?'

Phil laughed. 'I doubt that, mate. He's too valuable. Harry provoked him, anyhow. But it's probably on his mind.'

The boy started to tear up and angrily swatted his face and sniffed. He smiled through it and said, 'Sorry.'

'What for?' Phil asked.

The boy shrugged.

Phil smiled. 'Mate, don't you worry. Just head inside, try again tomorrow.' Phil tousled his hair and walked away, turning by the steps to ask, 'How're those boots doing?'

'They're great,' the boy said, and he watched as Phil walked along the path and up the stairs back to the deck. When Phil passed the boy's father, he stared at the man's back. His father didn't notice, and kept flensing.

Over the next week, the boy woke each morning determined and went to sleep sore, defeated, angry at himself, angry at his father. The cycle was making him sick with doubt. Sometimes, in his deep exhaustion, he would sob on his couch under the blankets. He knew he would give up, if it were an option, and felt ashamed of this weakness. Understood his father and resented him all the same.

The next day the boy was still at work on the hose, aiming the water low, when his father approached him. The sun behind him shone and the boy squinted through it and saw a smile. 'Mate. We're done.'

The boy breathed a sigh of relief and smiled, and his father shook his hand, grinning wide. The other team members walked by him and though they said nothing he saw that he had earned a small amount of respect and felt pleased.

The men leaving the deck greeted those starting their shifts with smiles and weary nods. The boy followed them and did likewise, handing the hose like a baton to the next bloke.

They headed into the mess hall and ate a large meal of spaghetti. The boy kept looking outside at the sun warped by the glass and curtains and the leaves that never looked so green. He ate well and didn't feel sick and his father laughed. 'You look pleased.'

The boy nodded. 'Didn't think I'd make it.'

'Ever?'

'Yeah.'

'Mate,' his father said, 'some things just take time.' The man swallowed, looked down at his knees. 'Not good, being soft, you know. Good you've finished your shift. Like me on the farm. Proving yourself. Changing who you are, yeah?'

The boy didn't respond, just kept eating until he'd finished everything on his plate, then rose to go put his dishes and cutlery in the tubs. He thought of his mother. He'd often helped her at the sink with the plates when it had been just the two of them. Difficult to think of her. Though he knew she would be proud of him – how determined he was, how sincere he was in effort – he felt bad because he'd not spoken to her for some time and had forgotten her completely while he worked. Like she'd never been. This ate at his sense of triumph, but he did his best not to let it. She wouldn't want to be remembered out of guilt.

After dinner he showered, and stared at his new reflection in the bathroom mirror, trying to discern what changes had been wrought.

As he stretched out on the couch and closed his eyes, he moved his weary limbs and tested his fatigued body. Not as bad as he thought it would be. Better than the previous weeks. There was an honour to his weariness now.

TWENTY-NINE

The boy soon found himself slipping into a routine. Though he had not yet touched a knife and the sight and smell of butchered whale still troubled him, he gradually became accustomed to working on the deck. He still hated the job, though. Each time a new whale was brought on deck he felt such sympathy for the carcass it was difficult for him to just stand there as Dan sliced out the eardrum and his father winched off the blubber. Each time a piece was ripped from the belly the boy winced and pictured the winch attached to his own stomach.

He kept a constant eye on Harry, who usually worked on the opposite side of the deck. He kept the whetstone he'd stolen in his pocket and whenever his eyes met Harry's he would think of it. If his father asked to use it to sharpen his blade, the boy would feel sick with anxiety as he held out the stone, sure his father would discover his deception. His father and Harry avoided each other as much as possible and the whole deck seemed thankful for it. Still, the boy dwelled on how quickly the violence had escalated before, and feared Harry would approach him and simply swipe a flenser across his stomach and watch his innards pool near his feet and laugh. Nothing his father could do would stop such swift retribution and he would be dead with his mother in the afterlife.

On the deck the boy watched the horizon as a breeze struck. A hand rested on his shoulder and the boy turned. 'Here,' his father said, and handed the boy a knife. It was sticky with blood and looked razor sharp up close.

'What do I do?'

'I want you to help Marshall here cut up the blubber.'

'Into squares?'

'Yeah.'

The boy nodded and regarded the blade. He kneeled beside Marshall, careful with his knife, and Marshall said, 'You know what you're doing?'

The boy shrugged. 'I'll just copy you.'

'You gotta be quick about it, the pace we work.'

'I know,' the boy said.

When the next piece of blubber was peeled from the whale they shuffled over to it and kneeled before it as though in prayer. The boy watched Marshall work. His movements were quick and deft as he sliced each piece into precise squares. Before the boy could say a word, Marshall said, 'Get in here. Start on the other end.'

The boy complied, but he was much slower than Marshall, and he had to keep looking up to make sure he had estimated the dimensions correctly. He had never touched the blubber before. It was like jelly: slimy, smelly, wobbly jelly. Hard to pin down, like eggshell in yolk. He made only a few cuts before Marshall had reached him from the other end and finished his work for him. He hadn't managed a single square. Marshall said nothing, but the boy could read the contempt in his eyes as he shoved the squares he had formed into the boiler hole.

While he worked the boy thought about Albert and how the dog might fare on this island. He also thought of how he had changed since coming to the island and wondered if his mother would have still recognised him. When he looked up from his task he noticed Melsom had appeared on deck and was standing next to his father chatting. He was wearing tan shorts the same as his father's and gumboots. He was pointing at the boy. The boy felt his stomach drop at this and knew he had been discovered:

they'd seen the whetstone, his father had figured it out, he was to be cast out.

The boy stood, terrified, and walked over. Melsom greeted him with a smile that warped his beard. 'You on the knife now?'

The boy nodded and then noticed his father's narrowed eyes. 'Dad just gave it to me today,' he said. 'To learn. I only just started.'

'Right,' Melsom said. He looked at the boy's father and raised his eyebrows. 'You sure about putting him on the knife, Walter?'

His father nodded, which lifted the boy's heart. 'He's been doing well, helping with the bones. He had a few weeks on the hose. Thought it was time to start him on something small.'

'And Marshall's double-checking everything?'

'Yeah,' his father said.

'Well,' Melsom said, 'best get back to it, son. Keep up the good work.'

The boy, dismissed, returned to his task. The knowledge that his theft remained undetected did nothing to silence the churning of his guilt. Like choppy water in his gut. Despite Melsom's praise and his father's pride, the blubber became even more sticky, trickier to handle. The boy exerted what remaining energy he had, and finished his shift with the other men. He ate and showered and tried his best to fall asleep quickly.

The next day the men were eating in the mess hall, the noise so loud the boy had to crane his neck to better hear what his father was saying. His father leaned forward and shouted something about the boats and Phil, across the table, sat back in his chair and nodded solemnly.

Then Melsom stood up and shouted, 'Right!' and the men slowly quietened. He took a moment, looking down, before he spoke.

'I'm sure by now you've heard the planes,' he said, though the boy had not noticed them. 'They've been doing their job, working hard, long hours, but there's still less whales here than we would've liked. You may have noticed there's been fewer coming in each shift.'

The men murmured then hushed again.

'You boys haven't been meeting your shift quotas, which hasn't happened before. So we're going to be lowering the quota to five whales per team per shift.'

Renewed murmurs at this, and it took some time before the men fell silent. His father said not a word but continued to stare at Melsom.

'And we're going to be sending out another plane. Now, I don't care if you make that quota in the first hour. When you've met the quota, you clock off. I can't keep paying you lot to drink coffee. Yeah?' He paused, took a breath. 'This season might last a little longer, so whatever you need to do to make allowance for this – call your family or whatever – make sure you do it. The phone in the office is always available. You need to be ready to stay an extra month this year, maybe two, which might lead right through Christmas. I know this bloody grates, but it's the way its gotta be so we all come out with a decent cheque at the end.'

The men reacted to this with groans and angry mutters.

Melsom waited for quiet before he spoke again. 'Keep a good attitude about it. This is the industry we work in. We're doing our best. We're going to have rough spots. Keep working hard and we'll be out of here soon enough.'

He looked as though he might continue, but instead he sat down and stared at his empty plate.

The men resumed their chatter and it seemed as though the anger had dissipated, or at the very least been buried until a later time. The boy, at the mention of the season being extended, had started breathing harder. He knew his father had normally been away four or five months a year and already felt deeply afraid that he might not survive until that time. That his father would be travelling home on that boat with the boy's own carcass towed behind. After his triumph at being able to last a whole shift, he had almost started to feel like he might make it through the whole season. Now, knowing the season might go right through

Christmas, the boy knew for sure he was in purgatory. Each day the same. Each day. Not a single day of rest. The boy took a mouthful of the meat on his plate, still breathing hard, and looked up at his father.

Phil said from across the table, 'Well, that's a bugger, eh?'

'It's not that bad,' his father said. 'People acting like some bloke got shot. Could be worse.'

'Never happened before, though.'

'I know.'

'So maybe that's it? For whaling I mean. Maybe we're done.'

His father shook his head and swallowed. 'It's just a mongrel season. If the numbers were dwindling, if there weren't as many, it would've decreased gradually. We've had a sudden drop. So it's probably something to do with the temperature of the waters. Or maybe the Japs have been getting more down in the Antarctic, scared the rest off. Who knows?'

The boy said, 'The Japs?'

'The Japanese hunt whales down in the Antarctic before we can get to them,' his father said. 'Bloody stupid, too.'

'Why?'

'The whales store up blubber while they're down there for their journey north, to breed. We get 'em on the journey, so they're as plump as they get. The Japs hunt 'em all through, so no telling how much blubber'll be on them. Waste of good whale.'

The boy looked at Phil, who was cutting into his meat.

Phil said, 'Normally plenty to go around but, hey, Walt?'

'Yeah. Normally.'

'Anyway. Who knows, right?' Phil pointed at the boy's plate with his fork. 'How's the whale, Sam?'

The boy looked down and swallowed the meat in his mouth. 'This is whale?'

Phil laughed. 'Tastes like steak, doesn't it?'

His father said, 'They serve whale steaks in here sometimes, just for fun. I've never liked the taste, myself.'

The boy looked at the meat on his plate and lifted an edge with his fork. It looked like beef. He cut off another bit and chewed. Before, in his ignorance, he had not tasted the ocean, but now he knew what it was the salt and brine of the ocean was more apparent. The steak was thick and chewy, but tasted okay. His new knowledge made it hard to eat, though. He pushed his plate away before he was finished.

Phil laughed so hard when he saw this that some of the men at a nearby table turned to see what was so funny. 'What's the matter, mate?' Phil asked. 'No good now?'

'I was finished anyway.'

'Sure you were,' Phil said, and winked.

The boy still did not like being teased. He looked at his father for his reaction, but his father just chewed and said nothing.

The boy went to fetch a cup of coffee to escape further mockery, and took his time about spooning in the granules. When he returned, the conversation had shifted.

Phil was saying, 'By the sound of things we might be getting a little more downtime this season. Might have to start hunting again. Can't remember when we last had time off here?'

'Normally too busy,' his father said. 'Four years ago?'

'Yeah, maybe. You want to come hunting, Sam?'

'Sure,' the boy said immediately, then regretted it. He'd been so thrilled by the invitation he'd forgotten what hunting would actually entail.

'Great,' Phil said. 'We just hunt pigs here, nothing serious. But it can be good fun in the dunes.'

His father said nothing but regarded the boy while chewing his whale, raising his eyebrows in question. The boy refused to answer.

The three men left the mess hall and stood out in the breeze beneath the cloudless sky and looked at the stars. His father turned to watch the men still working on the deck and said to the boy, 'You want to see a movie? We have time before we start.'

'Where?' the boy asked. 'Here?'

His father smiled. 'They screen movies here sometimes. Let's go see what's on. You coming, Phil?'

'I think I might try to fit in a nap, boys, but I'll see you on the deck.' Phil raised a hand and walked away.

His father put an arm around the boy's shoulders and together they followed an old path around the mess hall. In the dark it was hard to see the leaves before they slapped into his face. They came to a room at the rear of the hall and entered.

There was a movie already playing, bathing its audience in a wash of light as they leaned back on plastic chairs. The air was cold and the boy saw an air-conditioner at the back of the room pumping chill despite the cool evening. They sat down beneath it, facing the screen. The movie playing was *The Magnificent Seven*. The boy had seen this film already the year before with his mother. He had never seen a film with his father before and found the man already removed from him. His mother had sat close beside him and whispered things to him, explaining the parts he might not have understood. His father maybe had more respect for him, or less empathy. In one scene a little boy told Charles Bronson that his father was a coward and Charles Bronson said all fathers were brave because they carried responsibility.

It was during this scene that his father leaned over and whispered to the boy, 'Did I ever tell you how I lost my fingers?'

In the dark the boy shook his head.

His father leaned closer and whispered, 'I lost 'em in New Guinea. Bloody stupid it was, too. Why I probably don't talk about it much, I guess. It wasn't during combat, or anything like that.' He shook his head. 'I slipped, fell, cut my fingers on a tree branch when I tried to catch hold of myself. And then I didn't get it checked out. Bloody stupid. Just being stubborn. Cuts got infected and by the time I got 'em seen to they had to come off.' The boy saw his father clench his broken hand.

His father looked up. 'Thing is, mate, you don't hear me going on about it. I could spend my time here complaining about my fingers, how it hurts to even grip the knife, but I don't. I just get on with what needs to be done. That's what a man does. Now I watched you when you started here, and before that as well, and you'd complain about every little thing. But here you've been keeping your head down, just doing what needs to be done, doing as you're told. I wanted you to know I'd noticed.'

The boy knew that this was as close to affirmation as his father would come. He looked at the man, whose eyes were still fixed on the screen. In the flickering projector light his face looked monstrous as the shadows played across it.

After a moment the boy asked, 'Are you going to lose your job because of the fight?'

His father shook his head almost imperceptibly. 'Don't be stupid, mate. We sorted it out. He's not working our shift anymore.'

'Does Harry hate you?'

'Probably. It doesn't matter.'

The boy thought about this. Maybe his father was right and it didn't matter.

The two of them watched the rest of the film and enjoyed the final shootout, but the boy felt sad when each gunman passed. Giving up their lives for a cause was a noble but silly thing. No blood need be shed at all.

THIRTY

A few days later they were informed they would be moving to the day shift. They knocked off that day at midday as usual and the plan was to stay up until midnight, but the boy only lasted till six o'clock. He woke up too early the next morning, around four, and struggled to go back to sleep. The snores of Steve and his father coalesced into a constant thrum and the boy knew they they were not going to wake for some time. He had eight more hours before starting work, and then he had to work a twelve-hour shift. He feared he wouldn't be able to make it through the shift and would have to revisit those feelings of deep shame and failure until his body adjusted to the new working day.

After tossing and turning for some time, he rose and went outside to look at the deck and watch the men who were toiling at his old shift. They looked busy but soon the last whale was flensed and the man at the chalkboard shouted and the men stopped work and stood idle. The boy saw Harry among them and realised he now felt less fear. The man was chatting with his colleagues as a few cleaned up. There were no more inbound vessels that the boy could see, but the men must not have met their quota yet because they didn't leave the deck. Some of the men sharpened their knives, and others levered up the planks of wood lining the deck and scrubbed them with soapy water from a bucket. The boy was surprised to see that the planks were laid on a concrete base; he'd assumed the deck was wooden the whole way through.

Towards dawn a chaser approached across the sea and the boy could see a small whale lashed to each side. The men on deck surged forth and stood at the top of the ramp and watched as the whales were unloaded.

The boy's father woke not long afterwards. He shuffled to the railing and leaned on it like his son and said, 'You want to get breakfast?'

The boy nodded. 'Yes.'

'How long you been up?'

'A while.'

They returned to the room and pulled on some clothes then crept out, shutting the door quietly on Steve's heaving bulk.

In the mess hall the boy served himself three rashers of bacon and two eggs on toast and his father added two hash browns to his plate. They carried their plates to a table then the boy went back to fetch two coffees. He set one down in front of his father, who had a mouthful of egg.

'Cheers, mate.'

'No worries.'

Phil, the boy saw, was seated at another table with his guitar in his lap and when he caught sight of the boy he smiled and came over. He sat opposite the boy, next to his father. Strummed.

His father said, 'Can't sleep?'

'No,' Phil said, and strummed again, a sadder chord. He looked at the boy. 'You sleep alright, Sam?'

The boy shook his head. 'Got up around four.'

'Four!' Phil said, and laughed. 'You're going to be walking around dead come ten o'clock tonight. Four! Bloody hell.'

His father smiled and the boy smiled with him. 'He does alright,' his father said.

Phil said, 'You been up to the dune yet?'

'What dune?'

His father shook his head and swallowed his mouthful. 'We haven't done anything yet.'

'But you told him about it?'

'No.'

'Oh, mate,' Phil said, and slammed a hand on the table, which made Sam's untouched coffee slosh over the sides of the cup. 'One of the biggest dunes in the world on this very island. Just down the shore a bit.'

'Yeah?'

'I could take him now if you like, Walter? Give you a bit of a break.'

The boy resented the implication that he was a burden on his father, but his father nodded and said, 'Sure. I might rest.'

'You want to go now, Sam?'

'What do I need?'

'Just what you got.'

They left his father still eating, Phil placing his guitar in the corner of the mess hall. The boy felt nervous about what would follow. He didn't really know this man.

They walked down to the beach and the sand was white and brilliant in the sun. Only the breeze reminded the boy that it was winter. He looked for sharks in the water but didn't see any trace of them. The boy took his gumboots off and scrunched his toes in the warm sand and smiled. With the boy carrying his boots, the pair walked along the shore, looking out at the moderate-sized waves.

Phil said, 'You surf?'

'No.'

'You want to?'

'Not really.'

'Good thing, I guess,' Phil said. 'Couldn't here anyway, 'cause of the sharks.' He bent down and found a small shell and chucked it into the water where it dimpled and was swallowed without trace. 'What do you want to do then?'

'Do?'

'You know – what's your passion?'

The boy thought about the life he had once led with his mother and his school life with his friends. What had he valued? 'I don't know,' he said.

'Well, that's alright. You're young.'

'Do you mean what do I want to do for a living?'

'Yeah, that. But also a hobby, a passion. Ideally that'd be what you'd pursue.'

The boy put his hands in his pockets and studied the man beside him, pondering the differences between Phil and his father, trying his best to measure his father with some generosity. Phil seemed interested in the man the boy would one day be; his father only in moulding him into some pre-determined shape. After a few minutes he asked, 'What did you want to do?'

Phil coughed out a brittle type of laugh. 'I wanted to – want to – play guitar. Get women. What the greats do.

Drink till I can't.' There was a spirit to his words that sounded fake even to the boy's young ears.

As they walked Phil grew more serious and his pace slowed. The water beside them a sparkling blue. 'I did want to play, for real. I wanted to write music that really said something. I sound like I'm full of myself, I know. But it's true. I wanted to write music. Not just the popular stuff, songs to dance to – real stuff.' He looked down as they continued along the shore.

'Why didn't you?'

'There's no money in it!' he said. That brittle laugh again. 'And I'm not that good. It's alright. I still do it. I played you my song about whaling, yeah?'

The boy nodded.

'I play here sometimes, for the guys. I do some gigs in the downtime. It doesn't quite pay the bills, but who knows? I might be able to quit this mongrel island for good in five or six years. Depends on how I go, if anybody sees me. I got a few fans around the place.'

'You don't like working here?'

'I don't mind it here. But I don't like it, no,' he said. Then he added, almost to himself, 'There's a big difference.'

On their right the trees thinned and the boy could see more white sand through them. They kept walking and the landscape beside them shifted. The dunes, when they came upon them, were made of the same dazzling white sand. They were so tall and steep they blocked the sun and the boy noticed that the sand beneath his feet was cooler.

'Wow,' the boy said.

'Yeah,' Phil said. 'They're pretty massive.'

They both just stared for a moment and marvelled. Then Phil said, 'You should climb them.'

'*Climb* them?'

'You ever roll down a sand dune?'

The boy laughed and realised he hadn't heard that sound in some time. 'No.' And then he remembered rolling down the hill, squeezed into a barrel, scared for his life. He remembered, too, his mother's hand on his back at the end of it, and his father's laughter. He understood his sense of loss more deeply now. It wasn't just that she was gone; it was that he was never going to be her son again, he would share no new experiences or moments with her. He cleared his throat.

'Mate, get up there,' Phil urged. 'Best time of your life, rolling down. You'll love it.'

The boy found himself looking at the dune. He didn't want to relive the memory of rolling down the hill in the barrel. He didn't want it diluted further. So he said, maybe in an effort to distract Phil, maybe simply to unburden himself, 'You remember that whetstone?'

Phil's eyes widened. 'Yeah?'

The boy breathed out. 'I stole it.'

Phil burst out laughing, almost leaping from the sand. 'I bloody knew you did!'

The boy turned away from the dune and said, 'I lost Dad's and I was just borrowing it. I was going to give it back but then the whole thing happened.'

Phil, still laughing, clapped the boy on the back. 'Why didn't you tell your old man?'

'Thought he'd be mad.'

'He would be,' Phil said. He sighed and turned from the dune and looked out at the ocean. He sat down and hugged his knees. 'My old man's the same, I guess. Still. Probably better to tell him. You going to?'

The boy shook his head. 'No. Not now. Not after what happened with Harry.'

'He'd probably just be mad for a bit and then get over it.'

'I don't want him mad at me when we're here until Christmas.'

Phil nodded, seemed to think on what the boy had said. 'You going to climb the dune?'

The boy shook his head. 'Not today.'

'Another day?'

'I gotta work.'

Phil laughed. 'Just like your dad, eh? Bottling stuff up.' He brushed sand from his knees then held out his hands. 'Help me up then.'

The two walked back to the deck in silence. The boy sneaked the occasional glance at Phil, whose very stride conveyed confidence and simplicity. He longed to place his feet on the ground in the same manner and, in the time remaining on the beach, attempted to do so.

THIRTY-ONE

The boy felt sleepy when they returned, but there was no way he could sneak in a nap, not given how long they'd been gone. He managed a coffee and made his way up the steps to the deck, braving the terrible sun and the bitter wind, to find his father. He had to squint when they started work and kept shielding his eyes with his hand. He took the knife his father had given him from his pocket and, while they waited for a whale, sharpened it with the stolen whetstone. It grated pleasantly and in the sun the water on it made the stone turn black and next to this the silver of the blade shone. When he finished he saw the men were bringing a whale up: the first whale of his new shift.

When the blubber had been ripped away he kneeled on the deck and carved it into squares, almost retching at the smell, which struck him anew in his fatigue. When did he wake up again? Was it four? He sweated and the droplets ran down his temples and nestled in his eyelashes until he blinked them away. His feet were throbbing inside the gumboots and his knees, too, were boiling. As the beginnings of a headache gathered at the base of his skull he looked at his father. 'Can I get a drink of water?' he asked.

'If you need a drink, get a drink, mate. I'm not your father out here, yeah?'

Chastened, the boy hurried down the stairs and along the path to the mess hall. There he gulped down two cups of cold water and looked at the other men, none of whom seemed to struggle the way the boy did. Panting, he ran back up the stairs to the deck. The first whale his father's team had handled had been distributed, the bones already in the hole at the back and the saw whirring.

Shielding his eyes against the sun, the boy said, 'I need to take a break.'

'We just started.'

'I know,' he said. 'But I can't see straight.'

'Bloody dune, knew you'd get sunstroke or something,' his father said. He looked at his watch then said angrily, 'We've only been at it an hour.'

'I know.'

'You go to sleep now you'll wake up when we're finishing. Then what good will you be tomorrow?'

'I just need to go and sit down for a bit.'

'Bloody hell,' his father said. He spat and shook his head. 'Go on then. Do whatever the hell you want.' He waved a hand at the boy in an act of severance.

The boy left the deck and retreated to the air-conditioned mess hall. He drank some more water but it just made him feel worse, the water sloshing in his belly. He groaned, sick with shame.

He went into the empty movie theatre at the back and pushed two chairs together so he could lie across them. Feeling tired and sick, he shut his eyes.

The boy opened his eyes with a start. He hadn't meant to fall asleep, just to rest for a few minutes. He shuffled upright, the chairs beneath him scraping, and ran outside. The sun was low over the water, the men still toiling on the deck. He dashed up the stairs to the deck. His father looked at him then turned back to his task. When the boy didn't move he looked again. 'What're you standing there for? Go see if Brian needs you on the hose. We're alright here.'

The boy walked away, almost glad of the rejection. It seemed as though in this world of his father's a single mistake would cost you. He had no idea how to make amends, or if it was even possible. The boy knew he would never measure up to his father's expectations and there was almost relief in that. Still, he wanted his father's approval, even though he found himself disliking who his father was, the stern way he had, his lack of empathy. This was to be his lot in life: working towards a goal not of his design.

He found Brian smoking and looking at the sun. The hose in his hand was sloshing water aimlessly. Brian smiled as he approached and said, 'Back down with the dregs, huh?'

The boy nodded and held out his hand.

Brian gave him the hose and walked away, laughing.

The boy still couldn't look at the sun, despite its diminished power as it sank towards the horizon, and so he focused on the ramp and the water he was spraying. He looked back at the whale his father's team was processing. The flipper broken and skewed beneath the body, torn off at the joint. The gigantic head. The baleen like a comb, etching a grin into the otherwise dour face. Slowly mutilated, the body stripped from the rear, behind the head was empty carcass and viscera. The meaning of the beast taken with its organs. A face without body.

The sound of men shouting alerted the boy first to his distraction and he turned and saw with alarm the winch had started and a whale's body was being hauled up the ramp. A man barged into him while running by and said, 'Mind your bloody job, mate.' The whale's body was skipping on the wood and it stuck and jerked like it had life in it still. The boy hosed beneath it and it soon slid more smoothly. Another mistake to add to his tally.

When the whale reached his father, Dan inspected it and cut out the eardrum. His father reached beneath it and ran his hand across the skin, having been witness to his son's error. His hand came away with splinters. He held it up for his son to see despite the distance. Reluctantly, the boy walked over. When he reached his father, his father held out his hand so the boy could see the jagged splinters plainly.

'Just go inside, Sam,' his father said. The words were uttered without anger, only deep regret.

The boy walked away. He heard some muttering from the other men as he passed. He had lost what respect he had earned. He had only cost these men time, and maybe even money due to the splintered whale flesh they would need to discard. It seemed unfair.

Back in the room, he checked his pockets as he undressed to shower and found the whetstone he had stolen. He threw it at the wall, making a sharp dent. Then he stamped on it with impotent anger. He grabbed his pillow from his bed and punched and twisted it; he wanted desperately to destroy something, to render it as useless as he felt. He yelled and screamed his frustration. Surely somebody must have heard him, but nobody came. He fought his pillow until his hands hurt and then he lay down on it and cried and wished for his mother to wrap him up and take him from this place.

The boy pretended to be asleep when his father and Steve returned. They did not appear to notice the mess of his tantrum or the new dent in the wall. The two men talked quietly as they readied themselves for bed and then went to sleep.

The boy woke the next day to find the whetstone, which he'd left on the floor beside the wall, gone. He sighed and resolved to stay to the end of the shift no matter what and not to dwell on what had happened. He would strive to prove the men's low opinion of him was undeserved.

The next few days saw him achieve this goal. He was quiet and attentive. He listened to the men when they gave him directions and promptly did as he was told. His father pretended not to be watching, but often the boy saw him sneaking glances. Within a week, he had earned back the knife. When his father handed it to him, he touched the back of the boy's hand, looked him in the eyes and said, 'Take care of this, now.' The boy felt sick inside, knowing he had earned this respect without integrity, having delib-erately changed who he was to please these men, but it felt so good to be loved that he said nothing and instead slept that night with the knife at the base of the couch and prayed to God for his strength of character to return.

THIRTY-TWO

The boy woke early, before the others, and pulled on his clothes and went for a walk. He came to the deck and went around it and stood on the sand of the shore. The sharks at the bottom of the slipway had grown in number and ferocity. The boy watched them churn the water. Behind him men worked on the deck and their noise was a steady drone of yelling and sawing. The sound of the plane overhead drowned out the birdcalls.

A whale was towed over by the dinghy and secured with the winch, and before it was dragged up some of the sharks took the opportunity to chomp on the carcass. There was a thrashing in the water and the blue turned to murky red. Surprising how bright it was. Then the whale was dragged clear of the water and the boy could see large red oozing sores lining its face as it emerged. One of its eyeballs was mostly gone and hung from the socket. The join in the jaw was wrecked with tearing and the jaw swung freely, whumping against the timber with each jerk of the chain.

A man stood ready with the heavier cable and was attaching it to the tail as the whale reached the flat part of the slipway when a shark leaped a good nine feet from the water and latched its jaws onto what remained of the whale's face. The man with the winch yelled out and two other men from above scrambled down the ramp, skidding on the wet. The shark was tearing at the whale's lips, its mighty tail beating like a hammer. The boy could see red oozing between its teeth and travelling along the length of it. He stepped closer.

A gunshot. The sound so startled the boy he ended up sprawled on the sand. The shark shook then without conscious motor control. Still with jaws clenched, a hole oozing more red from the top of its head. Its eyes far blacker than the whale's. Dead before it died. To the boy's surprise Harry stood above it, one hand holding a rifle to the sky and the thumb of his other hand hooked in his belt. He looked like someone from a movie poster. He bared his teeth and muttered loud enough for all to hear, 'Bloody buggers.'

The shark was still attached to the whale as the winching began anew. The two animals, paired in death, were levered over the lip of the deck. The boy watched the men as they gathered around the shark, clapping Harry on the back. They kicked at the dead shark. Some put their gloved hands near its mouth to lever open its jaws. Another man ran over with his flensing knife held high and handed it to Harry, who bent down and severed the head. He had to saw into the flesh of it, and the bone, far tougher than a whale's hide. Eventually the throat was exposed and a steady sucking of blood and seawater could be heard even from where the boy stood. The men all laughed at this and kicked the carcass some more. The boy glanced at the sharks gathered at the bottom of the slipway; they had no idea of the fate that had befallen their friend.

Once the head was clean off, Harry held it aloft for the world to admire. The men cheered as if he was holding a trophy. Blood leaked onto his forearms. The rifle slung across his back. He left the deck with some of the other men, perhaps to find a place to store the trophy. Meanwhile, the whale was fitted with a different winch and hauled further up the deck. One man took the time to roll the body of the shark down the slipway with a series of kicks. Back in the water, its comrades found it quickly and sank their teeth in amid the thrashing of their tails. The mess and sound of their feast, teeth snapping and water churning, made the boy want to step closer so he might witness the violence. But he didn't.

THIRTY-THREE

Three shifts later he was cutting blubber beneath the powerful sun. The day had been unusually busy and they were almost at their quota with the sun still up. A few more shifts like this and Melsom might bump the quota up again, they might be out of here come mid-December. Five more months, probably more, the boy would have to endure. Would he feel pride in himself at the end of his time on the island? Would he still *be* himself?

His father was sitting on a milk crate, drinking water from a glass bottle. The shirt he wore was stuck to his back with sweat. It was the first time the boy had seen his father reach his limit for work. A whale was wobbling before them, flensed by the others on his team.

His father waved at the boy with the bottle, beckoning him closer. 'You want some?'

The boy shook his head.

'You want a go?' His father nodded at the carcass.

'Flensing?'

'Yeah.'

The boy looked at the cavernous maw and said, 'I don't want to stuff it up.'

His father smiled, took another sip. 'So? Go slow. We're way ahead. For once.' He craned his neck. 'You boys alright if Sam has a shot?'

The other men nodded. The first turned back to his task but the one named Tommy sat down beside his father and laughed. 'He can do the rest of the bloody thing if he wants. Marshall!' he called to the man who was etching lines into the black rubber. 'Take a break! Sam's going to have a crack.'

Marshall wandered over and collapsed onto the deck beside the others. He grinned at the boy. 'Just need a beer now.'

The boy's father smiled. He picked up his flensing blade and and handed it to the boy. 'Alright. Have a go, mate.'

'What if I stuff it up?'

'I'll tell you to stop.'

The boy approached the whale and studied the glossy skin before him, ran his hand along it. Smooth and slippery like soap. He hefted his father's long-handled flensing knife and shifted the weight. He punctured the skin slowly and found it slipped in as though he had carved into a slug. He had watched his father and the others and thought he knew how to proceed, but now he stood before the whale he found none of the knowledge at hand. Blood flowed heavily from the eardrum wound and the boy worried the creature's heart still thumped within its chest. The underbelly had been already stripped of blubber and skin, so surely if any consciousness remained the creature would have given its melancholy call or bucked them off then.

The boy stepped towards the open sore from which the flipper had swung.

He judged the distance to the next cut from where Tommy had left off and slipped the blade in. It went right in up to the wood. The curved blade swished easily up and down. The boy dragged it down too quickly because it caught inside the whale on unseen impediments. His line went crooked and he fought to wrench the long-handled blade free to redo it. His father watching all the while with creases in the corners of his eyes. The other men beside resting silently, letting the boy fail or succeed on his own.

He reached the midway point where his blade travelled into white and stopped. He found one of the side winch hooks and attached it to the top of the flesh the way he had seen the other men do, standing on his tiptoes to reach. Then he walked back to the winch and cranked it, struggling to keep it steady.

The blubber was torn off too quickly and lumps of white remained fastened to the carcass. The thing that hit the deck looked about half of what his father normally managed and rippled like the ocean. He looked at his father.

'That's alright,' his father said, standing. He inspected what remained in the whale. 'Good for a first go.'

'You make it look easy.'

'It is easy,' his father said. 'But it takes practice.'

His father picked up a knife and helped the boy scrape what blubber remained off the whale. The other men stood and joined them. The boy did two more strips on the underbelly and found himself stepping inside the whale to reach, as he had seen the other men do. The smell engulfed him but he found himself capable of withstanding it, and the innards and meat became a blurry mess and so less repulsive. The last strip he completed was decent and he looked at it proudly. He carved the blubber into squares and kicked it to the boiler beneath.

They finished their shift in the early evening, the sun recently set, and joined the night shift team in the mess hall for dinner. Not since the beginning of the season had all the men been gathered so. They were not served more whale. The boy lined up and a heap of steaming spaghetti and sauce was put into his bowl. The boy sat beside his father and listened to the chatter of the men around them.

Harry stood up halfway through dinner at his table and held aloft the white bone of the shark's jaw. It was enormous. The men cheered and clapped and most raised their glasses in a gesture of respect.

'Don't need to glorify killing things,' his father said, as the hall returned to its normal volume of chatter.

'But you kill things every day.'

'I process things. And no part of those whales is wasted. Not a scrap. Butchering animals for fun ain't right.' He shook his head. 'You kill an animal for food or for your work. What an arsehole.'

The boy remembered he had promised Phil that he would go hunting and now felt hesitant. 'But I said I'd go hunting with Phil.'

'You do what you like, mate. Better you learn by doing sometimes. I don't know the truth to everything,' his father said. 'You want to hunt?'

The boy thought. 'I don't know.'

'Or do you want to feel like you're one of the guys?'

'I don't know,' the boy said. 'Probably.'

His father smiled and in a sad way said, 'Do what you reckon's right.'

The boy thought about what his father had said as he ate. He said finally, 'I don't like how you treat Albert.'

His father smiled and took his time before he answered. 'Yeah? In what way?'

'You're too mean.'

'How am I mean?' his father said. His voice had gone quiet.

'You threw him into a tree.'

His father stopped spooning spaghetti and sighed. 'When?'

'Before we left.'

'Well,' his father said, and appeared to consider this for a moment. 'You're right. I shouldn't have done that.'

'Why did you?'

'Was I drunk?'

'Yeah.'

'Then that's why.' This admission of guilt, not coupled with any sign of significant remorse, angered the boy. His father added, 'But I don't think I'm mean to him otherwise.'

'You are.'

'How?'

'You want him to learn stuff he can't learn. You want him to attack people. He's not like that.'

'He can learn it,' his father said. 'That's the problem. Let me ask you this: what's better for him? Pushing him a bit, cuffing him when he gets it wrong so he learns? Or letting him grow up half the dog he could've been 'cause I was bloody soft? The dog doesn't know what's best for him. I do.'

'But you don't have to do it like you do.'

'And how would you train him, mate?' A hard edge to the *mate*. 'He wouldn't get trained. He'd bark and get into stuff he wasn't supposed to. You gotta be hard sometimes on your loved ones. Things gotta have a use.'

They finished the rest of the meal in silence. The boy was trying to remember how his parents had been before his mother had fallen ill. They had blamed one another for slights both perceived and real, normally at night-time, once the boy was in bed. His mother would sit up and wait for his father to return from the pub where he worked when he wasn't flensing. The boy had heard their voices through the walls, his own name mentioned often. It was difficult to work out what positive effect his father thought being hard on his loved ones had, because whenever he'd spoken harshly to the boy's mother, she had screamed back and the resentment between them had only grown. Or maybe this man was just a man who often grew angry and after his anger justified his behaviour, hiding behind imagined ideals.

When his father was away working at Tangalooma his mother had been warm and kind. She'd walk home with him sometimes after school, and dawdle with him as he daydreamed. While his father had been working here, the boy realised, his mother had been fulfilled, happy, respected. The marriage was sturdier without the people.

THIRTY-FOUR

They shuffled their plates into the plastic tubs and stood outside in the darkness as men ambled from the mess hall. His father rubbed his hands over his skull and looked up at the stars and then back at the boy. Without a word he pointed to the theatre and the boy obediently turned in that direction.

When he pushed open the door, instead of a movie he saw Phil standing in front of the screen holding his guitar, the strap draped across his shoulders. He was lit by a single spotlight. A microphone stood before him and cast a shadowed line down the middle of his face. He was dressed differently: flared jeans and a purple shirt that was too tight around the shoulders and the gut. Most blokes in the audience would have laughed if he'd walked on deck dressed in such a manner, but here in this different place it would seem he was appreciated. The atmosphere was solemn. The men chatted quietly among themselves and kept glancing at the stage, waiting. Phil looked nervous and kept shifting his feet and looking down at the guitar strap, fiddling with the end of it. The boy sat down beside his father. He smiled at Phil through the darkness but Phil gave no sign of having noticed.

Phil stepped forward and said, 'G'day, boys.'

This was met with loud applause and the chanting of his name.

Phil waited for silence before he continued. 'Cheers. Just got a few songs, that's all.' He looked as though he might say something else and the pause before he did so was awful. Then he stepped back and strummed his guitar with a sweep of his hand.

He strummed a few chords too quickly and the sound became distorted. The trembling of his hands on the neck was easy to see in the harsh light. He fingered a chord and switched to another and said loud enough for them all to hear, 'Oops,' which generated quiet laughter. He kept moving doggedly onwards.

Soon he started singing. His rough voice suited his songs, giving them an air of integrity. He seemed more comfortable singing than playing. The boy was struck with the realisation that this was what Phil loved to do, was how he wanted to express himself, but even so he remained mediocre. It seemed that all the will in the world could not make up for a lack of talent.

After five or six songs of variable quality, Phil announced that he was done and the men stood and cheered as though they were drunk. Phil was clapped on the back as he walked offstage and the boy could hear the men congratulate him and proclaim this gig his finest. Phil nodded and smiled at their praise.

The boy went outside when the movie started, leaving his father still seated inside. Phil soon walked out with his guitar case swinging and lit a cigarette before he noticed the boy. He grinned and walked over.

'Sam,' he said and shook the boy's hand formally. He leaned back against the wall and propped up a leg behind him. 'What did you think?'

'It was good,' the boy said, and decided quickly to be honest, because he liked Phil, and thought he deserved the truth. 'I think it could have been better, though.'

Phil raised his eyebrows. 'Really? How? What could be better than that?' He laughed.

'You know it could have been better,' the boy persisted.

Phil sat down on his haunches with his back against the wall. He sucked on the cigarette. 'Yeah, I know.'

'You just gotta do it more, I reckon.'

'That wasn't my first time.'

'I know,' the boy said. 'I just think you got to get more confident playing, that's all.'

'I know I do,' Phil said. A drag on the cigarette. Then he stubbed it out in the dirt. 'But you liked the songs?'

'I liked 'em alright.'

'And they felt real?'

'Yeah.'

'Alright, good. I appreciate that, I do. I appreciate you being honest.' Phil cocked his head to the side. 'You reckon I just gotta gig in front of people more?'

'I guess so.'

'But the songs are good?'

'I think some bits could be worked on. But yeah.'

'Alright,' Phil said. He seemed content.

The boy said, 'Can I ask you a question?'

'About music?'

'About marriage.'

Phil really laughed at this. When he was finished he said, 'Yeah? I'm not married, you know. Nor likely to be anytime soon.'

'But do you think it's good?'

'Is marriage good?'

'Yeah. Would it be a good thing to do? Or aim for?'

Phil exhaled. 'I guess it's like any other thing, mate. It is what it is. It is what it is to you. What do *you* think of marriage? Your opinion is worth as much as mine.'

'I don't know.'

'Then maybe that's what you gotta answer for yourself.'

They stood there together a moment, the man and the boy. Eventually Phil extended his pack of cigarettes and raised his eyebrows at the boy and jiggled them. The boy shook his head.

'I gotta shower, mate. I stink like I been working all day. I'll see you in the morning, though, yeah? Hey . . .' He paused to light a cigarette. 'Maybe if we make our quota early tomorrow we'll go hunting after? I'll tell the boys.'

The boy nodded and Phil walked away, leaving him alone in the dark beside the theatre, which hummed behind him with film-speak. The boy thought about what Phil had said about marriage, thought too about his father's vows to his mother on their wedding day and how little that aligned with his actions over the years, and then realised that men can say one thing and do another. This thought struck the boy with its profundity. He had to sit. Startled he had not thought it sooner.

THIRTY-FIVE

Phil, Steve and two others walked along the beach towards the giant dune with shotguns slung across their shoulders. The boy did his best to keep up.

One of the men in front of the boy turned to Steve and said something low in what sounded like Norwegian, but the words were carried off by the breeze before the boy could be sure. The water beside them was brilliant blue and the setting sun made the light dim enough so that the boy could see through the surface to the shifting sand beneath.

They stopped near the giant dune, shrugged off their rifles and sat. A couple lit cigarettes.

Phil called the boy over to him with a wave of his hand.

'You know what this is?'

'A gun.'

He laughed. 'What sort of gun, dickhead?'

The boy smiled at the insult, hiding his fear. 'A shotgun?'

'That's right. You ever handle one?'

'No.'

'You ever shoot any type of gun?'

'No.'

'You know how it works?'

'You pull the trigger.'

'That's right. You pull the trigger. You point it at what you want to kill and you just pull the trigger.' Phil smiled and ruffled the boy's hair, and the boy was reminded of his father, who now sat alone in their room. 'It's a twelve-gauge Browning, and it's new.' He nodded at the other men. 'The ones these boys are carrying are liable to go off accidentally at any moment given how old they are.'

'Shut up,' Steve said. 'You've been bloody going on about it since we got here.'

'Worth going on about.'

Steve shook his head and smiled and went back to rolling his cigarette.

'Brownings are made in Belgium,' Phil said, 'which is sort of right across the North Sea from Norway, where Gazza here is from.'

The man he indicated towards looked like he exercised regularly, the shirt he wore much too tight and stretched over his arms like cling wrap. He nodded at the boy.

Phil continued, 'The twelve has a hell of a kick on it, so you want to hold it up to your shoulder or it'll leave a bruise, let me tell you. You can load rounds in the bottom here.' He inserted a bright red shotgun shell into the chamber and the click it made was somehow satisfying. 'And you're ready to go.'

'Can you show me?'

'Now?'

'Yeah.'

'We don't have many rounds, mate. Wait till we're out there, yeah? And if we don't see nothing I'll still let you shoot it. Don't worry about it.'

'Can I hold it?'

'Sure.'

Phil un-chambered the round by hauling back on a silver lever on the right side of the weapon. It was spit out onto the sand and he was quick to grab it and brush the sand off with his fingers. He gave the shotgun to the boy, who was surprised at how heavy it was.

Phil said, 'You can load five rounds at once. The extra four that aren't in the chamber sit there.' He pointed at the wooden grip.

The boy wondered how loud the weapon might be and if it would sound at all like the rifle Harry had used to shoot the shark. He wondered how much damage it might inflict. A growing excitement in his fingertips he felt ashamed of. He thought about what Albert would look like at the end of it, what his little dog body might look like all spread out over the floor of the small shack he and his father now called home. Plastered to the crappy door. He shook his head free of such thoughts, but they kept on. Who he had been was so different from who he was now. Such violence had never before been a part of him. Why had such an ugly thought crossed his mind? Why did he not feel worse about it?

The men stubbed out their cigarettes, then they rose and continued on down the beach. The water lost its brilliance as the sun sank lower. Soon it was black and without form, there was just the sound of it percussive beside them. The men laughed and talked about all manner of things and the boy tried to listen but found he was more interested in the waves. The stars above him were bright but weren't reflected in the water. In full dark the division between sky and ocean was only visible through this difference.

They came to a point – Comboyuro Point, Phil called it. Far out to sea the boy could see red lights drifting over the water, what might be a chaser. He pointed it out to Phil and Phil said, 'That's *Kos Seven* probably. Long way out, too.'

The boy nodded, satisfied with his eye.

Phil switched on his torch and swung it back into the bushland. There was a concrete structure a short distance away.

Phil wriggled the beam. 'We'll eat in there.'

The men walked towards it, the boy trailing behind.

The concrete hut had a small lip that overhung a slit window. There was an entrance around the back. Inside reeked of possum and other animals. Spray-painted on the wall the name Dan. The boy was amused to imagine the Fisheries bloke had been here before them and, like a child, had scrawled his name on the wall. There was a swear word near the floor. The men sat on the dirtied concrete, which was dense with leaves. They pulled their sandwiches out of the backpack Steve had carried and ate.

'What is this?' the boy asked.

'The sandwich?' Phil said.

'The place.'

His eyes took in their surrounds. 'It's called a loop control hut. The government put it here during the war.'

'Which war?'

'The second one.'

'Why?'

Gazza spoke up. 'They run big cables beneath the ocean to Bribie Island, over there.' He waved an aimless finger. 'Three big cables in a big loop. They used it to detect enemy submarines. If they attacked Brisbane they'd come through here. They wanted to be ready.'

The boy nodded. He finished his sandwiches before the other men, who seemed in no hurry. He stood, shuffling leaves, and looked out the slit. Bribie Island was lit up in the darkness. He looked left towards the mainland, tried to see his own home and maybe his boat in the darkness. He knew it was hopeless, but he looked all the same. He imagined slinking through the waters in a black submarine and what it would have meant if Brisbane had been attacked in his father's lifetime.

They soon left and headed further inland on no discernible trail, slogging uphill through thick bush.

One of the torches soon lit on an old dirt track and they turned onto it. Both sides were walled in with foliage. The constant sound of insects squealing. There were cane toads lining the path, small breathing lumps of wart. The men kicked them viciously. The men stepped silently and the boy did his best to tread quietly with them. The stars completely shrouded by canopy. There were all manner of animals in the night making sounds, rustling leaves. None of these sounds gave the other men pause, but the boy wished he too held a torch, sure he'd be emboldened by its clarity.

They walked for a while before heading off the trail again and finding an old fallen tree with which Phil seemed familiar. The men squatted behind it and looked out over the top. The boy mimicked them and waited to be instructed but no instruction came. They waited. Before them, down a slope, sat a waterhole, serene and placid. The moon reflected in the surface of the water became muddied and lost its power. Hard to see much else. The men took occasional glances over the top of the log but otherwise remained still.

After what felt a long while the boy asked in a whisper, 'Is this all we do?'

'Yep,' Phil answered. Implied in his tone was the instruction to stop speaking.

The boy obeyed and concentrated on the grass beneath his boots. There was a stick by his feet and he picked it up and turned it over in his hands like it was some ancient relic. He knew there had been Aborigines on the island at one time and he wondered if any of them had handled this stick, if it had any history at all. He drew dinosaurs in the mud between his legs, drawing on memories of his youth. He used to pride himself on how straight and even the ridges were on his stegosaurus. He was not as capable in the dark.

They waited a long time.

A sudden movement made him sit up straight and look.

Phil had unshouldered his shotgun and propped it on the tree. The other men sat motionless and the boy did too. Phil's eyes roamed quickly. His finger on the trigger tensed and loosened. The boy strained to hear what it was that had made the men stir but heard only silence.

Soon the shotgun was lowered and rested carefully against the fallen tree with the butt in the earth. Phil said, 'Thought I heard something.' He spoke in a normal tone, all hopes for concealment abandoned. He stood and brushed the dirt from his pants.

Steve said to the boy as both stood, 'Pigs normally forage here at night. They do sometimes, anyway.'

The boy looked at the serene water. He climbed over the log and waited for a reprimand but none came. He stepped closer to the waterhole and looked again at the moon's muddied reflection. He wondered if there were any fish. There were a few toads moving at the edge, fat blobs. The boy retreated to the log and looked at the shotgun and almost picked it up, but he didn't dare. He looked at Phil. 'We could shoot a toad,' he said.

Phil laughed. 'There'd be nothing left. You that desperate to shoot the gun?'

'I'd like a go, yeah.'

'You know, we normally spend all night doing this. It's barely midnight. You gotta be patient, hunting.'

'Come on,' Gazza said, and stretched his back. 'We could get home at a decent time.'

'We're getting bloody old, eh?' Phil said. 'You sure you just want to quit? The other hole is just down a bit.'

The men groaned so that Phil finally laughed and said, 'Alright, alright.' He turned to the boy. 'You want to shoot a toad, hey?'

All the men joined the boy's hunt for a big one, laughing. Steve finally found one and shouted and the others found him hunched over with his hands on his knees looking at it. A big one, barely breathing by the look of it. It leaped away as they stepped closer and then sat still. It would look scared, the boy thought, if toads knew how.

'Bloody pests,' Steve said and nudged it with his boot. Then he stepped back.

Phil handed the boy the shotgun but did not relinquish his grip. 'Careful, mate,' he said. 'It's loaded. You just gotta squeeze that trigger and it'll fire. So do not ever point it even close to another person. Ever. You hear me? You don't want to drop it facing a bloke and shoot his face off. Yeah?'

He let go his hold and the boy handled it gingerly. He was afraid of the power he now possessed.

'Just make sure you hold that stock against your arm. Then you want to squeeze the handle near the trigger. Don't yank on the trigger like it's some toy 'cause the gun'll buck and you'll miss. Well. You probably won't miss like this.' And he laughed.

The boy levelled the weapon at the toad and shifted it into his arm but found he was too small to handle it correctly. He breathed out and squeezed the stock and fingered the trigger, shaking. He squeezed harder still.

An explosion. Dirt and mud sprayed into his eyes and he felt tremendous pain rack his shoulder. Confused, he dropped the shotgun and shrieked. Surely he had killed them in his carelessness, surely it would fire.

The men were all laughing as he brushed his eyes free of dirt. Still fearing the gun would go off he skipped out of the way and collided with a tree. He fell forward, landing on his side, then scrambled to his feet. The men's laughter exploded anew.

Phil was doubled over laughing, hands on his legs and covered in mud. In fact all of them were covered in dirt from head to toe. Steve was leaning against a tree, laughing so hard his back shook.

The boy looked at the crater in the dirt. The toad had been wiped from the land's memory. There were no more toads near the waterhole. In the moonlight little else had shifted, besides the boy's position among the men.

The boy felt ashamed that his first thought had been for his own life rather than the lives of the others. His shoulder throbbed, but he wouldn't mention it. Once Phil had collected himself he walked to the boy and put a hand on his shoulder. The boy so resented it he almost shrugged it off.

'It's alright, mate. Thought that might happen.'

The boy was near tears and so didn't move. His arms were folded, enduring their laughter. 'You brought me out here to make fun of me.'

'Mate,' Phil said. 'Come on.'

The boy shook his head. 'Give me a torch. I want to go back,' he said. Now he was crying and even though it was dark and the men couldn't see, he still felt more shame.

'Come on, mate.'

'Give me a torch.' He extended a hand.

Phil handed him the torch and the boy stomped away. He left the shotgun in the mud and could hear Phil picking it up as he walked off. One of the men was still laughing, maybe Steve.

He shone the torch at his feet and found the path, and then a bit further on the loop control hut. From here he retraced his earlier steps to the beach. He jogged along it a short way before running out of breath. Soon he found himself seated on the sand studying the water and thinking of the sharks that were most likely beneath the fathomless depths, studying him in turn. If he were to wade in and then be eaten, that would certainly shock his father into confronting Phil. Maybe some of that demon the boy knew inhabited the pit in his father's gut would burst out and smash Phil's face in. Phil himself would feel the guilt forever. This poor dead boy he'd teased so harshly.

Without real thought the boy stood and strode into the water. It splashed up his thighs cold, then he was on his stomach swimming. Quickly he imagined large dark shapes cruising nearby. He swivelled and looked for the telltale fins bearing down on him. The shark carcass, the headless grey floppiness of it, and its evisceration, kept playing over in his mind, and he found himself realising what he was inviting. Their teeth sinking into his flesh, dragging him under. He struggled back to shore, pumping his arms, the fear a cold wrench in his sternum. Soon he was on the beach again, shivering, hugging himself, crying. He walked home slowly, torch in hand, telling his mother that he was sorry he had tried to be cruel when she'd raised him to be kind.

THIRTY-SIX

When he woke the next morning his father's bed was already empty. Steve was asleep and looked the same as he had the previous morning. Now the boy knew, though, that beneath his jovial exterior beat a tormenting heart. It was probably the same with most men; internally they were different from the face they showed the world. It made the boy doubt everything.

He showered and thought back over his actions of the night before. He peeked out from the bathroom to ensure Steve was still asleep before stepping into the main area to dress himself. As he dressed he found beside his couch the torch, a reminder of his shame. He picked it up and handled the cool metal. He clicked it on and off and ran his fingers up the grated side. When he turned it on again he levelled the beam at Steve, which cast a shadow of his heaving mass onto the wall and made him seem an ogre.

He found his father in the mess hall. Waiting a moment before he walked over to join him, he watched the man's back, his steady breath.

His father smiled at him as he sat opposite. 'You have fun last night?' he asked.

The boy shrugged. 'I guess.'

'What time did you get in?'

'I don't know.'

'It sounded early.'

The boy looked at his father, who grinned. The boy said, 'What time is it now?'

'It's around nine.'

'How long have you been up?'

'An hour.'

The boy took a sip of his bitter coffee. 'What have you been doing?'

'I've just walked a bit,' his father said. He sat back and put his hands in his lap. 'Breathed a bit. It was nice, to be honest, not having you around. Not meaning offence by that.' He waved his hand. 'I just need a break now and then. Not used to constant company. Never have been.'

'Taking it all in?'

'Yeah,' his father said. 'I really like it here.'

The boy found himself envious of his father's relaxed demeanour.

'Did you see they've changed the quota again?' his father said, and arched his eyebrows in the direction of the corkboard near the doorway. It didn't escape the boy that his father was relating to him as a colleague.

'Have they?'

'They've upped it again. Higher than it was when we first got here.' His father shook his head, clearly unhappy with the decision. 'We're slipping. We're way down in number.'

'So we'll be working full shifts again?'

'Looks that way.'

The boy nodded and pretended to think before he said, 'How come you never talked about this place with mum?'

His father breathed out heavily. 'Don't know.'

'Did you?'

'We talked about it a bunch when you were little. She came out here a few times, too. You did once when you were really little.'

'How old was I?'

'Around four, I guess.'

'Did you have me on the deck?'

'No,' his father said. And laughed. 'Your mother would've shot me. Way too bloody. No. I remember we went for a walk through the forest up near our room – you know the path that runs behind? I remember holding your little hand and looking at the birds up there with you.' His father smiled at the memory, which gave the boy heart. Then his face dropped. 'Your mum just didn't like this place as time went by. Can't blame her, really. I was gone five or six months of the year and bloody useless for the rest. She pretty much had to raise you by herself. By the time I caught up with what was new, or the routine, I'd be back here again. She was good for putting up with it like she did.'

The boy said, 'Do you still think about her?'

'Mum?'

'Yeah.'

'Yeah,' his father said. 'Sometimes.'

'What do you think?'

'I don't know, mate,' he said. He sighed. 'What's with the questions?'

'I don't think about her as much as I used to.'

The boy looked down and then looked up again as he felt his father's hand rest on his shoulder.

His father said, 'That's fine, mate. Doesn't mean you don't love her.' His arm was stretched across the table and he'd half stood to make the distance. He sat back down. 'Think about what she'd want you to be doing, mate, and you'll do fine.'

The boy hesitated before saying, 'She wouldn't want me here at all, though, would she?'

His father reacted in a way the boy hadn't expected. He smiled. 'You know,' he said, 'I guess you're right about that. I'd be skewered over hot coals if she knew I'd brought you at all.'

'Then why'd you bring me?'

The father sighed. 'I'm trying here, mate.'

The boy said nothing. They sat, the two of them, isolated and together, until his father got up and walked outside. The boy finished his meal by himself. His father was doing his best, it would seem. The boy looked out the window as he scraped the remains of his food into the waste bin. Maybe he was the one who needed to be kinder. He sat back down at the table and one of the men from his father's team sat down opposite him and chatted to him about the weather as though the boy were his equal, and fishing, asking if the boy liked fishing, what he fished with, how often he fished. The boy chatted amiably with the man until, despite his doubt, and despite what had happened the previous night, he felt he was finally a peer.

THIRTY-SEVEN

On deck later that day the boy had Phil's torch in his pocket and as they awaited another whale, making its slippery way up the ramp, he rubbed the metal of it and felt ashamed. The whetstone again. Though this was different. This would be so easy to amend. He could walk over now and return it and apologise. But the boy had been the one who had been slighted. To apologise felt wrong. Phil should say sorry first, but the boy knew he wouldn't. Brian, who the boy looked to for solidarity, was no longer hosing, replaced by another man the boy did not recognise. The boy saw Phil nearby and as he touched the torch he kept an eye on him, as though the man might somehow divine his anger. If Phil turned, for whatever reason, the boy always looked away and pretended to be busy with whatever task lay before him. He wanted to apologise for being stupid and hand the torch back and change his behaviour and fix the whole damn thing. Phil was his friend, after all. The boy could trust his reaction, couldn't he? But as the words formed in his mind he started feeling sick in the throat, he started to feel angry, and confused. He feared that Phil might try to bridge the divide that had formed between them and so avoided him, such was his anger, but he also longed for Phil to do so. This internal conflict grew steadily as he worked.

The whale approached, the metal winch grating behind the boy, and the boy noted immediately its smaller size. Where normally the whale would tower over him, this one only came to his eye line and he could see the top of his father's head over its body. Dan stabbed it near the eye. The boy watched the process with a cold detachment that astonished him. Dan removed the eardrum, held it up to the light and shook his head. 'Bit young, this one,' he said. 'Shouldn't've brought her in.'

'How young?' his father asked.

'Fifteen,' Dan said.

'Mmm.'

'She even looks small,' Dan said. 'They should've been able to tell.'

'Hard to tell from deck until they've got the harpoon in.'

Dan shook his head as he measured the carcass with his bright yellow tape then yelled out the dimensions to be inscribed on the chalkboard. 'You shouldn't be keeping this one.'

'Yeah?' His father said.

'No, mate. Too little. Won't get you more than a few barrels anyway.'

His father crossed his arms. 'Well, what do you want us to do?'

'I know you've been struggling.'

'I know.'

'No use wasting her now she's dead, is there?'

His father didn't move and simply remained with his arms folded, regarding the man with a cold expression. Finally, he said again, 'What do you want us to do?'

'Process her,' Dan said, and sighed heavily. 'Just watch it, yeah? And I'll have to report her to Melsom.'

'You don't have to tell me.'

'You're right,' Dan said. 'I'll talk to Melsom. They shouldn't've brought her in.'

His father's team went to work, sinking their blades into the whale's flesh, and Dan wandered over to Phil's team who stood idle, awaiting the next catch. His father's team worked quickly, attaching winches. The spurting of blood in this beast was heavy and fell like raindrops near the boy's feet and quickly sloshed into the blood gutter, where it pooled like gravy. The boy, on his knees, bore witness to the blood as it travelled while he cut the strips of blubber into neat squares. His hands and knees were slowly soaked in whale gore. He wiped his hands on his shorts. The blond hairs covering his calves grew a dark, sticky red. The sun was high and in no time he was sweating heavily.

They saved the baleen and readied it for scrubbing and shoved the bones into their hole. Then they stood and talked quietly. Phil's team had before it a whale now and Phil was so intent on his work that he didn't look around. His focus unflinching, his directions assured and confident. The boy read intent into all that he did. Each angry stab of the flensing knife, each slosh of blood across his hands. Each action could mean something or nothing at all. The boy wondered if, after he'd left in such disgrace the night before, the man had thought about him at all.

They worked into the late hours and spent their idle time waiting for whales and doing little else. His father seemed content, though irritated by the low number of whales. He kept mentioning it, rubbing his hands together, looking out to sea, sharpening the knife with the stolen whetstone. The boy kept touching the torch in his pocket, which only made him sicker.

Midnight came. The boy was pleased he had made it. He shot a glance at Phil, who was packing up and laughing with his crew. Most of the men headed to the mess hall and the boy hung back a little so he wouldn't risk running into Phil even as he felt childish for doing so.

He was the last to enter the mess hall and stood at the back of the line of men. Instead of coffee the boy poured himself a glass of milk and found some biscuits in a basket. He carried them over to their table and, when he was seated beside his father, dunked the biscuits into the milk. He waited until they were proper soggy before he rushed them to his mouth. He could barely keep his eyes open. The other men didn't look as tired as the boy felt, not even his father, so after he was finished he excused himself and walked from the hall.

Phil was outside waiting and the boy almost walked by him, pretending not to see. Phil said, 'You gonna avoid me the rest of your time here, mate?'

The boy didn't look up but he stopped walking. 'No.'

'Come on, mate,' Phil said.

The boy looked up and saw Phil, his questioning eyes, his arms spread in appeal. 'It was just a bit of fun. Bloody hell, you're just like your old man, hey? Stick up the arse.' Phil looked as though he regretted saying this, but didn't retract it. 'You got my torch?'

The boy said nothing. Then, 'I dropped it.'

'Bugger, mate.' He scratched his head. 'Where?'

'On the beach.'

'On the way back?'

'Somewhere, yeah.'

'Bloody hell, mate. That wasn't yours to lose.' He breathed. 'You gotta pay for it, for a new one. Yeah? Or you just lying to me, like you lied about the whetstone?'

The boy only looked at the man with what coldness he could muster and realised he was mimicking his father.

Phil said, 'Can you take me to where you dropped it?'

'Not really.'

'Why not?'

'I don't remember.'

Phil shook his head. 'Don't remember.'

The boy said nothing and after a moment Phil walked away, still shaking his head and muttering something that was swept away on the wind. The boy watched the man round the corner and disappear into shadow. His lying felt somehow right to him, like Phil deserved it, like now he had something over him.

He trudged to his own room slowly. There was nobody in the room when he entered, so he found himself confronted with how adrift in the world he felt. He showered and changed and turned the lights off and stretched out on the couch. Steve and his father still had not returned, so the boy put his head beneath the blankets and flicked the stolen torch on, and off, and on. He flicked it into his eyes and blinded himself purposefully. He found the more he had to blink the better he felt. As he blinded himself, his guilt was assuaged.

THIRTY-EIGHT

A few days later he stood on deck with his father flensing another whale, the operation now routine for him, almost mundane in its rhythm. Phil had ignored him the past few days and now the boy watched the man work, wondering at this childish exclusion. His hand against the slippery hide of the whale steadied him as he stood to flense and he, because of his divided attention, was careless with how he flicked the knife. He struck his splayed fingers. The knife ran sharp against the knuckles, scraping ugly bone. He was quick to drop it and squeeze the hand but the pain seared deep, then deeper. He dared not cry out at first for fear of exaggeration, but soon the blood leaked through his knuckles and his squeezing hand turned white. He saw the blood dripping from his wrist mix on the deck with the blood of the whale. So he cried out and stumbled to his father.

His father took one look and pried off his clenched hand. The boy wept, not caring, finally, what the other men might think.

'Now, now, it's okay,' his father said. He took a quick look at the cut and then allowed the boy to grip it once more and encouraged the grip with his own, so their hands were coupled together as though in desperate prayer. Then his father held the boy's cheeks in his hands and forced the boy's eyes to meet his own, which conveyed calm certainty. He led the boy to the gate. All the men about them looked concerned and moved aside to let them pass. Steve shook his head and grimaced and clucked his tongue. Phil didn't look up as the boy was ushered by. They walked down the steps, still coupled by the hand.

The boy began to feel faint and he nearly stumbled into a wall. Despairing, he crawled from the footpath onto the grass. The tears welled in his eyes again and he blinked them away angrily, ashamed by his lack of fortitude.

'Let me look again,' his father said softly.

The boy shook his head.

'Come on, mate. Let me see.'

The boy peeled his hand away and gazed upon the wound himself. A deep angry gash ran across three of the fingers on his right hand. There was white visible in the gaps, gleaming beneath the blood, and the boy stupidly tried to flex the knuckles. The wound reopened and spilled its bright colour anew. He cried, and held his hand to his chest.

'Come on, mate,' his father said. He put his hands beneath the boy's arms and tried to lift him but couldn't without the boy's cooperation.

When the boy next opened his eyes his father was no longer there. Just the grass, laid out like carpet. Beyond that the mess hall. The boy shut his eyes again and wished himself to a different time. He talked to his mother. *Please, come back.* It felt as though she had only just died; the feelings, the thoughts. With his eyes shut he imagined her holding his throbbing hand and stroking it in that way she had. Soon he stopped crying.

His father clomped down the steps from the deck with three other men following. One of them was Phil, who offered the boy a sympathetic smile. The four men crouched around him and bore him up by his limbs. They carried him to the main office, a place the boy had never entered. They crashed through the door and turned left, and there before them was a bed covered in brown vinyl. The boy was gently lowered onto it, and then the men filed out, each in turn placing a calloused hand on the boy's knee. Phil was the last to go, and he put his hand on the boy's shoulder. He looked like he might cry. 'You'll be right, mate. Don't worry.' He left.

His father moved over to the boy and gripped his shoulder. 'I gotta go get the doc. You'll be alright?'

The boy nodded. 'I think it's stopped bleeding.'

'Just keep pressure on it and I'll be right back.'

The boy rolled onto his side and looked everywhere except his hand. It throbbed. There was a plastic tub in the corner full of kids' toys despite the lack of children on the island. There was a bookshelf crammed with medical books and some of the spines had been sodden with water at some stage because they peeled at the edges. A red telephone gleamed on the desk. Beside the desk was a white basin. He could hear his father in a distant room speaking on a telephone. His muffled voice through walls a comfort.

He soon returned and sat in a low chair beside the bed.

'Doc won't be long,' he said.

'How long?'

'Not long.'

The boy sniffed. 'Can I have a drink?'

'Yeah, mate.' His father stood, arched his back, a picture of calm. 'What do you want?'

'Just water.'

His father left the room, returning a few minutes later with a glass bottle full of water cold from the fridge. The boy drank as his father held it to his lips. He felt loved, and at the same time sad that it took such a dramatic event to arouse his father's affection. His father's hand on his head, the bad one, stroking his hair.

'What's going to happen?'

'You want me to have another look?'

'No.'

His father smiled and sank onto the chair. 'I don't know, mate. I don't know what will happen. I'd say you're done working this season.'

'Will you get in trouble with Melsom?'

His father shook his head. 'No. It was an accident.'

'But it's his fault.'

'How is it his fault?'

'I'm not supposed to be here, am I?'

'You can be here. What makes you think that?'

A shrug. 'I don't know.'

His father sighed. 'It's just an accident. I'm surprised you're not more concerned with the welfare of your fingers.'

'What do you mean?'

His father lifted his own crippled hand and squeezed the missing knuckles.

'I could lose my fingers?'

His father laughed. 'No, I doubt it.'

They stopped talking. The boy wanted to read one of the books to take his mind off the throb in his hand, the throb behind his eyes, but wouldn't ask. His father waited, drumming his fingers. A while later the doctor walked in. The boy had never seen the man before and wondered if he had been flown in especially.

'So what happened?'

'Sam just cut his hand.'

'With what?'

'Does it matter? He had an accident with a knife.'

'I need to know so I can give him antibiotics, if he needs 'em. Though I guess he'd need 'em anyway.' He rubbed his temples with his thumb and forefinger. He looked up again and tried to smile. 'Alright. Give me a look.'

The boy removed his hand from the cut. The blood was dry and dark in the wound, which was clean across his middle three fingers. The blood had dried down his forearm. He dared not moved his hand or flex his fingers.

'This is a mongrel cut,' the doctor said. He breathed out and the breath struck the sensitive skin near the wound. He had a large belly, this doctor. 'Flensing knife, right?'

The boy nodded and the doctor looked smug.

His father said, 'What's going to happen?'

'He's not grabbing anything with this hand for a bit,' the doctor said. He was twisting the boy's wrist and looking at the wound from all angles. 'We'll have to drown it in soap and dry it and get him on some antibiotics. Which we don't have here.'

'He'll have to go back to the mainland?'

'Yes.' The doctor turned to look at the boy's father. 'We'll get him on the boat and you'll have to take him to a hospital over there. I can give him one pill here, but we don't stock much. I can wrap the wound and stitch it, too, that's fine. But he'll have to get to a real hospital so it doesn't get infected.' While he spoke the doctor moved to a cupboard beneath the basin and took from it a clear plastic tub. He added soap and tested the water's warmth before filling it up. He brought it back and looked at the boy with empathy. 'This might hurt a bit. Okay?' He put the tub on the bed beside the boy and had him put his wounded hand into the water. The doctor very calmly massaged soap into his wound. It stung just as he'd expected. The soapy water turned pink.

The doctor soon withdrew the boy's hand and patted it dry gently with a brown towel. The blood ran in rivulets down his forearm. He said, 'Bit tough, your son, eh?' to the boy's father, winking at the boy while he did so.

The doctor bent over the hand which now lay sprawled on the bed. In the same cupboard that had housed the plastic tub he found a small kit, which contained a needle and thread and a sachet of sterilising liquid. He threaded the needle with wiry black and coated it in the liquid and expertly jabbed it into the skin of the boy's finger. He yanked it through the wound and pulled the thread through carefully afterwards. The boy could feel the fibres of thread inside his skin. He decided to shut his eyes. His father found him a toy gun in the crate of kids' toys and the boy levered back the mechanism and fired the impotent gun at the wall. He didn't look at his fingers again until the doctor patted his knee. His fingers now a sight. Black, jagged ridges. As though he was holding barbed wire. He ran his good finger up and down across it and winced as he struck each one.

The doctor regarded his handiwork with satisfaction. 'Looks good.'

The boy's fingers were then wrapped in flesh-coloured cloth, tight. Pressed together in such a way, it looked as though the boy had grown a flipper. He found he could bend the knuckles a little, though it hurt.

The boy and his father walked back to their room, and as they passed the flensing deck on their right the boy could hear above the sound of work. His absence had not affected the men at all. They walked up the stairs and entered their room and then stood silently. After a moment, they began to gather the boy's things, scooping his clothes from the floor, finding his toothbrush. The boy noticed, though, that when they'd finished packing his things they did not start on the father's.

'Why aren't you packing?'

His father sighed and sat on the bed. 'I'm going to have to send you back by yourself.'

'What?'

His father looked up. 'Don't talk to me like that. We need the money, mate. And you're a big bloke now. You'll be alright.' He searched his pockets and then stopped. 'I'll give you some cash for a taxi, enough to get to your grandparents' place, and you can tell them what happened and they'll take you to the hospital. Make sure you go, you hear me? Don't just get there and forget about it or think it'll be okay.' He waved his crippled hand before the boy. 'This was infected and I did nothing and look what happened. Yeah? Promise me.'

'Of course I'll bloody go,' the boy said.

His father softened. 'You'll get to see Albert again, at least.'

'You're not coming?'

'No, mate.'

The boy stared at his injured hand. 'You can't just abandon me when it suits you.'

'I'm not abandoning you.'

'Yes you are.'

His father said nothing and then stood and lifted the boy's suitcase. He shoved open the door and nodded with his head for the boy to follow. 'Come on. We'll say goodbye to everybody.'

'No.'

'You being a sook, then? Fine.'

They walked down the steps, both angry, the boy refusing to glance back at the room he was now leaving behind. He looked at his feet and heard the birds and the men working without him and the sound of the winch hauling a whale. Then the sound of waves. They came to the jetty. The boy hadn't been here since they'd first arrived.

The *Norman R Wright* was waiting for them. The man behind the wheel nodded gloomily as the boy stepped aboard. His father threw his suitcase in after him then fished in his pocket for his wallet and took out a wad of faded purple notes. 'Here.'

The boy accepted it, sullen. 'I just go to Grandma and Granddad's?'

'Yeah.'

'This'll be enough?'

'It'll be heaps,' his father said. He looked at the boy's bandaged hand. 'Still hurt?'

'No.'

'I'd come with you, mate, if we didn't need the money.'

'No you wouldn't.'

His father looked at him then and compassion was so clear behind his eyes the boy almost forgave him. His father wanted to form words. His mouth moved a bit, then he clammed up. He only said, 'You be good.' He added, 'You'll be better off without me, anyway. I'm only screwing every-thing up.' He turned and walked slowly back along the jetty.

The boy watched him go with tears in his eyes and then shouted, 'You know I stole that whetstone, right?'

There was something to his father's gait. Too slow maybe. The man didn't even turn, just replied, 'Yeah, well, that's that, I guess.'

'I wanted you to be fired,' the boy shouted, though it wasn't true.

His father didn't acknowledge this. He just kept walking away, each step another towards total abandonment of his son.

The setting sun ruined the colour of the sea. He looked over at the factory. The men on the flensing deck were working hard. He couldn't see Phil. Brian hosed the slipway as another beast was cranked up, its skin warping in the heat. He watched three of the sad animals travel up to the deck to be butchered. Still the boat didn't leave. 'What're we waiting for?' the boy asked finally.

'Might be somebody else coming. We don't leave till seven.'

The boy sat on the wooden bench. His father could have waited with him at least. He looked again at the deck as the towering lights flickered on and illuminated the men beneath them. Not a one had noticed his absence. The flensing deck functioned as it always had. The boy was left feeling utterly worthless.

THIRTY-NINE

1958

The boy was outside on his tyre swing in the dark, staring at the stars. Inside he could hear his mother hard at work in the laundry. She was clanging on something and swearing loud enough so he could hear her through the walls. Occasionally a cloud would move over the stars, but the boy kept staring, trying his best to remember their location, so that he knew where they were when they re-emerged.

After a while he went inside to get ready for bed. As he was brushing his teeth he saw out of the corner of his eye something dark in the corner of the ceiling. A huntsman was splayed out as large as his fist, and at first he was shocked into stillness, not wanting to startle it. When it didn't move, he resumed brushing his teeth, spat, keeping his eyes fixed on the spider. He feared that if he lost track of it, he would wake in the middle of the night to find it in his mouth, biting his tongue with its fangs. But it never moved.

He walked backwards from the bathroom and peered down the hallway. His mother was hard at work still in the laundry. She would be of no help. He ran to the kitchen, found a glass, grabbed his father's discarded newspaper from the kitchen table and ran back to the bathroom. The huntsman still hadn't moved.

He had to stand on the bathtub edge in order to reach it. It was a risky proposition and he teetered wildly before finding his balance.

Up close, the huntsman appeared strangely hairy. He carefully placed the cup over the spider, and as he did he accidentally severed one of its legs. It didn't appear to notice, though, and remained still inside its new enclosure. The severed leg dangled from the wall now and swayed from some unseen thread. He wondered what a spider's scream might sound like. The boy manoeuvred the newspaper beneath the glass and allowed the spider to stand upon it and then lifted the glass with its new inhabitant and new lid into his hands. He stepped carefully down from the tub and regarded the spider. It betrayed no emotion and remained motionless, despite its missing limb and imprisonment.

The boy walked the spider to the front door and left the glass and its lid on the front doorstep, took a step back, and knocked it over with his foot. The spider at first did nothing and the boy continued to watch. Soon, though, it struggled from the glass and scurried into his mum's garden. The boy picked up the glass and put it on the sink ready to wash and felt immensely proud of his accomplishment, until his mother called to him from the laundry.

'Sam? What're you doing?'

'Nothing, Mum.'

'Can you come here, please?'

He went down the darkened hallway, the laundry dull yellow with dying light. He found his mother lying beneath the mechanical mangler with her hands all oily.

'Hey, sweetheart. Why'd you go outside?'

'I just caught a spider and I put him out the front.'

'Can you give me a hand up?'

He did. His mother stood and wiped her hands on his pants and looked at the mangler and said, 'Your bloody father said he'd fix this thing next time he was off.'

'But he didn't?'

'No. No, he didn't.'

'Can you get it working?'

'That's what I've been trying to do. I'm sick of doing the washing by hand in the sink.' She looked out the window to the dark outside. 'Let's go get him.'

'But he's working, isn't he?'

'Well,' his mother said, 'I think it's about time he came home.'

In the dark, the pub was a beacon of life. The lights glowed brightly and as they stepped from the car the boy could hear the sounds of laughter, of singing, coming from inside. The windows were thick and frosted over and as they walked by the boy craned his neck to see his father behind the counter but could not make him out. His mother strode up to the door and shoved it open with her fist. The boy followed her inside. Immediately he saw his father behind the counter, grinning at a customer. He then turned and pulled a tap to fill a glass with beer.

His mother pushed through the crowd towards the bar.

On seeing her, his father's grin faltered.

'Liz?' he said.

'You got a minute?' she said. She had to yell over the noise of the men. The boy could barely hear her.

'Not really, Liz, no. I don't,' his father shouted back, pouring another beer.

'Well then you can bloody hear it in front of all these people.'

His mother's yelling only somewhat diminished the talking of the crowd. The men closest to her had turned to look but then returned to their conversations, perhaps wanting to avoid witnessing whatever embarrassment was to follow. The boy stood at his mother's side, afraid.

'You said when you were home you'd be home, Walt. And you're never home and when you are you mope around like a beggar.'

His father's face contorted and then he shouted, 'Well what do you want me to do, Liz, hey? We have to bloody eat somehow.'

'I want you to come home and be with us for a change. What was the last thing you did with Sam? Just you and him?'

'We were going to go fishing,' his father said. He'd looked down as he'd spoken and the boy had to strain to hear the words.

'You've been home for four months now, Walt, and you haven't done anything. You'll be gone again in two more months.'

The men around them had grown uncomfortable and had shifted away.

His father shook his head and said, 'Go home, would you?'

'Sam's growing up without you, Walt. You always said you wanted to be a dad and now you are one and it's bloody sailing by without you. He needs you. Come home and spend some time with us. And fix the bloody mangler before another Christmas comes.'

His mother then turned and stalked away. The boy took a moment before he followed her. He watched his father as his head sagged down into his chest and he tried to meet the man's eyes and smile at him to let him know that everything was okay. His father never looked up; never gave him the chance.

FORTY

1961

The *Norman R Wright* grunted through the water. The lights of the city towards which they were bound became thick, like rope, as they drew near. The boy sat in the cold breeze. He opened his bag and pulled out his jacket with his undamaged hand and struggled to pull it on. The stars dull behind the clouds. The lights of the city joined together, mottled like shells underwater swept up in sand.

They soon came to the jetty they had launched from two months earlier. The boy left the boat without speaking to the captain, who turned the boat around as soon as the boy's feet were firm on the jetty. The boy stood and watched it move away from him through the black water.

The boy looked at the money his father had given him. He pulled the torch out of his pocket and turned it on and looked at the water. The beam pierced the top and struck the sandy bottom. There was nothing there worth seeing.

He walked. He came to the street. Some cars passed; none of them were taxis. The boy thought about hitch-hiking but he didn't know how. As he stood watching, a car honked as it passed and startled the boy. In the car park to the right he could see Phil's car, but it was of no use to him. He walked beside the road to the left, up a hill, carrying his suitcase. As he passed under each streetlamp he felt exposed and hurried his steps.

He turned back to gaze at the water, saw the *Norman R Wright* in the distance, the lights hesitant in the water like faded paint scratched into wood. He thought about what was before him, what choices he had. His whole life he had been without options and now he had been left on his own. His father had forfeited what right he had to direct his son. So. The choice was now his. He would not bend himself to his father's will.

Before him, stretching to each side, was a busier roadway. He walked to it and stood on the footpath, nervous. A faded black-and-white taxi rounded the corner. He raised his good hand and waved. The taxi braked and swerved, causing nearby cars to honk. The driver leaned over and wound down the window closest to the boy. 'You need a ride?' The boy nodded. 'Where to?'

The boy didn't know where he wanted to go, just knew he didn't want to go to his grandparents' house. So he said, 'Just up the road a bit.'

'How far?'

'Why?'

'Need to know if it's worth my time.'

The boy said, 'Five minutes.'

'Bugger it. Get in.'

The boy climbed in the front seat after securing his suitcase in the boot and once the window was back up the traffic noise muted.

The driver sat there and regarded the boy. He raised his bushy eyebrows, his fingers drumming on the steering wheel. 'Well?'

'Just drive up here,' the boy said, pointing.

'You got money?'

The boy brandished the wad of notes.

The driver clucked his tongue. He pulled into traffic, cutting off another bloke, seeming oblivious to the verbal thrashing he received. He laughed as they sped away and the boy was tossed to and fro as though he were back on the boat, doing his best not to collide with the driver. He gripped the seat with his hands, the bandaged one throbbing.

The boy recognised the neighbourhood they came to, the familiar service station on his right, and sighed in relief. He asked the driver to make a right turn, then a left, then directed him to pull into Phil's driveway.

The boy said, 'How much?'

'Ten pounds.'

The boy thought this figure much too high, but didn't dare argue. He handed over one of the notes, which the driver pocketed. The man grinned. Then the driver popped the boot and got out to remove the boy's suitcase. The man got back behind the wheel and reversed up the driveway. The boy was briefly blinded by the headlights before being enveloped in darkness once more.

By moonlight, the boy shifted his suitcase beneath the staircase, then ascended. He looked through the darkened windows of Phil's house with his hands cupped around his eyes and couldn't see a thing. He fumbled for the stolen torch and switched it on and shone it through the window. There was no sign of life within. The boy couldn't remember if Phil had mentioned housemates. His bandaged hand was throbbing greatly now and he wanted to tear off the bandage and let it be soothed by the cool breeze, but he didn't.

There was a pot plant, uncared for and dying, sitting on the verandah near the boy's feet. He picked it up with his good hand and hefted it through the window, the shattering of glass loud amid the silence. The boy covered his ears and looked around desperately. It would be hard to explain his presence here if anyone came to investigate. In the silence that followed his vandalism he waited for somebody to cry out, to point at him, arrest him, but nothing happened.

With his bandaged hand he shoved the remaining glass of the window into the room; it made no sound as it rained onto the carpet. He then crawled through, careful not to cut his hands. His shoes crunched against glass as he landed on the carpet. He stood. Silence in the house and the musty smell of an old rug. Dead plants. The boy had no idea how he would re-secure the house when he left again, but didn't care enough to dwell on it. He found the car keys where his father had left them in the bowl on the kitchen bench and pocketed them.

The torch. He held it up and toyed with the idea of placing it on the kitchen bench and leaving a note for Phil explaining what he had done, but in the end he decided not to. He left quickly through the door before he changed his mind.

The car smelled old when the boy got inside it. He put the keys in the ignition and turned. He knew to open the bonnet and let it idle a bit. He watched the engine crank and the machinery whirl about itself and knew nothing about what made it work. He just watched and made sure the spinning things continued to spin. They did. After five minutes he was satisfied, so he slammed the bonnet and moved to sit behind the steering wheel again. He had never driven the car before and felt daunted by the prospect. He looked at the stick shift and pressed the pedals. He revved the engine and heard the brakes squeak. Once he'd found the clutch he pressed it in and changed gears like he'd seen his father do. He revved as he did so but he let the clutch out too quickly and the car stalled and leaped forward. The boy turned the key again and worried he would run out of fuel. The car sprang to life and he started the process once more.

An hour later he had managed to get himself to the top of the driveway. He looked at the street before him and felt elated and proud of his accomplishment. He turned the engine off and just sat there in the relative quiet and looked at his bad hand and knew he had done well. After a moment he turned the engine back on and took the handbrake off and coasted down the hill, riding the brake the whole way down. He stopped at a stop sign and a busier road buzzed before him. Beyond that, the Brisbane River snaked through the dark, and on the river cruised a ferry lit up like a small township. The boy had to lean forward to see over the dashboard properly. He kept grabbing the wheel with his damaged hand and wincing with the pain. He watched the traffic surge by and waited for a lull.

When he felt confident he turned onto the road and accelerated. The engine revved and he moved forward. Worried what the other drivers would think. He shifted up gears when the engine whirred too heavily and stopped at all the stop signs with pedal brake and handbrake both.

He stopped at the service station he had recognised earlier and walked inside.

The man behind the counter looked old and grumpy. 'You want a fill up?'

The boy nodded.

'Pull her up closer then.'

The boy walked back outside and started the car and stalled it as he tried to move it forward. He looked at the attendant, who looked embarrassed on his behalf. He managed it on the second go. He got out and while the attendant outside grumbled over his car he helped himself to a Mars Bar and pocketed three more. The attendant returned and went to stand behind his counter and looked at the boy, whose mouth was now covered in chocolate.

'You old enough to be driving?'

The boy nodded. 'I'm small for how old I am.'

'How old are you?'

'Eighteen.'

'Yeah? You're not fourteen and just know the legal age enough to tell me a fib?'

'No. I'm just small.'

The attendant smiled and rang up the chocolate and the fuel on the cash register. It dinged as he opened the drawer to retrieve the boy's change. 'Just don't crash or nothing.'

The boy put the change in his pocket with his good hand. 'I know.'

'Where you going?'

'Gympie Road. Up north.'

'You know how to get there?'

The boy shook his head. The attendant squinted and gave him thorough, though hurried, directions. The boy did his best to memorise what he was told and when he climbed back into his car and put the Mars Bars on the seat beside him he felt more confident.

He pulled into traffic. At the first set of traffic lights he unwrapped another chocolate bar and was forced to scoff it when the light turned green. A man behind him revved loudly before he took off and the boy laughed at how reckless he was being.

The traffic thinned as the night grew longer. Soon he was alone on the road, the tar softened by his headlights, which shifted as he adjusted the wheel. Trucks dotted Gympie Road when he finally found it. He stayed behind one, which helped him to regulate his speed, and he felt happy and hungry. By this stage he had lost all feeling in his bad hand.

He knew the way to his grandparents' house well and and found it easily in the dark. He parked on the road out front and sat in the car and looked at the windows. His grandmother's lace curtains billowed in the breeze in their living room, like ghosts without purpose. There were no streetlamps. He remembered entering the house all those weeks ago immediately following his mother's funeral. It looked no different then.

He opened the car door and didn't shut it. He stood and put on his jacket. Before him now his choice in plain sight. He jumped the fence and glided beneath a tree. Footsteps without sound. He kept an eye on the curtains. Their movement kept tricking him. If his grandmother's face were to emerge from the darkness he knew he would be terrified and unable to explain himself. His granddad's snoring grew deeper as he walked beside the house and the familiar sound gave him comfort. The garden seemed more overgrown, as though his grandmother had stopped tending to it altogether. In the dark the flowers were without colour and with their dead arms they sprang up from the garden and tickled his neck and made him think of spiders.

He headed out back and unlatched the gate, grimacing at the sound, and walked into the yard. He looked around. Next to the garage was Albert, who upon sighting the boy sat up and started wagging his tail. He jerked forward on his leash, causing a racket. The boy raised his finger to his lips and tried to shush the pup. He'd grown much bigger in the two months the boy had been absent. The boy was sad he'd missed it. He was surprised the dog had recognised him at all; he had by now spent more of its life with the boy's grandparents than with him. This made him anxious. He kneeled down when he drew close to the dog and cuddled him to his chest. When he leaned his face down he shut his eyes and mouth and received a vigorous licking.

He undid the leash and led the dog to the gate and walked him quietly through. He hurried past the house and to his relief still heard the rhythmic grunt of his granddad. He looked at the window and imagined there his grandmother's placid face and how she would regard him in his theft and isolation.

He hurriedly bundled the dog into the car and drove off into the night.

FORTY-ONE

His mother's grave looked healthy enough. Grass dotted the top, so long now it needed mowing. Almost as though she never was. The stone itself felt natural, like it had grown organically from the earth. By now she must be bones. She must be bones and nothing more. A skeleton down there beneath the soil piled on top, her son's handiwork. He considered digging her up and giving her her freedom. Taking her skeleton someplace else with no idea where they'd go. Maybe to their old home. Where would she go? If skeletons could fly, he imagined his mother would be one and her wings would be skeletal but still capable of flight.

A bat in the night looking down, angelic. Wings squeaking like his granddad's gate. The boy looked at the earth and smudged it with his shoe. It started to rain. He hadn't noticed the clouds.

FORTY-TWO

It was still pouring when the boy and his dog arrived at their shack in the middle of the night. At least he thought it was the middle of the night; he had no way of telling time. The headlights of the car illuminated the old barrels still dormant beneath their tree. He left the car in neutral and slammed the door and ran to the dumpy building. Somehow, the shack had withstood the weather. For a moment he was terrified he'd forgotten the key to the lock on the shack door, but then he remembered it was bundled together with the car key so he ran back, getting soaked, and stopped the engine. Hastily, he unlocked the door and shoved it aside. Swamped instantly upon entry with the smell of food turned bad. Possum faeces dotted the floor and both their beds. A hole near the ceiling, bent corrugated iron, leaking rain. The food they'd neglected to store effectively was torn to shreds. The cans were okay, but strewn about. His father's toolbox still carefully arranged in the corner. The boy brushed everything down with the back of his good hand. He took the mattresses outside into the rain and shook them. When he brought them in and shone the torch upon them they were still coated in animal hair.

He brought Albert inside and lay down on the mattress, wet, and pulled the sheets up over himself without undressing, still clothed in what he had been wearing on the flensing deck. The night was warm enough despite the rain for the boy to kick the sheets off. He soon stood and took off his wet clothing and lay back down.

The dog was restless beside him and kept wandering around the shack and snuffling at the decay left by possums and probably rats. He got into something, rustling his nose in a packet. The boy stopped him with a firm word and stood as he went unheeded and threw what the dog had been interested in outside for whatever else might find it.

In bed, he switched on the torch and studied his damaged hand. He unwrapped the bandage. He tried to press his fingers together, but found he couldn't. The stitches were black and in the torchlight reflected small beads of water. His fingers warped and white from pain and moisture.

He did not sleep well and woke with a start to the sun already caking the corrugated iron near his feet. His surroundings were messier than he had thought. The rain outside had stopped and through the tin he could hear birds trilling. A kookaburra barked. Albert was resting on his father's bed with his tongue out, his ears down. The boy sat up. On the wall were thin bars of sunlight that shone through small gaps in the iron. It made him feel as though he were in prison.

His hand looked okay with the bandage off. The fingers had lost their mortician's white. He still couldn't squeeze them, though, and they were stiff and swollen. The wound was deep and ragged. A picture of hell. What demons would do to mortal remains.

He opened the door. The sky was bright blue and cloudless. He went to the toolbox and rummaged around till he found the matches, then he went outside and started a fire. It was a struggle with the damp wood, but he managed to find a few drier pieces at the bottom of the stack. He shoved in a can of baked beans. He would have to go to the shops for bread and water. The beans burned but he ate them anyway, sharing with Albert.

He walked through the jungle, Albert unleashed beside him, until they came to the beach. Only the day before, he had been on that island that sat on the horizon. He squinted into the sun. Impossible to see anybody, or anything. He thought he saw the *Norman R Wright* making its way through the meagre waves but it might have been any ship of any size.

He found his little boat where he had left it, mostly buried beneath the leaf litter. Still in one piece. In the small sections not covered by leaves, bird crap mottled it white. He frowned at this.

Back at the camp he loaded the dog into the car and climbed in himself. He reversed the car back onto the road and headed into town, past the familiar farms and buildings. As he entered town he grew anxious when he saw a cop car on his right. He tried to sink into his seat. He drove a distance away from the shops then parked and walked back. In the grocery store he bought supplies with the notes his father had given him. He stocked up on bread, beans, spaghetti, some apples, some bait for fishing. He filled the jerry can from the tap behind the pub he and his father had used. The jerry can was almost too heavy for him to carry in the heat and with his injured hand. He had to stop several times to drink and breathe and flex his hand a little. It still hurt and the stitches bristled. There was no hospital nearby that he knew about and so he walked back to the nearest shop, leaving Albert in the car, and asked the man behind the counter, 'Where's the hospital?'

The bloke said, 'Nearest hospital is ten minutes in that direction.' He pointed.

'Thanks,' the boy said, and turned from the counter.

'How old are you?' the man said.

The boy stopped walking. 'Thirteen.'

'And where's your dad?'

'Home.'

'Where's home?'

The boy paused for a moment before he said, 'None of your business.'

'It kindly is my business, thank you. Don't you know how to speak to your elders?'

'It's none of your business, sir.'

The man grunted. 'Reason I ask is that he still owes me for the corrugated-iron sheets he bought here a few weeks back. Was that three months ago, now?' He grinned, displaying white dentures. 'Thought I didn't recognise you, didn't you?'

The boy looked around and realised he was in the hardware store. 'I'll tell him.'

'He owes me a bunch. Had a whole story, too. Figures.'

'You calling him a liar?' the boy demanded. He didn't know why he felt he needed to defend him; his father was a liar and had been one to the boy especially.

The man said, 'It's not that. But he isn't here, is he?'

The boy breathed and did his best to release what anger he held. 'How much?'

'Does he owe?'

'Yeah.'

The man ducked behind the counter and produced a stack of white paper. He spread the pages out in front of him and sorted through them until he found the one he was looking for. He held it from him and squinted at it like the old man he was. 'He owes twenty-two pound.'

The boy had nowhere near that remaining. 'I don't have that on me. I got ten left.'

'Didn't expect you'd have it. Put that away, son.' The boy had produced his now-small wad of notes. 'Your old man's name is Walter, right?'

'Yeah.'

'Walter Keogh?'

'Yeah.'

'You tell him,' the man said, 'that he needs to pay soon or I'll be calling the cops into it.'

The boy nodded and opened the front door. Above him a bell dinged. 'Can I go now?'

'Go on.'

The boy walked back to his father's car and climbed in. Albert, on the seat beside him, licked his gunky hand and the boy yanked it away and scolded him.

He drove for ten minutes in the direction the man had pointed and passed a solitary gaunt cow, which eyed him glassily.

He found the hospital, a huge cream-coloured edifice topped with a big white cross on a green background. He contemplated going in.

He squeezed his hand and found it moderately better. Maybe if his hand rotted off his father would repent.

He sat a while, then drove on.

FORTY-THREE

Outside, Albert – tied to a tree – barked at some uncatchable prey as inside the boy tried to sleep. The corrugated-iron shack baked in the afternoon sun. The boy placed his injured hand on the cold concrete floor to draw the heat from it. Then he put his cheek against the floor. The dog kept barking.

After a while he stood and shoved the door open and stormed over to the dog, who cowered before him. He swung a hand and struck the dog on its snout. 'Knock it off!' he said.

The dog, his tail between his legs, cowered.

The boy stomped back inside. The throbbing heat in his hand was almost unbearable.

Once his breathing had slowed he stood and went back out to the dog, who greeted him with a wagging tail. He already seemed to have forgotten the boy's violence. The boy got down on his knees and the dog jumped on him and licked his face and the boy bowed his sorrowful head. 'Sorry, mate.'

Later, he let the dog off his leash. He found one of the fishing rods and a spool of line stored under a cloth behind some food tins and collected the bait he'd bought. He and the dog set off through the jungle towards the beach.

The sun set and he found himself enshrouded in thick black and the sounds of insects grew loud, almost overwhelming. The dog seemed unaffected. The boy turned on his torch and found the beach and sat upon it. He took off his shoes and felt the sand between his toes. Moreton Island lumpy and black on the horizon. The lights of Tangalooma reflected in the ocean, blurry stars shifting with the tide. There were no chasers inbound. As the boy wound the line onto the reel by torchlight he thought of his father and the other men, including Phil, working on the deck.

When he'd finished winding the line he threaded a sinker and tied a hook. He baited an entire whiting and stood and and hurled the fish into the waves then sat back on the sand. Albert trotted over and curled up on his lap.

He jabbed the rod into the sand so he wouldn't have to hold it, but soon he saw the top of the rod snap quickly down so he pulled it from the sand and jerked back. Whatever had been going at his bait was gone. He reeled it in and found his bait missing, so he rebaited and stood, then cast out again. This time he held the rod steady as he felt the first few tugs. He then pulled back sharply and felt something alive answer on the other end. He reeled it in. The silver fish was bright in the dark and surfaced slowly. It flapped about on the wet sand as the ocean licked at it. He shone the torch at it and its scales gleamed with water. A small bream. Holding it aloft, as triumphant as if he'd caught something much larger, he smiled at Albert, who failed to return his enthusiasm.

They walked back to camp with the fish and the boy was careful as it swung from the line not to allow the irritating spine or fins to touch the dog or himself. It kept flicking its tail.

When he reached their camp he looked at the fish and realised he had no idea how to fillet it and he didn't want to try, so he wrapped it in aluminium foil. It kicked at its confines and ripped the silver sheet. The boy wrapped it tighter. He contemplated cutting its head off, like Harry had cut the head off the shark, but he loathed the sound of its wet sucking still, so did not want to hear it. He would let the thing drown in oxygen. Albert sniffed it curiously and the boy hung the still-hooked fish from a tree, draping the uncoiled line from a branch. It swung silver and looked ornamental.

In the dark, with the help of the torch, the boy built a fire. Each action took him much longer than it should on account of his hand and he had to wedge the torch beneath his armpit to steady it. He toasted bread on a wire coat hanger then slathered it in butter and Vegemite and ate it, tearing off bits for the dog. The silver fish had stopped kicking and the boy knew he had not given it a good death. He watched it sway in the breeze.

After dinner, the boy and dog retired to the shack. The boy was exhausted and he stared at the roof as he drifted off to sleep and thought about whales and the life he had so recently forfeited.

In the morning, the boy emerged early from the shack and saw the remains of the fish dangling from the tree. Its guts had dripped onto the dirt and had then been dragged away, judging by the tracks leading into the jungle. Some of the slime still dangled from the spine of it, which was yellow and translucent with the sun behind. The dog came out of the shack and snuffled at the dirt. There was no trace of the aluminium foil. The boy untied the eviscerated carcass of the fish and chucked the remains in the still-smouldering fire. He stirred it into life and watched the fish head sizzle and the eyes boil, the liquid dripping from them, sizzling as it struck hot coals. The boy didn't cook his beans, but ate them cold on bread.

With Albert in tow he headed back to the beach and repeated his efforts with the fishing rod. He stood at first but when no fish took the bait he sat down in a mood. Moreton Island was without solid shape behind the low-lying clouds but when he squinted the boy could see the white of the dune he'd declined to roll down.

Albert played near his feet, and he patted the dog and fondled his ears. Albert soon rolled over and presented his white belly and the boy accommodated him with a lengthy scratch. One of Tangalooma's chasers headed towards the open ocean beyond the island. Next time he would ask to go aboard. He would ask to handle a harpoon and he would prove himself. He shook his head and sighed, struggling to understand his own motivations. He hated the place but wanted to brave it. He hated the men but wanted their respect. His father's especially.

No bites or nibbles. He reeled the bait in. Untouched. He hurled it out again, further this time, secured the rod between his legs and waited. If he had more cash he would buy a piece of plastic pipe and wedge it in the sand and leave the fishing rod standing, which would allow him to roam freely on the beach, maybe have a swim. If he had more cash he might work on his boat.

A fish finally struck and the rod jerked. The boy reeled it in and the fish at the end was mightier than the bream. It was an ugly flathead, brown and misshapen.

He carried it back to camp and he stood the rod up against the shack with the fish dangling. He felt bad leaving the fish to die in the sun with its lip stretched out on the hook but when the boy looked closer he saw the hook had been swallowed by the fish whole and had lodged inside it. If he tried to pull it out he might drag up the guts, killing the fish that way, watching its own innards splash onto dirt. The boy empathised. He quickly cut the empty tin of baked beans with tin snips from his father's toolbox and unfolded it and washed it with soapy water and dried it with one of his shirts. As he worked he had forgotten his poor hand. It was looking better and felt better.

He slapped the fish, still gulping air, onto the tin and set to severing its head with a knife and a hammer. He bashed in the knife, which squinched against bone. The fish barely struggled but its tail continued to wag forlornly. The boy found Albert mimicking the fish, probably hoping to be fed. He kept crunching in with the hammer until the head was off and the fish was out of its misery. The tail kept wriggling for a bit. The neck bone and muscles were pink, white, warped. The boy studied it carefully. Such a mess. His hands were covered in blood, some fleshy bits clinging to the stitches. He wiped them on his pants and rinsed them with soap and water and did his best to fillet the fish with no clear idea how. He cut down either side of the spine. The guts were brown and red and oozed like snot between his fingers. He found what he thought was some meat but it was bristled with bone. Hard work with his gimpy hand. Eventually he procured two strips of grey flesh. He rinsed the flesh again and then fried the meat in a pan with the skin still on and watched the grey turn to white. It looked as it should. The dog seemed hungry so the boy fed him some beans.

By the time he ate his fish it was lunchtime; the job had taken most of the morning. The fish was salty and feathery in texture but he enjoyed it immensely, satisfied with his work. He had to pick out the bones from each mouthful. When he put his fingers in his mouth his stitches caught on his teeth and yanked at the wound and the pain in his fingers sprang to fire. He abandoned the fish to the dirt in his haste to stand. He held his hand to his mouth and blew warmth in until the pain dwindled. His hand was not mending on its own. The dog sat beside him wagging his tail, watching him yelp.

FORTY-FOUR

The next morning he awoke to a knock on the makeshift door. He sat up with a start. The dog had his eyes open but didn't move. The boy blinked away sleep and stood up and called, 'Who is it?'

'Police. Can we have a word?'

The boy rubbed at his eyes. 'Sure. Give me a minute.'

He dressed, Albert watching blearily from his father's smelly mattress. His leather shoes as they squeaked on reminded him of his mother's funeral. The room reeked of sweat. He shifted the door aside and blinked at the daylight. A police officer was standing with his hands at the small of his back, gazing towards the jungle as though he had never before seen a tree. He turned at the sound of the door scraping on dirt and smiled.

'You Sam?'

The boy nodded. 'Yes.'

'You living here?'

Another nod.

'Your dad in there?'

'No.'

'Where's he?'

'He's working.'

'Where?'

'Moreton Island.'

'And he's just left you here, then? On your own?'

The boy shook his head. 'No. He told me to go to my grandparents.'

'Mmm,' the police officer said, and leaned forward on his toes. 'Why're you here then?' He walked closer, and when he was nearer to the boy he crossed his arms. He had on a hat with a brim. He looked at ease.

'I didn't want to go to my grandparents.'

'Why not?'

'Look,' the boy said, and breathed. Albert scurried out between his feet and dashed to his water bowl and the boy used the the time it took to chase him and scoop him up to carry him back into the shack to gather his thoughts. There was no telling what the police officer wanted, and nothing to be gained from trying to run, not with him standing right there.

When he was standing before the police officer again, he asked, 'Why're you here?'

The officer grinned. 'I'm here to talk to your dad.'

'He's not here.'

'You said that. I know. I'm here to tell him that he needs to tear this building here down, and that he's going to be arrested if he doesn't.'

'Arrested?'

'You can't put up a building like this – or any sort, really – just wherever you like. This is government property.'

'He owns this property.'

The cop laughed and tipped his hat. 'You can't own this property, bud. This is a campground.'

The boy looked at their shack in all its decrepit solitude. 'What's that?'

'This is a campground. Not a popular one, and not a popular time of year besides. Otherwise there'd be caravans and tents dotted all over here.' He waved his hand at the muddy expanse.

'He owns this land.'

'No, he doesn't.'

'Well,' the boy said, 'he paid for it.'

'If he did he was scammed. Either way he'll have to tear this thing down –' the officer nodded at the shack '– and he'll have a to pay a fine, at the least.'

'He paid for this land. He said so.'

The cop said, 'He a liar, your old man? I don't mean offence by that, but some men are given to lying.'

The boy glared. 'He's not a liar.'

'You sure?'

'I'm not a liar either.'

'These questions pissing you off?'

'A bit, yeah.'

The cop laughed. 'Alright. What I want you to do is come with me.'

'Where to?'

'To the station. And we'll call your grandparents.'

The boy looked about himself and at the remains of his fire. 'Dad'll be home soon.'

'When?'

'Today,' the boy said.

'You lying to me?'

'No.'

'He'll be home today?'

'Yes.'

'When?'

'Later. I don't know. He said he'd come back today.'

'You said before he thinks you're with your grandparents.'

'He'll come here after he sees them.'

'And he'll be home later today?'

'He said that, yeah.'

'So if I just sat here and waited I'd see him?'

'You could come back later. I'll tell him you want to see him.'

The police officer grunted, finally annoyed. 'If I come back later and he's not here, then you're coming with me.'

'That's fine.'

'And I'll take you to your grandparents. And I'll ask them to call me if your father shows up. They his parents?'

'No.'

'Do they like him much?'

'I don't know. I suppose not.'

'Where's your mum?'

'She's dead.'

The cop looked at a loss for words. He frowned and tipped his hat forward.

A pause. 'How'd she die?'

'You're a bit bloody personal,' the boy said.

He breathed hard after this, worried the cop would be angry, but the cop just laughed. 'I suppose. I don't mean nothing by it.' He sighed. 'My mother, rest her, died a few years ago.'

'How?'

'She was just old.'

The boy said nothing to this, though he wanted to offer sympathy. Hard to know what was stopping him.

'Anyway,' the officer said, 'I'll be back later. You can bring your dog too. You sure you don't want to come now?'

'No, I'll wait,' the boy said. After a moment he added, 'Thanks.'

'How'd you get out here by yourself?'

The boy didn't answer.

The cop looked around and saw the car. 'You didn't drive that here, did you?'

'I did, actually.'

'You're too young for that.'

'I know.'

'You drove it anyway?'

'Yeah.'

'You going to do it again?'

The boy shook his head. 'No.'

'You sure?'

'Yes.'

The cop shifted dirt with his feet. 'Alright. I guess if you need me, just wait for me to come back.' He looked like he wanted to continue speaking but didn't know what to say. So he climbed into his car and wound down his window and as he moved away he stuck a hand out and waved. The boy waved back.

As soon as the car was out of sight the boy sat down in the shack and cupped his chin in his hands. He looked at the dog as it tussled with a blanket. The stitches were starting to hurt again.

His father. He was done with the man. That had been the final damning thing. There was no more trust to break.

He grabbed the hammer from outside, still grimy with fish, and from his father's toolbox he took the rusty saw. He hurled the toolbox out of the shack, and the mattresses and blankets and food, and stuffed it all inside the car. The mattresses needed squishing and struggled to fit and in his rage he shoved them in. Albert was positioned between the back and front seats and licked the boy's hand happily despite his confinement. The clothes that had been in his suitcase were pressed against the front window. When he was done he regarded the now-empty shack and understood what it had meant to his father, and that he had most certainly lied. He understood, too, that it was now his duty to destroy it. His rotten, absent father. He would prove himself and he would do so now.

Breathing heavily, he strode forward and, without thought for his wounded hand, tore the door from its position and hurled it into the dirt. In the car, Albert whimpered.

The boy kicked at a wall. The way it crumpled beneath his shoe gave him satisfaction. He kicked again and heard the corrugated iron clang, the noise tremulous in the otherwise near-silent day. It almost startled the boy from what he intended. He kicked again and again. The walls caved a bit but were held in place by the roof and the posts.

The boy found gaps beneath the walls and slotted in the saw horizontally and moved it back and forth against the upright wooden beams, but at that angle it was slow going. He went inside and kicked at the wood until he realised that if the wood were to give way with him inside the roof would fall on him. So he went back outside and sawed until one corner gave. There was a sound of splintering wood. He was sweating badly but would not cease. He only stopped to drink some water and offer some to Albert. He wound down the window of the car so the dog could get some air and he gave him some of the leftover beans.

With some more work he managed to make one side collapse. The wood groaned as it toppled. The roof fell on the wall and then came off completely and whomped into the dirt. He pulled it upright and leaned it against a tree. The corrugated iron his father never paid for sagged in the top right corner, bent with his efforts. There were birds nearby and the familiar kookaburra laughed so close it felt to the boy as though it were on his shoulder.

He went back to the shack and pushed over the other sides, which gave way easily now they had no support. Soon all that remained was their misshapen concrete slab. The boy thought about how he might destroy it, too, but could think of no easy way, so he left it.

He thought about putting the roof in the wheelbarrow but knew it wouldn't fit. With some effort, he pulled the roof through the jungle. It wasn't heavy, but it was certainly awkward. The dog he left in the car with the window down.

When the iron caught on a root he leaned against a tree and wiped his brow free of sweat before continuing. Emerging from the jungle, he heaved the roof and lost his grip and fell back. He jarred his wounded hand as he fell and he groaned and sat up. He held his hand to his chest and then just sat and looked at the roof and the beach and the water, which was a dull blue today.

After a while he stood and flexed his hand. The stitches pulled and it felt as bad as it had two days ago. It was starting to turn white again.

He turned and heaved the roof to the water's edge so that the tide sloshed over it. He looked over at Tangalooma with the tide against his shins. His father was there, completely ignorant of everything, having decided the boy's fate. He clenched his injured hand despite the pain. The water would not stop him.

He returned to the camp, let the dog out of the car and gave him a good scratch on the chest. Albert bounded about him and got down on his forelegs and growled, at play. The boy swatted at his face and shoved him to the dirt and for a moment he was lost in this diversion and gave all of himself to the dog. Soon, though, he returned to his task, and with the dog's encouragement he dragged the three remaining walls of the now-defunct shack to the beach, each one as much of a struggle as the last.

He piled the sheets one on top of the other so that when he was finished he had formed a corrugated-iron sandwich. He lashed them together with rope, threading it between the sheets of iron. It ended up looking like a Christmas present coiled in ribbon. He then retrieved the two empty barrels from the camp and and rolled them through the jungle. He tied these to the sides of the boat, his knots haphazard but serviceable.

This hard work in the sun almost did him in. He was getting sunburned, he knew. He took a break to drink water from the jerry can and eat.

When he was finished he went to the car and found some of the paint his father had stolen with his lies and carried it back to his new boat. On the side, on a piece of wood, he painted his mother's name, Elizabeth, in messy letters. He stood back and admired his new creation. Then he turned towards Moreton Island. Given the distance, he knew it would take him some time to traverse the channel, but he also knew he was capable. There was no doubt within him. On his way back to camp with the dog at his heels he spared a look at his old boat and realised just what qualities in him had shifted in so short a space of time. His motives were no longer innocent. He was now grown.

His muscles aching, he sat down near the car and ate bread with Vegemite and looked at the rusting cement mixer, which had gone unused for two months. 'We're going soon,' he said to Albert, who lay near his feet.

The dog scratched at his own ear and then panted and looked the boy in the eye. He was getting dusty, so when the boy finished eating he patted Albert's coat down and dirt billowed from it like smoke.

He found the wheelbarrow and righted it. He threw in all of his canned food, the jerry can, the bait, his fishing rod, and he wheeled this pile to the beach. After stacking everything neatly in a corner of his vessel he knew deep down that these items would not brave the sea for long, and so he returned to his father's toolbox, found an appropriate spanner and brought it back to the beach. He undid the nuts securing the wheelbarrow bucket and levered it off the base. He secured the bucket to the raft with more rope and then placed the tins of food and the jerry can inside. The rod he secured to the vessel with more rope, thankful for his father's over-preparation in this one area.

The sun was starting to set and shaded Moreton Island a deeper grey. He dragged his old boat onto the beach and with a few kicks managed to snap it in half. He waded out into the ocean with one half and scooped at the water. It caught nicely and would make a good paddle.

Before he set off he made sure of his direction. The sun was almost down, and the many clouds were tinted a dull pink. The boy feared the cop would emerge from the jungle at any moment. He kept looking around, nervous. Tanga-looma's lights still weren't on. There were no ships. The boy breathed out.

'Right,' he said. He pushed his new raft out into the ocean without any assurance of its buoyancy, but he found it floated and floated well, the barrel on each side bobbing in the water. His leather shoes now soaked, he jumped aboard, and felt the wind. He called the dog to him but Albert just watched anxiously from the beach, so the boy had to leave the boat and fetch the dog.

When he returned, it had floated out a bit and the boy waded to it through heavy water, cursing his carelessness. When they reached the boat the boy threw the dog on first. Once they were both aboard he tied the dog's leash to the wheelbarrow. Then he turned to face the island once more. The sea sprayed him with each passing wave and cooled him pleasantly.

It was not easy getting out to sea but the boy assumed the going would become easier once he had gone beyond the breaking waves. He had to work hard with his makeshift oars. They were too big, he realised, and he regretted making them. They pulled at the back of his arms with each stroke, but they did carry power and he made some headway.

It was truly dark when he made it beyond the break. His boat bobbed at ease and he lay back. He looked at his home, the beach, as he passively drifted from it. The cop hadn't shown.

Albert seemed ill at ease and kept shifting about the boat, shying away from each small spray of water, barking. The boy did nothing about this beyond allowing the dog the time to adjust to its new surrounds.

FORTY-FIVE

The lights of Tangalooma became a steady beacon in the darkness. As he rowed and rested and rowed, the boy grew tired and realised he had not fashioned something on which he might sleep. He was afraid that if he slept untethered he would roll off the boat and wake thrashing in the ocean with sharks beneath him, wondering what this strange shape above them was. They of course would eat him quickly. He knew the sharks would be as violent towards him as Harry had been to their kin. He imagined they would exact their revenge on him.

The stars above dotted the black sky, the clouds blotting them like spilled ink, and beneath them all, reflected in the water, were Tangalooma's lights. There was little else. Albert had lain down on his front paws and looked into the ocean with canine enquiry. The boy took his torch from his pocket and switched it on. The light bounced off the gently rippled surface. He couldn't see beneath. No shark fins, though.

He spent some time on his back, listening to the waves slap the boat beneath him. The ocean thumped like a heartbeat on the corrugated iron. All the teeming life beneath him united in that rhythm. If he shut his eyes he felt at peace with the water and himself. Swallowed by something bigger than he, a life eternal. If he were to be eaten at least he would become a part of this.

When he woke the moon had shifted. The clouds now much more numerous. He sat up. Beneath him the vessel was bouncing up and down violently. He gripped the iron. He went to the side and saw the waves rising and falling in peaks and valleys. Beside him, Albert was yipping in terror, scampering from one corner to the next, doing his best to ward off the water splashing over the side. The boy hadn't noticed the rain, barely noticed it now.

The boy remembered playing in the bath when he was little, shoving his toys into the water and watching as they submerged, rose, struck the sides of the tub. This was what he now felt: an untethered chaos. There was a chance the boat would upend at any moment and those sharks he so feared would be at him in the dark. As the blood pulsed from him in whale spurts it would attract more feeders and mix with the ink of the water until all that remained of him was salt. He flattened himself against the bottom of the boat, attempting to weight the craft evenly on all sides. He went up and down with the swell, and his good hand turned the colour of the bad from the strength of his grip. The dog barked wildly, adding to the boy's apprehension.

The next wave saw one end of the boat dip beneath the water – the end he gripped with his throbbing hand. He felt the salt against the stitches and yelled out in pain as the water sloshed up his forearm. The sea itself was near silent. The only sound the dog, his breathing, his heart, the light rain upon the iron.

As he went down again he held on and as the boat came up he swivelled around to see better. In this motion he accidentally struck Albert with his arm, and the dog flew into the water with a yelp.

The boy plunged his hands into the ocean but could not see the splashing of the dog or any form of his body beneath the black. The boat went down into a trough, and as he searched he felt the end begin to tip, so he held on once more. As the end of the boat went under, he felt something beneath him collide with the vessel. The boy knew immediately what had happened, and felt his stomach heave. As the boat went up again he saw in the dark the shape of his dog floating near the surface, motionless in the water.

He paddled towards him, straining, and finally was able to seize the pup by the scruff of his neck. He heaved the dog aboard. The dog's limbs were still.

'Albert?' the boy said. He tugged at a leg. The paw flopped back onto the tin.

Carefully, on his knees, he bent his head to the dog's chest, so that he might hear Albert's heart. The boat still careening. Praying for a heartbeat. Praying for a heartbeat.

He sat back. There was blood between Albert's teeth, a small dent above his eye, and the pupils were unfocused. Though the waves continued to batter the small vessel the boy no longer noticed. Albert was his friend. His only friend, now. And he had done this. He held the dog up to his chest and put his face into Albert's fur and breathed warmth into the cold, dead skin. He tilted his head to the sky and wailed, angry and alone, breathing in what remained of Albert's spirit.

It was some time before the waves calmed a little and the boy, grieving, still on his knees, looked at the sad wet body of his dog. He thought of flicking the torch on to better see what his adventure had done to his friend. But, for the shame, he couldn't. Instead, he turned the torch on and shone it at the barrow bucket. He extracted a can of baked beans and prised open the lid with a knife. He ate the beans with his fingers in the dark and his wounded hand stung. He turned the torch back on and threw the empty can into the barrow.

He sat down and put one hand upon the dog, hoping to feel the rise of his chest, the thump of his heart, and breathed. Hoping for a miracle. Then he leaned back on his hands and looked at the stars.

He realised he should drink something, but filling his mug with water from the jerry can was difficult as the boat continued to rock and he was worried that he lost some water over the side in the poor light. Only when he'd finished the cup of water did he look over to Tangalooma, one hand still resting on his sodden dog. The island was further away then when he'd last looked. He realised his boat was adrift. The shore he'd abandoned was a distance from him but even with the distance he could see in the low light how quickly he'd travelled. He grabbed an oar, kneeled near the dog, and tried desperately to alter his course, but after his torment his whole body ached and would not respond despite his efforts. The lights continued to recede no matter how hard he paddled. An immense strain on his back. He cried. Finally, he knew he could no longer continue. Moreton Island's lights still glinting on the horizon.

He abandoned the oar and sat back down and watched as the lights forgot him. His father and Phil were at work maybe, unaware of his plight. He was sure now he had no value. His one contribution to this earth was this, his dead friend. The dog's fur clumped between his fingers. The dog's ears now without life so soft to touch. The tongue out. He was no better than his father. A man who, despite his good intentions, left only pain in his wake. Now that he'd accepted this it almost silenced his despair.

He finally lay down, Albert in the crook of his arm, and studied the clouds and the stars. They didn't move. Still the rhythmic thump of water. He stayed this way for a long time.

FORTY-SIX

The sun was drawn forth, pulled up on strings of silver and red. His eyes felt salty and tear-sticky when he opened them. Seagulls circled and squawked above him. He'd grown used to the silly creatures at Tangalooma but had never watched them closely. One landed now on his boat and waddled about, its footing unsure. It stared at him, cocking its head from side to side. It hopped nearer to Albert, almost standing on his belly. Half of its left leg was missing, crippled like the boy. The boy, on his stomach, inched closer to it. It flapped its wings and rose, squawking angrily.

He sat up and looked at his mangled hand, avoiding looking at the dog. Thick yellow pus oozed from the wound. He picked at it with his good hand and winced at the fresh pain. Soon it was bleeding. The blood dripped into the water and diffused quickly, but even so the boy swished it away with his hand to avoid attracting sharks.

The morning was already hot enough to warrant the removal of his jacket. He placed it carefully over the barrow. He had a drink of water and found the jerry can was still more than half full. He didn't eat anything despite his hunger, because he knew there was no telling for how long he might be adrift.

He didn't know what to do with the body of his dog. It felt wrong somehow to put him in the water. In the fresh light, the dent near his eyes was severe and the boy was surprised there wasn't more blood. It was hard to look at. He supposed the dog's brains must now be squished, like what they did to mummies in Egypt with the hook up the nose.

He untied the fishing rod and put the loose rope in the barrow. He baited the hook with some tuna from a can and let the line trail behind him in the water. He sat on the edge of the boat, Albert's body at his back, and dangled his feet in the water. The sun above him made him regret not bringing a hat. As he sat he looked at the barrels lashed to the sides of his makeshift vessel and remembered rolling down the hill in them and the laughter of his parents.

His family. One member now dead behind him. Another in the earth.

A while later the line drew out and he let it dance beneath his outstretched wounded hand. He lifted it cautiously and at the next tug he hauled upon it and felt the fish. He grabbed the reel and wound it in.

A large flathead, lethargic after its brief fight. Its gills bellowed as they were soaked in oxygen and it mouthed words unknown. The boy slapped it down upon the iron and plunged the knife into the base of its skull. He removed the head and threw it in the water, then cut strips off its back. There was no way he could start a fire on his small vessel and he did not want to eat the fish raw, so he took the empty baked beans can from the night before and stuffed the flesh in there. He put it in the barrow and covered the barrow with his jacket and hoped it would stay cool enough. He would eat it if he became desperate. He knew that soon he would.

Something he hadn't counted on was the heat of the corrugated iron. He had to keep sloshing water beneath himself so that he could sit still for even a short amount of time. He couldn't rest his feet on it, the heat even ebbing through the black soles of his shoes. He worried that Albert's body would fry like bacon in a pan.

Moreton Island like a torn piece of paper, a mark on the horizon. The mainland in the distance as he drifted.

He hadn't bothered paddling in an age. He tried for a moment and soon gave it up for hopeless. He sat back and looked at the island and, near it, on the horizon, the smoke of a ship. So tiny. Smaller than his fingernail, which he held up for comparison.

His isolation began to unnerve him. He might fall off and drown and there would be no one to bear witness. He might fight a shark, with both his good and corrupted hands, and win, and eat its remains, and no one would ever hear of his courage. Under the boat, the water turned a murkier colour, and the boy wondered if what he saw was the ocean floor. Maybe the water was really only waist deep and if he were to jump in he would touch squishy bottom with his toes and he would be able to drag his boat back to shore. He stared for a long time, trying to figure it out. A few times he tried paddling for shore, but found he grew no closer and tired quickly.

The sun bit into his skin and the boy braved it as long as he could before he took his jacket from the barrow and draped it over his head. Then he removed the remaining food from the barrow and, cradling his dog's body in shaking arms, placed it reverently inside. He gently covered the dog with the cans, careful not to further bruise him. He sat back. He'd had no idea how much he'd miss shade. He lay down on his back, the jacket over his mouth and eyes. His breath became hot. 'Bloody hot,' he said.

'Bloody stinker.' He kept repeating these phrases, growing steadily quieter, until he was silent once more. Then, with a burst of energy, he screamed into the jacket. Nothing effected. Hard to determine if he was even alive.

He flung the jacket aside and grabbed one of the cans of spam and opened it, and scooped the oozy meat into his maw. He looked at the fish flesh in the baked beans can, already pungent. He considered throwing it overboard but knew it would be useful in future for bait.

There was no plan. Nothing he could do. He sat on the boat for hours and shifted as his legs grew too hot and watched the sun and breathed and said nothing. He thought always of the dog and what it must have been like for him in his final moments. Did he doubt the boy loved him? Moreton Island was no longer visible. No other boats or land. Fear settled in him and he was almost relieved by the knowledge that he too would surely die and they, the dog and boy, would be united in death.

He rolled onto his front and the iron soon cooked his stomach through his shirt. He looked into the water. He searched for his mother down there, for life of any type. Her face seemed further from him now and was difficult to summon amid the sweeping water. The colour of her eyes had been green. She had dimples when she smiled and when she frowned. Her nose had been slightly crooked. She hugged too hard and sometimes yelled at his father and when she did her dimples disappeared and in their place a thick rosiness. She too was imperfect, and perfect all the same.

The sun went down quickly and there was no brightness suffusing the sky to welcome the boy this night. In the dark he found relief from the sun, but then his hot skin became much too cold. He covered himself with his jacket, which scraped against his skin painfully.

In the dark, with the torch wedged between his legs, he picked at his hand. Taking his knife, he cut the stitches and pulled them out, the sensation like bugs beneath his skin. The wound had mostly healed, but he couldn't quite bend his fingers. It felt no better.

He slept. When he woke there was a noise near his boat. He didn't want to wake up properly so he continued to doze, but when he realised what he'd heard he sat up and looked about. Beneath the water a large shape moved. With the moon behind and the stars on the horizon, he saw clearly the silhouette of a large tail flicking up and then thumping against the water before retreating beneath the surface.

The boy grabbed an oar and paddled, trying to get closer. He pulled his knife from his pocket and readied it, feeling frantic and peculiar.

The whale surfaced again nearby and announced itself this time with a water spout, and the boy felt the drops fall like rain against his burnt face. The creature was so close he could almost touch it. A miracle. He stretched out his hand. The whale gave no sign that it was aware of his existence. The boy longed to see its eyes alive. He paddled closer.

The whale sank again and the boy held the knife tightly in his wounded hand. He relaxed his grip and as the whale came near to the surface once more, bellowing, he studied what he held, he studied what violence had been impressed upon him.

The next time the whale surfaced the boy was sitting back on his boat, hugging his knees to his chest. He only watched and listened. The knife he had put away.

It turned on one side in the moonlight and waved a flipper. It rolled over. The boy never knew the beast alive could be so wonderful. He didn't pursue it when it retreated from him, and he didn't shrink away when it turned and came towards him. He had no fear for himself or for his boat. He just watched.

The whale slipped beneath him and emerged on the other side of the boat, spouting water, free in purpose and in spirit. The droplets struck his burnt skin. The whale's white belly shone in the moonlight and it bellowed, shooting water. There was no second-guessing its own nature. It was what it was. He tried to imagine perpetrating the violence he had earlier felt upon this beast and robbing it of its life. The boy felt remorse, and shame, that he had helped

363

butcher this beast's family. He whispered, 'Sorry, mate,' and really meant it.

Watching the whale stirred him. He felt within him his spirit return. It filled the water surrounding him and went towards the whale and returned to him. He breathed and looked at the sky and watched the whale and felt no urge to do anything else.

When the whale had glided away from him in the dark, he lifted the cans from Albert's body and stacked them on the boat. Then the boy lifted his dead dog and held him. He put his forehead against the dog's fur and rubbed it back and forth. Then he lowered the body into the ocean. Albert's eyes were open and unseeing, but the boy saw within them the possibility of forgiveness. He knew he had made a mistake and that his friend had paid for it. He knew, too, that there was no fixing it. As he watched Albert sink into the black and lose his form within moments, he knew the dog was alive. His mother's words about the afterlife were true. He knew the dog's body would become food for a shark or some other ocean creature, and he knew the rightness of it.

In the morning he looked to the west, towards the mainland, the sight of which had been a reliable comfort to him as he drifted, but he couldn't see it anymore. All that surrounded him now was tremendous ocean. All the peace the whale had brought him during the night was forgotten in his panic. If there was no land, there was also no direction in which he should paddle, even if he were to muster the strength. His arms were failing him and his crippled hand was talon-like in its rigidity. The muscles in his forearms and his legs were aching and cramped.

The corner of the boat slipped beneath the water as the vessel bobbed and sank, a little deeper each time. There was no way to right it. The barrow was still mostly full of cans and the jerry can was perched atop and he still had his knife and Phil's torch. His mother's name on the side of the boat had faded from the sun and the salt water and now looked a blurry mess.

With his oar he swept the water off the boat as it gushed over the corner. Frustrating work that had little effect, but it was nonetheless important and necessary. He sat back on his jacket to insulate himself from the already boiling iron and had some asparagus from a can. It tasted foul and he feared the can had been punctured somehow and the vege-tables within rotted, but he couldn't find any hole. He set his fishing line and had a drink and kept sweeping water from the boat.

'Damn it,' he said aloud, after hours of silence. 'Damn it.' Then, 'Please come back,' with thoughts of the whale and Albert both.

He sipped from the jerry can and caught no fish and swept away the water and passed the day in this way.

When the sun began its descent, he took stock. Half the cans he had started with remained, and he still had the soggy flathead fillets. The jerry can was almost half full but that was because he had not been drinking enough, and he felt light-headed as a result.

He considered his situation. Every action he might take from this point forward was futile. It felt pointless to even try. Still, he had to. It was no longer a case of mere preservation. He had settled in his mind that God must exist because of the whale and because his mother had told him so. So God must be real and his mother must be in heaven and must have sent the whale. He almost wished for his death so that he might see her, but he knew that she would not want him to give up and so he baited his line, stretched his legs, swept the water.

The sun had not long disappeared when something tugged his line and he yanked on the rod. He started to reel it in but found it to be a fighter and so gave it some line and let it tire itself out. His limbs were weak and he kept shaking his hands to ease the ache as he worked the reel. He waited for the fish to become settled in its death before he really hauled it in. As it got closer to the boat he realised he had hooked a shark.

In the dark it was a black formless shape beneath the water but there was no doubt what creature it was. Probably a gummy. It was as long as one of his oars and its tail swept from side to side but it had lost most of its will. He got it beside the boat and let it sit there as he decided what to do with it. With his arms as dead as they were he was uncertain about his ability to lift it onto his vessel. Uncertain too about how to skin the thing, though he knew well enough how to kill it. With one hand steadying the rod he found his torch with the other and shone it on the shark. It didn't startle and regarded him with reverence, this maker of its death. Its eye was black plastic and without soul, though the boy was sure there must be one in there somewhere. He risked his safety to reach out and pat it. Its skin rough, like sandpaper, caught on his fingertips as he stroked it.

He undid one of the many ropes that kept the barrow secure and looped it around the shark a few times. He heaved on the ropes and braced his legs and got the shark aboard, then lashed it to the wood. As he worked the ropes he accidentally embraced the shark. It didn't struggle and the boy saw in the shark's apathy his own desire just to lie down, accept his fate and be done with it.

The boy waited for the shark to die a peaceful death; he refused to cut off its head and end its life prematurely in that fashion. This method of death was more respectful, he felt.

He knew when it had died because its eyes looked different. He tentatively poked at one of them. There was no response. He imagined what it would be like if the boat were now to sink. He would wrap his arms around the shark and they both would drift to the bottom of this dark ocean and at the bottom his ears would pop and he wouldn't hear anything but he would look at the shark and feel comfort. But the boat didn't sink. He stood, wobbly on his feet, and left the shark alone.

With his knife he later carved up the shark by moonlight. Difficult work holding the torch, so he squinted through the black until his eyes adjusted. Now he cut the head off and to his relief there was no gurgling of blood or beating heart. The boy had waited long enough and the shark was truly dead. Without its head it was no longer itself. The head went in the water. He yanked out the intestines and heart and other offal and flicked it into the ocean and washed his hands in the salt water. He was unsure if he could eat shark without cooking it. He put some of the meat, with the skin still on, in his mouth and it tasted of ocean. He chewed and found it tough and unpleasant. He managed to swallow, though, on account of his hunger.

The night passed slowly with this work. The scab on his hand kept cracking when he bent his fingers and oozed yellow fluid which in the dark looked like pale custard. He ate a bit more of the shark and felt sick. He drank water, growing anxious as the water level in the jerry can dropped. He he'd been told, possibly by his father, that a man could drink his own piss if he were desperate. He thought about peeing into the empty spam can but instead he went over the side into the water.

The whale had saved him; of this he was sure. He sat and looked up at the sky, supported by his aching hand. He would make it back to land, and things would be different now. He knew it now to be true. Like the whale had extinguished all doubt.

FORTY-SEVEN

He slept for some time, and when he woke the sun had risen and he could see land. A current was pushing him towards it and he quickly sat up and grabbed an oar and began to row. He made slow progress and soon realised that his rowing was having little effect. He lifted the oar back onto the boat and watched the land and willed for it to come closer. It did. It seemed to grow in expanse and then he saw trees and was surprised by how much he'd missed their greenery. The shore stretched out golden and the sun lit the sand.

The waves increased in strength and and he rose up and down with them, each one pushing him forward. Soon, in his exhilaration, he grabbed an oar again and rowed and rowed. Finally he was in charge of his own fate!

He surged forward and soon the beach was so near he was tempted to dive off the boat and swim for it, but he felt such fear he didn't try. Then the boat threatened to capsize in the surf so he was forced to risk it. Panic in his heart and limbs. He couldn't touch the bottom and so he clung to the boat with both hands clenched tight and the waves were upon him, dunking him underwater. He tasted the ocean and it stung his eyes. He let go of the vessel and struck out, propelled forward by the waves at his back.

He crawled onto the beach and, with the ocean still lapping at his legs, rested his head on the sandy mud and breathed. His sore hand was burning and pumped to the rhythm of his heartbeat. He rolled onto his back and looked at the sky. Maybe he was in heaven and soon his mother would walk down the beach towards him, holding Albert in her arms.

He sat up and then stood on wobbling legs. The boat was still adrift but was coming steadily closer. He looked at the barrow still half full of food and water and he considered retrieving it, but was so weak that instead he sat down again and waited for the decision to be made for him. Hugging his knees to his chest, teeth chattering. The boat came closer. He stood and waded into the ocean. When he was waist-deep in water he grabbed the boat and dragged it ashore. The activity left him breathless and he had to lie down for some time before he could stand again.

He untied the barrow and dragged it up the sand to a shady spot under a tree. He splashed his face with some water from the jerry can and drank half of what was left. He found the knife still in his pocket and used it to stab into a can of green beans and consumed it all, foul juice included. The torch in his pocket was now dead but still he would not discard it. Then he sat and watched the waves catch the side of the vessel made from the old shack. Those barrels had belonged to his mother. He was happy to let them go.

The boy managed to doze fitfully beneath the tree, not waking properly until it was dark. It was freezing. His fingertips felt frozen and the fingers gashed with the flensing knife had no feeling left in them at all. He tried to squeeze them shut and couldn't. He touched them with his good hand and found they felt like overripe bananas. He rubbed at his eyes to remove the sand that had become embedded in his eyelids and then considered his situation.

Where he had washed ashore was a picture. Even in the night the beach was soft and lush. The water was dark but still inviting. The trees were bright green even moonlit. There was a steady breeze. But he was shivering from the cold and had no change of clothes nor any way to dry what he had on. He had no way to start a fire. 'Bloody stupid,' he said, and was surprised at the quiver in his voice.

He took off his shorts and the leather shoes that, absurdly, he was still wearing. He removed his brown socks – they were dripping wet – and flung them aside, so he was left in just his undies. Teeth chattering, he piled sand over his legs and torso, and almost at once lapsed back into sleep.

The first thing he was aware of when he woke, still in the indomitable dark, was his infected hand. The numbness had been replaced with a terrific pain, terrible and cutting. It was a wonder he had managed to sleep through it. He gripped it and groaned, then tried rubbing it with his good hand, which only made it worse. Some of the soft scabs peeled away and he felt fresh blood trickle down his forearm. By moonlight the blood resembled ink. He needed to do something. He needed to get help.

He strained his ears for some sound of civilisation but heard nothing beyond the breeze rustling through leaves, and insects, and waves. There were no lights that he could see. There were no fires on the beach indicating the presence of campers. There might be people further up the beach, though equally there might not be. Still, he had little choice but to try.

He pulled on his still-wet clothes and shoes. There was no easy way to carry his food and remaining water. He tried to cradle the barrow in his arms, but the pressure on his injured hand caused an intense wave of pain. With the knife he punctured a tin of baked beans cut around the lid until he was able to bend back the top. After devouring the contents, he filled the empty tin with water and pushed the top back down. He tried to pocket it and struggled with the size. He ended up placing it between the band of his shorts and his hip, securing it with his belt, making sure it remained upright. It did if he walked carefully.

He set forth, leaving behind his oars and his boat, and the rest of his food and water. Knowing this effort was his last. He carried the torch in his good hand. As he walked down the beach, struggling through the soft sand, he swung the torch like a club. In the trees there were no sounds beyond the breeze but he pictured creatures there all the same.

He walked for a long time, until the sun rose over the horizon and shone into his eyes. He stopped and spat and sipped at the water. The sun came up slowly and in the distance were grey clouds. He was hungry now, and regretted not bringing any food with him. There was nothing on the beach to eat and inland there were only trees and he was sure the leaves would provide little sustenance.

As he sat and watched the sunrise he gradually became aware that over the waves he could hear the sound of traffic. It was distant and hard to make out, but as he walked closer to the trees lining the beach the sound became clearer. A highway, or something like it. The low rumble of a truck engine far away.

Immediately he ploughed into the jungle. There was no clear path, just a dense wall of trees and vines and bushes so impenetrable that he almost lost heart. He wanted to give up, but he knew he couldn't. He yanked at the vines and pushed aside branches. He said to his mother, 'I'm alright,' and was sure it helped him somehow. He had no feeling left in his wounded hand and both hands were dark red with blood. There was a cut near his eye, too, and the blood streamed down his face so that he tasted the iron on his lips.

Finally the foliage began to thin. The land dipped down and then climbed back up and in the basin there was a puddle of stagnant water. He stopped and drank a little from his can – the liquid tasted faintly of beans. Then he walked down the sandy slope, splashed through the water in his already sodden shoes, and scrambled up the other side on his hands and feet.

Now he surged forward. Desperate to make it. If he found no people soon he would never find them. He fought through the obstacles with renewed ferocity. He was King Kong in the city, tremendous and powerful. He kicked at puny trees and they snapped like matchsticks. The vines and leaves peeled away like paper. He felt no more hesitation. He knew nothing but his will to survive.

He had no way of telling for how long he had been walking and he didn't care. He scrambled like a dingo through the underbrush, his breath loud in his ears. No longer human, but animal. If he did not make it, then he would die an animal and the memory of his mother that he alone held would die with him.

The sun had traversed the sky and it was almost dark again. Through the leafy canopy, the sky was the colour of blood. He sat, leaning awkwardly against a tree, and pulled his can of water from his hip, but when he brought it to his lips the can was empty. He hadn't realised how thirsty he'd become until he he could not have water. He wanted to cry and smack his hand into the earth. He tried, but his limbs were so weak his hand only thudded lightly and his impact on the world was naught. The sound of traffic was inter-mittent but close by. He couldn't summon the energy to continue. He watched the sky turn from blood to lavender and then black.

As his breathing slowed he listened with care to the sound of his body. His hand was numb and he knew he would lose it and become his father even in his death. He fell asleep but not really. The canopy of leaves above him swayed with breeze like waves upon the ocean and he knew if he swam in them he would be dead. Maybe there were people there swimming in them now.

Staggering to his feet he was surprised to see the head-lights of an oncoming car through the trees. He tried to force his legs to walk and found they wouldn't move.

'Come on,' he said. One foot forward. The other foot. He grasped at the tree limbs that blocked his path with his whole body. He leaned on each tree as he passed, then pushed off from it to propel himself forward. As he stumbled along he realised he had lost his knife and his torch. No matter. This effort before him was all that was left.

He pushed up a hill and then he was beside the road in darkness. There were white reflector posts lining each side. He touched the asphalt reverently with his foot but dared not touch it with his hand for fear if he were to bend down he would fall down and be unable to get up.

The next vehicle to round the corner was a truck. Its lights were on and blinded the boy so that he shielded his eyes with his good hand, and with his poor hand he waved.

The light and the sound increased. He heard braking, then a horn, and squinted into the light. The truck was slowing on the road before him.

The truck driver swung his door open and stepped around the front of the truck. He yelled, 'You there? You alright?'

A car swooped by behind him. The boy tottered forward.

'You alright?' the bloke said.

The boy nodded. 'I guess.'

'You look like you been hit by a car.'

The boy nodded again. 'Feels like it.'

The man looked at the boy in the glare of the truck's headlights. 'Bloody hell, mate. You're burnt to a crisp.'

'I know.'

His eye fell on the hand that hung awkwardly by the boy's side. 'What you do to your hand?'

The boy managed a croaky, 'Hospital, please'.

The man's eyes widened at this request. 'Sorry, mate. Of course.' He opened the passenger-side door and helped the boy into the cabin.

The shutting of the door behind him was a relief as the pressure of the wind and the noise subsided with it.

The driver pulled the truck back onto the road. 'I'm Mark,' the bloke said.

The boy felt sick and suddenly desperate for sleep. He shut his eyes and leaned back. 'Sam,' he said, then asked, 'Where am I?'

'Near Noosa. You know where that is?'

The boy nodded. 'I didn't come far.'

'Where you come from?'

'I launched near Moreton Island.'

'Launched what?'

The boy heard the question but couldn't supply an answer. He kept his eyes shut and allowed sleep to take him.

FORTY-EIGHT

When he woke he was in a hospital lounge, draped across some dark green vinyl chairs. The truck driver, Mark, must have carried him in. He looked around at the linoleum floor, the panelled ceiling; Mark was talking to a nurse at reception. The boy shut his eyes again and waited.

Mark's voice. 'They'll be here soon.'

The boy opened his eyes. 'Who?'

'The doctors. They'll come look at you soon.'

'Thank you.'

'No worries.' Mark stepped backwards. 'I'll call later, see how you got on.'

'Are we still in Noosa?'

'Yep.'

The boy shut his eyes and leaned his head back. When he opened them again Mark was gone and he was alone apart from the nurses who moved about with their heads down, concentrating on tasks that did not concern him. There were no other patients waiting. He wanted water and before he could ask a nurse approached.

'I'm going to get you a wheelchair, alright, honey? And we'll get some fluids in you.'

'What's wrong with me?'

'Well,' the nurse said, 'you're clearly dehydrated and your hand is quite ugly. We'll be getting some fluids and some antibiotics in you, I think.'

'Will I lose my fingers?'

She laughed at this. 'You're a long way off losing your fingers, honey. Don't worry about that.'

The wheelchair was brought in by another nurse and the two of them lifted him into it. He was wheeled into a white room and lifted into a bed. A needle was stuck into the crook of his left arm, with a tube running from it to a plastic bag full of clear liquid. He imagined he would feel this coldness course its way through him from within, but instead he felt nothing besides a faint queasiness. The nurse who'd called him 'honey' patted him on the head and told him not to worry and both nurses left.

He waited. The doctor arrived and inspected his hand. 'This hurt?' he said as he put a pin in different parts of the boy's flesh. It hurt far worse than normal and the boy struggled not to snatch his hand away. The doctor held it firm. He seemed pleased and he smiled at Sam without meeting his eyes.

The boy asked, 'What's happening?'

'What's that? Oh, you're going to be fine, son. Just need some antibiotics to clear up the infection on your hand. And we're going to hydrate you and feed you for a bit. How'd you get so burnt?'

The boy looked at his feet. They didn't quite reach the end of the bed. 'I was fishing and got lost.'

'Lost?'

'I was out at sea for a few days.'

'Days?' The doctor, who had been fiddling with the plastic bag, turned to look at the boy. 'By yourself?'

The boy nodded. 'I lost my dog.' He sniffed and with his good hand wiped his nose.

'Sorry to hear that.'

'Yeah. Me, too,' the boy said. The moment Albert died, the dent in his skull. The boy shook his head, clearing those thoughts, and instead chose to remember who Albert had been. The roll down the hill. His family. He sighed.

'Good thing you made it though,' the doctor said. 'Good thing.'

'I guess.'

'Son,' the doctor said, 'if you were adrift for a few days, you're darn lucky to be alive, let me tell you. People go without water for less time than that and fare much worse.'

'I had water.' The boy tried to smile.

The doctor returned the smile and said, 'Just keep that hand on your chest for a bit now.'

'Will I need more stitches?'

'It's a bit late for stitches now the wounds have healed. We'll just let it heal itself. We'll keep it clean and wrapped up for a bit. It'll heal alright, but you'll have a scar down there . . .' He traced his pen across the back of the boy's three fingers. 'Don't worry about that though. It's a good thing.'

'Yeah?'

'Yeah. Ladies dig scars. Makes you seem mysterious.'

The doctor soon left and he gazed around the bare room.

Eventually a nurse came with food. A hot plate with a brown plastic lid. Beneath were mashed potatoes and over-cooked meat. He ate it all without pause. She watched him, clearly fascinated. Soon she said, 'You called anybody yet?'

He swallowed. 'To say I'm here?'

'Yes.'

'No. Not yet.'

'You want to? We would have, but the man who brought you in didn't leave any details about you.'

'Do I have to?'

'You will in the morning.' A motherly smile. 'You can wait until then if you like.'

He nodded and smiled. 'Thank you.' He leaned his head back and studied the ceiling.

In the morning he found someone had placed a phone on his bedside table during the night. He dialled his grandparents' number then held the receiver to his ear.

'Hello?'

'Hi, Grandma.'

'Oh, Sam!' she exclaimed, and immediately began to sob. She was talking, too, but the boy couldn't understand what she was saying.

'Grandma?' the boy asked.

'Sam. Sam.' And she sobbed again.

The sobs were replaced by another voice. 'Sam?'

'Dad?'

His father's voice cracked. 'You alright, mate?'

'I'm okay.'

'Where are you?'

'Noosa hospital.'

'Yeah?' his father said, and sniffed. 'I'm on my way. Right now. Just stay there.'

The boy had forgiven his father on the boat, he realised, but had not yet begun to trust him. He hadn't forgotten how he had been abandoned, again and again.

'I love you,' his father said. 'Alright?' There was a moment during which his father might have been waiting for the boy to respond, but the boy said nothing. Instead he hung up.

The boy leaned back in his bed and the nurse soon came and collected the phone and offered him a sad smile.

The boy waited. There was nothing of interest on the ceiling or in the movement of the nurses and doctors in the corridor outside his door. He went to the bathroom and relieved his bowels for the first time in days. The smell of disinfectant stuck to him, the smell of his mother's death. He climbed back into bed and pulled the blankets up and shut his eyes but couldn't sleep, the thought of his father's arrival frightening him. His father had not sounded angry, only relieved, but there was no telling what the long drive might do to his demeanour. The boy found himself growing resentful that his father would be angry with him, that the man would dare, but then he felt forgiveness, and pity. He, too, had made mistakes.

Around an hour later his father rushed into the room. He threw himself at the boy, wrapping his arms around him and holding him tight. His father's crying shook his whole body as though all that he had kept within was finally given release.

Soon his father pulled away and slumped into a chair. He wiped his eyes and laughed and sniffed. 'Never cried like that in my life.'

'Not even when mum died?'

'Not even then. So, what happened?'

'I got lost,' the boy said. 'I'm fine.'

'How're the fingers?'

'They're alright. The doctor said I just needed rehydrating and antibiotics.'

'Should've just done what the doc on Tangalooma said then, yeah?' His father clearly meant this in jest but the boy did not take it that way.

He said, 'I lost Albert.'

'What?'

'I lost Albert,' the boy repeated. 'I was out at sea and I had him and in the night he fell off. He ran into my boat. And it's my fault. I shouldn't have taken him.'

His father looked at the boy. It did the boy good to see the solemnity written in his father's features. 'That's alright, mate. People make mistakes.'

'No, it's not alright,' he said.

His father stood and again wrapped his arms around his son and whispered to him that it was okay. The boy was relieved that his father had accepted what he had done to the dog and felt the weight of death lifted from him.

FORTY-NINE

The doctor gave them some advice about how to care for the boy's wounded hand and handed them some tablets in a small grey packet, then the boy and his father bundled the boy's still-sodden clothing into a rubbish bag provided by a nurse and left the hospital.

The boy was surprised to find their car in the car park without all of the possessions he'd stuffed in it before he left their camp.

'Where's all our stuff?' he asked.

'Your grandparents' place,' his father said. He unlocked the boy's door and helped him in, then walked around the car to his own door. As he opened it he said, 'Except the tools. They're in the boot.'

The boy smiled. 'You found the key?'

'Yep.'

'Where did I put it?'

'You don't remember?'

The boy shook his head.

'You'd put it under the tyre like we used to when we went fishing.'

His father turned the key and the old thing sprang to life and they bumped out of the car park. The boy leaned his head against the window and watched the world he'd forgotten wash by him as his father drove on in silence.

Eventually his father said, 'So what happened to you?'

'I don't know.'

'Why didn't you go to your grandparents like I said?'

The boy countered, 'How come you're back?'

His father drew a long breath in and released it. 'I only stayed a few more days after I sent you back. Realised I'd made a mistake. I couldn't let you . . .' He stopped. He kept his gaze fixed on the windshield as they made a turn. Then, 'It's hard. Since your mum died I thought I'd just sort of fold you into my life. Like another layer, another job. You know? You'd end up just like me, life wouldn't change. I didn't realise that of course it already bloody had, whether

I wanted it to or not. You're not me and I gotta look after you a bit now. It's not just me on my own anymore.'

The boy said, 'You looked after mum.'

His father's voice was quiet as he said, 'No. I didn't.'

They were silent for a time and his father did not press him further about his journey and the boy was sure he'd never really tell it. Soon the boy said, 'Why'd you lie?'

'About what?'

'About buying the land.'

'Oh,' his father said. 'That why you tore it down?'

The boy nodded. 'Plus I was mad at you.'

His father laughed at this. 'Yeah?'

'Yeah.'

They turned onto another road and soon they were passing farmland, stalks of sugar cane standing green and strong.

His father said once they'd passed, 'I went stupid when Mum died. That's all. I did lie. I know I did.'

'I know you did.'

His father looked at him and then back at the road. 'I didn't sell our house, either.'

'You lied about that, too?'

'I know, mate. I just . . . After she died, I went into our room and I just sensed her there, you know? And I was bloody gutted she wasn't alive. And so I went stupid. Bloody idiot to keep running from her.'

'Why the shack?'

'Why build a shack?'

'Yeah.'

'Couldn't tell you.'

'You know you broke the law?'

His father nodded. 'How'd you find that out?'

'A cop came by and asked after you.'

'He did?'

The boy nodded. 'We should go see him.'

His father said softly, 'Yeah. We should.'

They went straight to the police station and walked in together. The policeman behind the counter was the same one who had visited the boy. He took one look at the two of them and grinned and came out from behind the counter and shook his father's bad hand. He looked at the boy's bandaged hand and instead of a handshake rubbed the boy's hair.

'Keogh,' he said. 'I thought you'd done a bloody runner, mate.'

'I did.'

'But you're back?'

The boy looked at his father.

'I am. So I gotta pay a fine or something?'

The policeman nodded and retreated behind his counter. He called the hardware store and asked about his father's outstanding debt. Then he asked if the man knew someone who could tear up a concrete slab and how much that service might cost. When the policeman relayed this figure, the boy's father took a roll of notes from his back pocket and paid it on the spot.

The policeman looked surprised.

His father said, 'Didn't want it on my back.'

Afterwards, they climbed into the car and drove back the way they'd come and then along the highway. They took their usual exit and passed through hills and came upon farmland. They soon reached their old home, on the old gravel street. The boy could see the tyre swing his father had erected standing lonely in the backyard. The front lawn of their house had grown long and as the boy got out of the car he saw it had grown to his knees and that his mother's carefully tended garden was now overgrown

His father swung open the front gate and stepped to the side to allow the boy to go through first.

When he went through the front door, he was immediately hit by the hospital smell of his mother's death and the boy understood his father's reluctance to return.

He turned and walked to her bedroom. His father's bad hand found his shoulder, a comfort. He fiddled with the bandages wrapping his own.

The old bed looked somehow sad.

His father said, 'I hate this place.'

'Why?'

'Just hate it,' he said. He walked in and sat in the chair that had faced their bed those many months and assumed the pose the boy had seen him in whenever his father had sat by his wife's side. He was slouched down and his foot tapped against the carpet. His father looked at the phantom image of his mother and the boy followed his gaze and did his best to see it too. His father said, 'I'm sorry, mate.'

'I know.'

'I'll do better.'

The boy nodded. He still wasn't sure that he could trust this man, but he tried his best to hope. 'I know,' he said.

He looked at where his mother had slept in her sickness and remembered her yellow colour and her eyes still green and present during her death.

They unpacked the car and then wandered about the house for a bit, then the boy went into his bedroom and collapsed happily onto his bed.

His father came to the door and said, 'We need to get some food. You want to come down the street?'

The boy and his father filled up a shopping basket at the grocer's and took it to the counter, and the store clerk who tallied up the cost, somebody the boy did not know, offered his father a sad smile of commiseration. His father nodded at this.

At home they cooked in the usual way and the boy understood more deeply what his father had been trying to escape. The kitchen's smells were a sharp and powerful reminder of his mother. The two of them sat on the floor in front of the radio, which remained off, and ate in comfortable silence. Afterwards the boy threw his clothes into the laundry sink and remembered his mother's efforts with the mangler. She was everywhere in this place.

That night, with his father asleep on the couch, the boy walked out to the backyard. He sat on the tyre swing and pushed with his feet and thought of Albert. There had been such joy in that pup.

There was a stone on the back verandah they had always used to prop the door open. The boy fetched some tools from his father's toolbox, still in the car, and under the verandah light chiselled Albert's name into the stone. With his damaged hand the task was difficult, but he managed it. He placed the stone on a fence post that overlooked the paddock adjoining their home. He patted it a few times and then, with his hands clasped before him, whispered his apology, and his love – to whom he was unsure. In his mind the dream of the whale.

ACKNOWLEDGEMENTS

A novel is never written in isolation. There have been so many people during my thirty-two years on this planet who have encouraged and supported me. If your name isn't here, don't worry; you're very appreciated.

David Myer, who wrote *The Whalers of Tangalooma*, was invaluable. This book would not exist without his input and generosity toward this new author.

Thank you Paul Stephens, Martin Winney, Nathan Dodd and Tiny Owl Workshop, who encouraged me when encouragement was hard to come by and made me want to keep going.

My agent, Gaby Naher, whose support and eye for a story made this book way better.

All the wonderful people at Allen & Unwin. You've all been so patient and kind. Siobhan, Ali, Rebecca, and all the unsung heroes who made this book as good as it can be; you have my many thanks. And especially Jane Palfreyman, who took this novel (and me) under her wing and then pushed it (and me) confidently from the nest.

David and Carolyn Thomas, my spiritual mum and dad. I wouldn't have had the confidence to pick up a pen without you gently and forcibly shoving me in that direction.

My mum and dad, who showed up to so many Sounds Like Chicken gigs it bordered on embarrassing. You've always been my biggest champions and I love you for it.

My family. My kids. It's an honour to be your dad. You are brave and wonderful. This book is for you.

And Lena. What a beautiful lady. The very best type of wife. You set me straight and pick me up when I'm down and encourage my creativity and love for Nintendo. I count my blessings every day that I'm the guy you're spending your life with.

And God. For everything.